BOB AT THE LAKE

R. MURPHY

Dear Margaret —
Enjoy your visit
with Bob and
Crooked Lake!
Roy

SOUL MATE PUBLISHING

New York

BOB AT THE LAKE

Copyright©2013

R. MURPHY

Cover Design by Christy Caughie.

This book is a work of fiction. The names, characters, places, and incidents are the products of the author's imagination or are used fictitiously. Any resemblance to actual events, business establishments, locales, or persons, living or dead, is entirely coincidental.

Published in the United States of America by
Soul Mate Publishing
P.O. Box 24
Macedon, New York, 14502

ISBN: 978-1-61935-412-8
eBook ISBN: 978-1-61935-287-2

www.SoulMatePublishing.com

To AMH and MFD,

with my love and gratitude

for your constant support

Acknowledgements

Many thanks go to the Wiltberger family of multi-award-winning Keuka Spring Winery for generously sharing their exhaustive knowledge of wines and winemaking with me. Any errors regarding wines in this book are absolutely my fault—I might need to do much more tasting research on our local wines! My heartfelt gratitude also goes to talented writer and neighbor Beverly Lewis for her deft and thoughtful comments on an early draft. Finally, my thanks to merry neighbor Barbara Pinneo, who's always willing to explore new wineries with me. Ready for another road trip, Barb?

Chapter 1
Bob at the Lake

"Trust me, it will hit you like a brick of gold."

That's Bob. He's my ghost. Well, not *my* ghost since I'm sitting here writing, but the ghost who lives with me. Other women probably get muscleman ghosts who can fix plumbing and take out the garbage, or romantic ghosts who set their hearts a-flutter. Me, I get a ghost who's middle-aged, plump, and who likes to lounge around the house in a silk smoking jacket from the nineteen-thirties. Not exactly the kind of ghost I'd ever imagined I'd get. I will admit, though, that Bob does make an amazing martini. A martini that, in fact, hits you like a brick of gold.

I found, unfortunately, the longer Bob lived at my place, the more I appreciated his skill with martinis. Which was probably not a great thing for my liver, or my relationships with my sisters, but what the heck.

Remember the Great Recession? According to the newspapers, some consumers seem to be wiping it from their memories, but it had a big impact on a lot of people, including me. That economy hurt. Lost jobs, lost houses, lost marriages, lost hopes—lives turned upside down in the flutter of a pink slip. People scrambling just to keep from drowning—couch surfing, penny pinching, living newly frugal lives.

Like millions of others, the economy sucked me into its undertow. In Nashville, my life had been moving along in a sensible fashion, even if it wasn't Cinderella happy. A big-girl job, a decent townhouse, nice-enough neighbors, the occasional date. Then, like an idiot, I decided to stretch a bit financially and buy a lake house in Upstate New York. I'd planned to rent it out during the summers and make money on it with an eye to retiring there a few decades in the future. My sister Katie and her husband have a summerhouse on the lake, and they were doing just fine with it.

After much to-ing and fro-ing between Nashville and western New York, I found a beautiful house on Crooked Lake in the Finger Lakes, three miles up the road from my sister, and bought it. What a place! Twenty-one windows; nineteen of them with spectacular lake views. (I know, because I've washed every one of them by hand.) The lake is gorgeous. My house is ten miles from the nearest coffee shop or grocery store but, for a rental vacation home, who cared?

Two Nashville job layoffs later, I cared. Those were tough, bitter months, and I decided to leave the south to live closer to my sister. There's nothing like getting kicked in the teeth a few times to make you realize how much you need family. So I sold the Nashville town house and moved into my lake house in the middle of a freak late-October blizzard. Of course. I remember sitting in the middle of my freezing cold living room with snow melting off the boxes and onto the tile floors. Have you ever cried so hard that you get little salt crusts under your eyes? I have, only about three times in my life. I don't recommend it.

So there I was, officially jobless, freezing cold, almost broke, facing winter in an isolated lake house miles from coffeehouse civilization while most of my neighbors were snuggling into their Florida homes for the winter.

In retrospect, that solitude probably sounds like heaven to some people. For me, who'd lived most of my life in cities, it was kind of terrifying. For one thing, it violated one of my central tenets: Always live within screaming distance of other people. Visions of broken legs and ax murderers populated my nightmares. The situation wasn't helped by the mystery novels I used to prefer, or the television shows I used to watch that seem to specialize in exploring horrifying new ways to murder single women every week. Notice the past tense on both of those pastimes.

At this point, it might be appropriate to interject a few words about me. Decades ago, people used to have a phrase for me: a woman of a certain age. Back then, everyone knew what that phrase meant: Young enough to want to *(fill in the name of your favorite venial sin here);* old enough to know better. The phrase implies a certain amount of polish, a certain amount of experience. A woman who's been knocked down by life, still has the energy to get off the floor, and has learned lessons from her fall. Back then, women of a certain age were hard-bitten newspaperwomen, or glamorous, mysterious divorce co-respondents in courtroom dramas, who wore elegant hats with veils down to their chins. I associate them with words like peplum, and negligee, and I know they were all blondes who wore daring designer suits and genuine silk stockings.

I wish I could afford to wear daring designer suits. Instead, my everyday clothes typically involve some form of denim. And, although my short, wavy brunette hair usually has some highlights of blond, the quantity of highlights tends to vary proportionally to my bank balance. The more money I have, the blonder I get.

I don't know how to assign a specific age to a woman of a certain age in the twenty-first century. It's especially confusing these days, when forty is the new twenty and fifty is the new thirty. I think it's mostly a matter of mind and experience.

Back to our story.

Technically, I guess I did have nearby neighbors. Mary and Stan, an unmarried couple (she was ninety-two, he was seventy-five) lived a few houses down from me on a spit of land that jutted out into the lake. Officially, he was her handyman; unofficially, who knew? At ninety-two, did it really matter? And then again, as a woman of a certain age, should I really have been making these judgments? While it was nice to have beating hearts in the vicinity, I didn't really want to rely on them for emergencies. Actually, I was kind of glad I could be here for *them* in case of emergency, which I thought was a lot more likely.

Kind of bleak, huh? It was a challenging time, but at least I had a few assets on my side. I've always been a freelance business writer, so there was some income there, and I could build on it. And I am a Taurus, a banker of the zodiac, so I tend to be good with money. In fact, I've always had a tough time deciding whether my three favorite words are: I Love You or Paid in Full. This internal debate probably explains a lot about my life, and why I ended up living (almost) alone by the side of a lake.

Another asset: I'm a hard worker. I can actually scare myself sometimes with how hard I work. These days, in an economy with ten percent unemployment, I'm not really sure if it's a valuable attribute.

Long days of unpacking. Unpacking, like so many things in life, always reminds me of making frosting. You put the water into the frosting mix and stir like crazy for several minutes. For what seems like the longest time, nothing happens. You're just stirring this messy bowlful of powder around like an idiot. Suddenly, though, the conversion happens. What had been a bowlful of mess flips into glossy, creamy frosting. Lots of effort, no progress for what seems the longest time and then *flip!* delicious frosting.

It's the same with unpacking boxes after a move. Tons of work with no visible progress for a long time and then *flip!* you have an almost moved-into house.

A few days after the move, I had to shift my focus from unpacking boxes to making money. (Speaking of making money, I'm always amazed at how many books and authors don't mention this little topic. How do writers support themselves? Do they all have spouses who pay the bills in their startup years? Do Mommy and Daddy carry them for decades? Are they writing after putting in full days at their real job? I've always been curious.

I almost think each chapter of a book should start off with a budget, or a financial anecdote on How I Paid the Bills While Writing This Chapter. Maybe a diet tip on how you cut back on eating while writing a certain section. Mine would probably start with *Take one package of ramen noodles . . .* How do you write if you've got no one else to pay the freight as you're starting up? Just curious.)

As I've mentioned, I have a small talent with money. And, some days, I think I have a small talent with writing. Put them together, and you have a writer who specializes in money topics. In my case, a writer who ghostwrites for the heads of several global companies on corporate philanthropic topics. I seem to be able to find that sweet spot of making a company sound as if it cares about more than its profit margin.

So one day around Halloween, I was rummaging around in boxes looking for some data I needed to write a CEO letter about my Ohio client's Community Chest campaign. I spent hours looking for those stupid papers and finally blurted out a few choice words I usually try to avoid.

"Gracious," a male voice behind me said. "My friend McGregor would blench to hear a woman using such language. And McGregor is not usually a blenching sort!"

I spun around, the coffee cup I held went flying, and the screaming started. Most of it came from me, but not all of it. Screams happen when you see a strange man standing in your living room, even if he does have mild, owlish features and wears a silk smoking jacket.

"Don't scream! Don't scream! I'm not here to hurt you!" the stranger kept yelling, as he flapped his arms in what I suppose he thought was a pacifying manner. He looked so bizarre, even harmless, that I eventually started calming down.

"Who are you? What are you doing here?"

"I'm Bob. I've been assigned to you. As to why, well, that's a complicated story."

Just then, I noticed a certain wavering quality to Bob. A certain shimmering, a transparency, as if he hadn't quite committed himself one hundred percent to this conversation.

"What's going on here?" I said, trying to get a little control over this bizarre situation.

"I'm Bob," he repeated patiently. "I've been assigned to you. I like to think of myself as a free spirit, but you'd probably call me a ghost."

There's just something about the word *ghost*. I could feel another shriek on its way.

"No, no, don't yell. I'm not here to scare you. I'm not one of those young, ill-mannered thuggish ghosts who throw furniture around and carry on. I'm here to help."

"Help? Help with what?" Have you ever tried to find third-gear in an old manual-transmission VW? Lots of fumbling around and false attempts? That's how this conversation was feeling.

"Well, for one, you've been complaining about the solitude," Bob continued. "I can keep you company."

"A ghost? For company? Are you nuts? How do I know you even exist? Maybe all this isolation has sent me around the bend. Maybe I've gone crazy."

"Oh, come on. You haven't even been in the house a month yet—it's too soon to go berserk. You have to have four or five snowbound winters before you can officially go nuts."

"You know this for a fact, huh? Good to know. I'll mark it in my calendar." I started to feel my atoms reassembling in their usual slots and mumbled a mantra to calm down. "A few deep breaths, a few deep breaths, and I'll get my balance."

"Good idea," Bob chipped in. "Deep breaths. I could mix up a martini for you if you like, or pour you a shot of rye."

"It's eleven o'clock in the morning, for Pete's sake. I'll pass on the alcohol. But you go right ahead. So I guess ghosts can drink?"

"'Each to her own, said the lady as she kissed the cow.' Of course I can drink. It doesn't seem to have quite the punch it had in my salad days, but it passes the time."

"Sorry, but I don't think I have any rye. I'm not even sure people still drink it."

"Amateurs. No problem, I carry my own." Bob reached into an inner pocket of his smoking jacket and pulled out a silver flask. "To new assignments!" he said, and threw back a healthy snort. "Ahhhhhh, now where were we?"

"You mean, aside from the screaming?"

"Exactly."

"I was trying to find some papers I packed when all of a sudden this middle-aged—"

"Hey," Bob interjected.

"Plump—"

"*Hey!*"

"*Ghost* pops up out of nowhere and scares the *bejeebers* out of me!"

After a short pause, Bob responded in a matter-of-fact

manner, "Well, the first few minutes with a new client are always the trickiest. Introductions are so dicey. I had one assignment who ran out of the house and just kept running. Not one of my better days."

"I didn't know this house was haunted." I was angry. Was I the out-of-town rube who'd been snookered by a sharp realtor? "I would never have bought this place if I thought a ghost lived here. Aren't realtors supposed to tell you these things?"

"The *house* isn't haunted, *you* are. I've never been here before, but I was assigned to you, and I found you."

"You said that before . . . assigned to me. Who assigned you? Why did they assign you to me?"

"I'm a little fuzzy on the details. They usually clear up as we move along. It's not that I do anything to you. We usually work something out together, and I get a little closer to retiring."

"Retiring?"

"Yeah, you know. Head toward the light, strum a harp on a cloud, blah, blah, blah. It's never really been my idea of a good time, but everyone else seems to go for it. Tell you what. We've finished our introductions and we've both probably had enough excitement for one day, so why don't I just toddle off, and we'll pick this up later."

"Toddle? What do you mean, toddle? Where do you toddle off to?"

"Again, part of the long story. For now, why don't we just say I have two locations. Here"—Bob waved his arms around to indicate my house—"and not here."

He vanished.

I plopped onto the sofa. "Ohhhh, crap, this is going to get weird."

You probably won't be surprised if I confess to being a tad jumpy for the rest of the day. But reading this over, I have to admit I'm impressed with my *sangfroid* in meeting a ghost. Especially considering that, of all things in the world, ghosts are the scariest things to me, right up there on the scary-o-meter with ax murderers and being broke. After I stupidly watched a horrific ghost movie a few years ago, I'd taken to locking my bedroom door every night. As my sister Katie very reasonably pointed out, any ghost could have just walked through the locked door. In my heart I knew she was right, but, still, it felt better locking the bedroom door. At the least, I figured it might delay any ax murderers long enough for me to jump out the window and run away.

Speaking of my sister, Katie, she has a summerhouse down the road with her husband Bill. When I described my assets a while back, I should have listed my sisters, because they give me the only real security I've known lately. Husbands can leave; jobs can vanish; houses can get foreclosed; but a sister is stuck with you forever. I have five sisters and two brothers. I'm particularly close to two of my sisters, Katie and Angela. They're as different as chalk and cheese. Katie lives in New Jersey. She's brunette, practical, very down to earth, disciplined, and works in the financial aid department of a local college. Angela lives in Mississippi, has long blond hair and immaculately manicured nails. She's spent decades of married life taking care of her family, while studying esoteric topics like transformational kinesiology and chakras.

For me, I get the best sisterly combination possible since they rarely have the same opinions. Yin and yang, black and white, Republican and Democrat, spiritual and pragmatic, liberal and conservative—I get to choose from a whole spectrum of options whenever I get in trouble. And I suppose most people would consider a rye-swilling ghost trouble.

The few times Katie and Angela have agreed on a situation, I know I have to take their opinions very, very seriously.

There were several worrying things about my Bob phone call with Katie a couple of hours later. I'd say the most worrisome was the long, pregnant pause when I told her about having a ghost. You could have driven a truck through that pause. And when she spoke to me in a soft, gentle voice after the pause, I became truly concerned. As wonderful as Katie is, gentle is not one of her strong suits.

"A ghost, Roz? Are you sure you didn't fall asleep? Maybe you were just dreaming?"

"No, the image was too vivid. I'm sure if I dreamt a ghost he wouldn't be wearing a smoking jacket. Where the heck would a smoking jacket come from? I think the last time I saw one Ricky Ricardo was wearing it in an *I Love Lucy* rerun. That would have been years ago."

"What have you been reading? Watching any old movies? Fred Astaire movies? I know you love them."

"No, I haven't seen any movies lately. I've been too busy with the unpacking, and I only figured out how to hook up the TV yesterday."

"I worry about you being up there all on your own," Katie fretted. "You need to get out more. You should take some time off and explore. Go shopping. Treat yourself to lunch. Go to one of the wineries for a tour."

Katie sounded so sure my ghost was imaginary, so solid in her conviction, that I did begin to doubt myself.

"Well, maybe, with all of this unpacking and trying to get myself straightened out with my writing, maybe I did just overdo everything. I'm sure you're right . . . I probably just dozed off or something. Yeah, good point about taking a little time off. I have been pushing myself hard."

"Roz, as long as I have you on the phone . . . I just put in for my vacation time at Christmas. Why don't you plan on coming to New Jersey for a few days then? Pop and Milly will be here, and Bill will be cooking his usual filet mignons. Amy will be home from college, too. It will be good for you to spend some time with family."

I agreed about Christmas. It'd give me something to look forward to. And, as always, Katie had a good point about me being inside my house and my head too much. So I decided to go out and have a little fun for a few hours.

Avondale, the small town ten miles north of my house, combines the best of a New England village with the money-magnet splendor of a resort. Sprawling, century-old Victorian mansions grace the oak-lined Main Street. Tucked along the edges of town are the tourist shops that cheerfully suck money out of the pockets of the unwary. Little stores selling homemade ice cream, customized mugs, fudge, fruit, vegetables, tee shirts, and lake memorabilia line the roads. Further out are the shops for the year-round residents— hardware stores, run-down grocery stores, and Mennonite-owned bulk stores full of bargain-priced meats and staples.

I headed toward the bulk store, one of my new favorite places. Young Mennonite girls, with their starched, translucent white caps, homemade pastel cotton dresses, dark socks and big, comfortable running shoes staffed the place, working the cash registers and stocking the shelves. They looked like exotic, delicate flowers with upside-down mushrooms on their feet. During the summer, the tourists packed the aisles, exclaiming at the lower prices and loading up their carts. Shelves there were full of the kinds of items that grocery stores don't stock anymore: preserving jars, containers of yeast instead of the little packages, dark molasses, exotic flours and cooking ingredients. Four different kinds of oatmeal—flaked, instant, steel-cut, regular. Vegetables right off the farm.

The Mennonites are very savvy business people. They'd opened a little coffee shop right in the store, bursting with homemade soups and baked goods. It was always full of people, either local farmers or tourists, and I'd started the habit of stopping in when I was in the vicinity. There's nothing like a good cup of coffee, and I admit I'm addicted. When I worked in Manhattan (before Nashville), I had a friend who'd lost her job. We'd meet for coffee once in a while, and to this day I remember her saying that, although she had tightened her belt in many places with her budget, she still insisted on buying her favorite butter and coffee. I liked that—austerity throughout, but a few good things sprinkled here and there to keep up the spirits. This is how I'd always describe budgeting to my friends: scrimp . . . scrimp . . . scrimp . . . *splurge* . . . scrimp . . . scrimp . . . *splurge* . . . and so on.

When I'd moved to the country, I'd decided to start baking my own bread. My ultimate bread goal is a sour, chewy rye. I'm a little intimidated by the recipes I see for this, though. They have such oddball ingredients, like instant coffee, cocoa powder, and mashed potatoes. As someone who lives on her own, I can tell you, mashed potatoes are not a huge part of my diet. That's why all I've baked so far are the more traditional breads—wheat, whole wheat, oatmeal. I do the whole thing by hand since I have the time. Now that I'm not saddled with that pesky little thing called a regular work week, I have nothing but time. Literally. Plus, I find kneading and throwing around the dough makes me feel good. I get all of my frustrations out and a little exercise too.

So I picked up some bread basics like flour and yeast at the bulk store, browsed through the cookbooks and the different kinds of pickles and jams, and the amazing selection of candies and snack foods they have there. I read once that Mennonites and Amish burn through 10,000 calories a day doing all their chores since they don't use many mechanical devices and, judging by the amount and variety of snacks at this store, I'd believe it.

As always, the coffee was excellent. But much as I enjoyed my outing to the bulk store, I couldn't put off returning home forever. My work deadline was calling. The drive home was lovely. All the drives around my house are lovely. You pass beautiful, cultivated fields populated with cows, cabbages, classic red barns, and silos. No matter where I go in the Finger Lakes, I feel like I'm driving through a fricking Currier and Ives Christmas card. Always, off in the distance, is beautiful Crooked Lake. Sometimes it's blue in the summer sun, or steel gray in winter, with mists rising in curls from its surface. Or, like that day, a fiery blaze of color reflected from the surrounding autumn leaves.

Finally, back in the house, caffeinated and full of great cherry pastry, I located the missing information I'd been looking for that morning and sat down at the kitchen table to get started on my CEO letter. Hours later I looked up (I love it when I get into the flow of writing. Hours can go by in what seems like seconds. Other times trying to write can be like getting a root canal.) I had that feeling in the back of my neck that someone was watching me. My scalp tightened, as if I'd had too much coffee. I looked up and, sure enough, there was Bob, shimmering by the kitchen cabinets.

"Oh, crap."

Chapter 2

The Nearness of You

"Crap," I repeated.

"Yeah, I heard you the first time."

"So you're really here. Nuts. After talking to Katie I became convinced I'd imagined you. A dream or something."

"Nope."

"Bob, we've got a problem here. I don't want a ghost. I don't want an advisor. I don't want spooky companionship. If I wanted to live with people, I'd still be married. I'd have lots of kids. I'd be like everybody else. I wouldn't be living alone by the side of a lake. I absolutely cannot be hounded by a ghost every day. I have work to do, and a life to live, and I don't really see how you can help me with either one of those."

"Sorry, kid, but I don't have any options here. Assignments are assignments. I'm here for the duration. You have your work, I have mine."

I sighed and pushed away my writing. Even tried putting my head in my hands for a few minutes, but he was still there when I looked up. What an enormous pain in the butt this situation was going to be.

"Can you at least tell me what this assignment of yours is? And who gave it to you, and why I should pay any attention to whoever did? Is it something that we can do really quick so you can get out of here?"

"As I said this morning, I'm not really clear about all of the details. I know people think life on the other side is full of information, but it really isn't. It's as vague as things over here most of the time. My knowledge is very spotty; just flashes of things. I imagine it's a bit like recovering from amnesia—just glimpses of random bits and pieces that don't usually make a lot of sense."

I could understand that. Goodness knows I felt like I was grasping at straws trying to figure out my life most of the time. And just when I thought I'd figured one thing out (like marriage or a job), it would vanish. As a result I could buy that things were just as confusing on the other side.

"All I can tell you about my assignment is that I'm supposed to help you with something," Bob said. "I don't know what you need help with, exactly."

I gestured toward the pile of boxes still stacked against the living room wall. "I need help unpacking. Can you unpack?"

Bob gave me this exasperated look that I would come to know well. "How am I supposed to unpack? I don't know where things go."

True enough, but I thought 'where things go' was skating the issue. "What can you do? Can you move furniture? Can you cook? Can you write? Can you bake bread? Can you convince my sister I didn't make you up?"

"I'm not sure I can do any of those things. I can talk, and I can make amazing martinis. I know those for sure, but I have to discover my other skills as we go along, just like you do."

Great. Just great. This whole encounter reminded me of that scene in the first *Rocky* movie where Rocky says to his two turtles, Cuff and Link, that if they could sing and dance he wouldn't be living life in his dingy little apartment. If Bob had a couple of amazing abilities, like picking winning lottery numbers or predicting the stock market, I could see that changing my whole life. But that would be way too easy. Of course.

"So you don't know why you're here, I don't know why you're here, and I don't know what I'm going to do with you. Typical. I think we're going to have to set some ground rules so we don't keep tripping over each other. Why don't you just go to your happy place for a while and let me think about this?" Bob vanished.

I took off my glasses and rubbed my eyes. Staring out the picture window at the lake, I took a sip of now-cold coffee and muttered, "Oh, nuts. Not again."

You might be wondering how I felt about this whole having a ghost situation. Would you be shocked if I told you my only reaction was that I wasn't surprised? Weird things have happened to me all my life. I wasn't surprised but I was, frankly, sort of irritated. So far I couldn't see any earthly benefit to coping with a ghost.

Two cups of coffee—okay, and a doughnut from the bulk store—later, I yelled, "Bob? Hey, Bob?"

He popped into the kitchen. Now that was kind of cool, having a ghost pop up when you called him. Kind of like having a well-trained puppy.

"Bob, have a seat. Let's talk."

He floated over and perched an inch off the kitchen chair facing me. His smoking jacket glistened in the afternoon light flooding the kitchen. Outside, the wavelets on the lake rumbled like the breathing of a sleeping kitten.

"It sounds like we don't have a lot of options here. You're not going to leave me alone, are you?"

"No, sorry about that, but I can't. I don't have to be with you every minute of every day, but I'll always be in the vicinity."

"Here's how I see things. You have to leave me alone when I work. You have to leave my writing alone."

"If I leave your writing alone, you can say anything you want about me. People won't know the real me."

"Real you? You don't exist! No offense, Bob, but if you're a ghost, you're dead. You're gone. All your friends are gone. All your family's gone. I don't mean to be nasty here, but let's face facts. Who's going to care if you've lost some hair and gained a few pounds in the afterlife? You have to promise to keep your mitts off my writing. If you're so uptight about telling your own story, write your own book."

Bob gave me a nasty look, and I gave it right back to him.

"What else?"

"No hanging around when I'm in the bathroom, or dressing, or in the shower. If I have a male friend here, you have to be gone. Not just invisible, but gone."

"As you so delicately pointed out, I'm dead. What you're worrying about here doesn't get to me anymore."

"Really? You don't get those twitches anymore? Those aches? That's too bad. Still, I don't want you hanging around during any intimate moments."

"Intimate moments?" Bob snorted. "I don't think there's been too many of them lately."

"Don't get snarky with me, buddy. I need your solemn ghostly oath on this, or it stops here."

Bob hemmed and hawed. "I have no interest in those so-called intimate moments. Don't worry about it."

"Promise?"

"I promise I won't be here for any intimate moments. Okay? Can you relax now? Jeepers. Has anyone ever mentioned that you're a real control freak?" Bob reached inside his smoking jacket, pulled out his flask, and took a sip.

"It's come up in conversation now and again, but I don't think anyone would blame me here." This was my house, after all. Wasn't I allowed to set at least *some* of the rules? "So that's what I need. What about you?"

"What I need is simple. We just have to talk once a day.

The more we talk, the more I'll get to know you and start to understand why I'm here and what we're supposed to do."

I slid back from my tense position at the edge of my chair and started to relax. Frankly, conversation once a day didn't sound too awful. After all, I was new in town and totally by myself most days, and writing is a very solitary craft. Shooting the breeze once in a while wouldn't hurt me at all. In fact, it might be kind of fun. Although I wasn't too sure what an alky spook would bring to the table conversation-wise.

"Here's the deal," I told Bob in a no-nonsense tone of voice. "We'll have dinner together every day that I'm at home." I paused. "How do we handle things when I'm not at home?"

"I'll be with you. I'm your ghost, not the house ghost. So as long as we talk every day, things will be fine."

"So you can come with me on trips? Weird. What do you do, ride shotgun in the car? Sit on my lap in the plane?"

"Actually, I have a very fine outfit for motoring, so a car trip would be fun. It's been a long time since I was in an automobile. I imagine they've changed quite a bit."

"Yeah. They don't have running boards anymore. Or manual transmissions."

"I'd like that. I don't think I was ever very good with machinery."

"Me either. Makes it very challenging these days, with everything computerized. Machines are getting so complex your refrigerator can tell you when your milk is starting to spoil."

"Refrigerator?" Bob frowned. "Oh, you mean, icebox?"

"I guess that's what they used to call it." I got up, went to the refrigerator, and started flapping the door. "It's got a freezer, too. For ice cream and stuff."

"Amazing! What's this?" Bob floated toward the living room and gestured toward the TV.

"It's a television. I can watch stories on it."

"Stories? You mean, like motion pictures?"

"Sure. And lots of other things." How do you explain sitcoms to a ghost? Or reality shows?

"I remember these a little bit. The pictures are in black and white, right? I remember a show where a fat man was always yelling at his wife."

"Sounds like *The Honeymooners,* from back in the fifties. Is that when you were alive? Or did you have an assignment then?" Obviously he hadn't had an assignment in quite a while. Why me?

"I'm not really sure. I don't remember any specifics."

"We can take a look at TV later and see if that brings anything back for you."

The next forty minutes found me doing an appliance tour of my home. Bob knew toasters, lamps, radios, washing machines, vacuums, and alarm clocks; was intrigued by coffeemakers and dryers; and freaked out by microwaves and computers. (Frankly, so am I, a little bit.) He burst out laughing at my exer-cycle and ultrasonic toothbrush. I decided to hold off showing him my leaf blower and cell phone.

"People have gotten a lot lazier since I was here last." Bob chuckled.

"I don't know about lazier," I replied, a bit defensively. "I think we're using our time and energies differently, that's all. Lots of women work outside the home, so we're always looking for ways to save time with household work."

"So people save all this time and energy by using machines to work around the house and the yard, and then they take that time to sit on a stationary bicycle or to go to a gymnasium to work off their energy. Sure makes lots of sense to me."

"Oh, be quiet! That's just the way it is. Nobody's asking for your approval," I muttered crabbily. Sheesh. Like I said, a pain in the butt. "We've got some time before dinner. Now, do you want to watch TV or not?"

We sat down. I picked up the remote and started flipping through channels. Reruns of *How I Met Your Mother, Everybody Loves Raymond,* shows on redecorating and renovating homes, history shows, travel shows, and the ubiquitous *Law & Order*. Of course, I came across a ghost-hunting show. I swear, some stations seem to be all ghosts, all the time. This one featured spectral footsteps and cold spots, and I flipped the channel quickly.

"Wait, wait, hold up, can't you?" Bob exclaimed, reaching for the remote, though I knew he hadn't a clue how to work it. I'd had enough trouble learning it and I'm from this century. Trying to control the remote must be genetically a male thing. "Wasn't that last one about ghosts? Let's watch that one!"

I stretched the remote away from his reach. "Sorry, but I hate ghosts. What do you think all that screaming was about this morning? I can't watch ghost stuff, even stupid ghost stuff. When you wake up by yourself at two in the morning, it doesn't seem so lame. Even Vincent Price horror movies scare me. Besides, you're nothing like the ghosts there, with their cold spots and footsteps. You didn't hear anybody talking about martinis on that show, did you?"

"Every ghost has their own assignment. We do what we have to do to get the job done. Thank goodness, I must have no abilities for those cold spot kinds of jobs. I'd hate to think what the aptitude test was for that one."

"Aptitude tests for ghosts. Right. That's a good one." I shook my head in exasperation. "I was in Savannah a few years ago, and I went to this house that was supposed to be haunted by a ghost kitten. Now what on earth kind of aptitude would a ghost kitten have?"

"You think every ghost is the same? We're as different as the beings still here, and we all get different kinds of assignments. Sometimes the aptitude tests screw things up, just like the army used to do in my day, but we do what we have to do."

"You are too much." I kept flipping the channels and hit Turner Classic Movies. They were playing one of the *Thin Man* movies with a dapper Dick Powell and an impossibly thin, impeccably dressed Myrna Loy.

"Stop! Let's look at this one for a while," Bob said.

We spent a few minutes watching Nick and Nora at a holiday party, and I started to get restless.

"I wouldn't mind seeing more of this," Bob said, so I left him on the couch and went to the kitchen to start dinner.

Twenty minutes later, I heard an odd tapping. The remote clicked off and Bob drifted in.

"I liked that movie. We should watch more of those."

"How'd you turn off the remote?" I asked.

"Oh, I just kept hitting it on the table until the TV turned off." Bob responded, somewhat breezily. "Was that all right?"

Great, just great, I thought. Scratch one remote.

I continued cutting vegetables for a salad. "Do you want any dinner? Do ghosts eat?"

Peering disdainfully over my pile of vegetables, Bob snorted, "You call that eating? No thanks. I'll pass. You don't have to feed me. Food, like sex, really isn't an issue for me any more. But I still enjoy a drink at dinnertime. Care for a martini?"

"Maybe one of these days. For now, I'll stick with a glass of wine with dinner. I'd better keep a clear head."

Speaking of wine, I live in the Promised Land of Wine. The Finger Lakes. God's Little White Wine Heaven. Because of our cooler climate and the hills around the Finger Lakes, this area is a natural for German-style wines, especially rieslings and gewürztraminers. There are more than twenty small family wineries nestled into the hills around Crooked Lake, each one making better white wines than its neighbor. About five miles up the road from me, Constantin creates sparkling wines and rieslings that make your mouth feel like it's playing hooky on the first day of spring. Bright, crisp, luscious—just writing this, my mouth is starting to water. Napa is great, but I live within twenty miles of some of the yummiest wineries in America.

When you live in White Wine Heaven, you don't waste a lot of time waiting to explore it. Several days after my move, even though I was still up to my ears in boxes, I went out to investigate the territory.

First on my list was Royal Egret Winery. Small, family-owned, in business for only thirty years, its rieslings were winning double-golds all over the world. I'd heard of it even in Nashville. So one crisp autumn afternoon, with golden leaves reflecting down the length of Crooked Lake, I drove into the hills. Royal Egret looked like a castle in Tuscany. Yellow bricks warming in the sunlight, ornate patios, windows gleaming from floor to ceiling in the tasting rooms perched over the vineyards that stretched miles down to the glistening blue water.

Since it was mid-week, the foliage-seeking crowds had thinned. Only one woman waited ahead of me to get into a tasting station. She was slender, with short gray hair and Delft-blue eyes.

We laughed as we reached simultaneously to pick up the last informational brochure from the rack outside the door.

"You take it," she said. "I've been here before. I was just going to read through it to pass the time."

"Thanks so much," I said, reaching for the brochure. "This is my first visit, so it will come in handy. So, if you've been here before, does that mean you live nearby? I'm Roz, by the way. Roz Murphy."

"Bev Miano." She smiled and we shook hands. "My husband and I live a few miles north. We've been here forever. Gino grows grapes, and we raised our two kids just outside Avondale. It's a wonderful place to raise a family. How about you?"

I laughed. "Well, I've lived here for all of three days now. Most of my stuff is still in boxes, but I've been unpacking for days and I needed a break. I've heard about Royal Egret for years, and I couldn't wait to try their wines. This is my first Crooked Lake tasting, and I'm kind of excited!"

"You should be. The wines here are outrageously good. I come to Royal Egret a couple of times a year to taste the latest releases and to stock up. Since Gino grows grapes, we get a nice industry discount, which is the only way I can afford this place."

People in the tasting room started to finish up and move along into the winery store. As tasting slots opened up, Bev and I moved into positions at the tasting bar, still chatting.

Our pourer was a pleasant middle-aged woman, Pat. Turned out Bev knew her. Turned out Bev knew just about everyone in the local wine industry. And she knew her wines, so I got smart real quick and followed her lead.

Pat handed us lists of the winery's offerings, which included descriptions and prices on each wine. Since Pat knew Bev, Pat waived the usual two-dollar tasting fee for each of us.

"I'll start with the drier, lighter whites and then move into the sweeter whites, then to the reds, if that's okay with you," Pat said.

Bev and I nodded. It's embarrassing to admit it, in these days of red-wine worship, but I have a hard time tasting red wines. I enjoy them when I'm eating a meal that complements them, but on their own, red wines usually taste unfinished and raw to me. The phrase "battery acid" comes to mind. It's hard to admit that in the middle of a tasting with other people around, though. I'm hoping, as far as reds go, that my palate is just not educated.

"Then we'll wind up with a taste of our newest sparkling wine," Pat continued. She leaned across the bar and lowered her voice. "Bev, since I know you like the fortified wines, I'll pour a port I bet you'll love. We don't usually pour the ports, but I have a smidge back here." Then she winked. I had lucked into the right company, that's for sure.

With Pat pouring only teaspoons of wine at a time, we worked our way down the wine list. Although I'd been worried about driving after the tasting, the samples were so small that I dropped my concern. I followed Bev's example at the tasting. First, I stuck my nose deep into the glass to smell the wine. Then I held the glass up to the light to check the color of the wine and swirled it to release more of its fragrance into the glass. Sniffed it again. All this before I even tasted it. When Bev took a sip of the wine, she kind of sucked in a breath of air with it and swished it around in her mouth. I couldn't quite figure out how she did that, and I decided not to try it in public for a while. With my luck, I'd start choking and cough wine down the front of my shirt.

But even in my own inexperienced way, I could taste that the wines were incredible. Hints of fruit, or slate, or citrus, or tobacco would explode in my mouth. It was like having a symphony unfold on top of my tongue. After trying five or six different wines, I stopped. I was on sensory overload. This was heaven, sipping new wines, talking with the pourer about notes of tropical fruit, oak, and grass while looking at a beautiful, shimmering lake, nestled in beds of grapevines. When the leaves were peaking in color as they were that day, the view made you feel like you were living inside a postcard.

While Bev and Pat talked about residual sugars, I drank some water and subtly swished it around my mouth to clear my palate. I glanced around the tasting room, taking in the light oak paneling, the shelves of wines, the customers, and the other pourers. I did a double-take and promptly decided that, as nice as Pat was, Bev and I had gotten the wrong pourer. On the far end of the room was a dark-haired, dark-eyed pourer with a golden tan—just my type. Think Tom Selleck or Colin Firth. Just my luck to be standing on the wrong end of the room. Drat. Resolutely I turned my back on Colin/Tom, and refocused on the wine conversation.

"Roz, did you want to try some of this port before I put it away?" Pat asked.

"You should. It's wonderful," Bev added, scribbling away on her wine list.

"Okay, sure, a little," I said.

Pat poured a thimbleful into my glass, but the port proved too strong for me, and it sent me into a coughing, snorting fit.

"Don't worry." Bev smiled as I hacked away. "It'll grow on you."

For now I decided to stay with the lighter whites. Bev reviewed her copy of the tasting menu, put together an assorted case, and gave Pat her marked-up list.

"You've still got your industry discount, Bev, right?" Pat asked.

"Sure do," Bev responded. She looked in my direction, where I was sipping water to recover from the port. "Can you do anything for my friend Roz here?"

Pat looked at me and winked. "Roz, when you go to check out, you tell the cashier that Pat said you could have the Friends and Family discount. That'll give you twenty percent off your wines today.

"Really?" I perked right up. "That's great, Pat! Thank you so much!" Twenty percent off? Why, maybe I could splurge on two bottles of wine instead of the one I'd originally budgeted to buy. Sweet!

Over the coming months, Bev, me, and Bev's discount would explore several of the local wineries. My first new acquaintance in the Finger Lakes (not counting Bob, that is) had turned out to be a lucky one. Fortunately, there are more than one hundred wineries in the Finger Lakes so Bev and I never risked running out of them.

Speaking of Bob, my glass of Royal Egret Semi-Dry Riesling in hand, I finally settled in to my dinner. And my dinner companion.

One of the benefits of being a business writer is that you get used to interviewing people and getting information out of them. Usually business executives are very forthcoming. They know what they want you to know, and they have no problem saying it. After years of working in corporate communications, I often thought I could get a tree stump to cough up information if I questioned it hard enough. So I wasn't really too worried about getting the scoop out of Bob.

"So, Bob, do you mind if I ask who you were when you were alive? I don't mean to get too personal but, after all, you are living in my house."

"Technically, I don't live here. I visit you . . . wherever you are. And, believe it or not, I don't remember my full identity from my body days. I remember 'Bob,' I remember being a writer of some sort, of always having people around, and some vague memories of motion pictures. As I said, things on the other side are pretty fuzzy. Just little bits and pieces of things. Nothing that would make a coherent answer."

I chewed another bite of salad. So far this interview, I mean conversation, was not going as planned. But I persevered.

"Do you remember what you did with motion pictures? By the way, we call them movies today. You said you wrote. Maybe you wrote movie scripts?"

"I really couldn't tell you. And I don't mean to frustrate

you. You can ask me any question you want, but I'm afraid, odds are, my honest answer will be, *I don't know*."

Unfortunately, at various stages of my life I've been in the same situation. You could ask me any question you wanted, and my honest answer would be, *I don't know*. I always found it a miserable place to be. It only happened when things were at their worst, when I'd lost a job or a marriage, and didn't know what I'd do next. All those transitions. I've always said, "Transitions are a bitch." I didn't like Bob's answers but I was starting, reluctantly, to understand them.

"I guess it makes sense, Bob. You probably are in a transitional stage, between life and death. Not a fun place to be."

"Don't over think it. It's not that bad, a little loosey-goosey, but so what? I just get to hang out. And once in a while, I help someone."

"What have you helped people with?"

"I'm not positive, but I think mostly I've tried to help them make a few changes, maybe not take life so seriously."

"Good luck with that, bub," I replied, stung. "We're wrestling with the Great Recession, with record unemployment and people losing their houses all over the place. Have fun selling a message of tra-la-fricking-la, life is wonderful. At least don't try selling it to me. Some days I think I'm hanging on by my fingernails here. If your only purpose is to be Jiminy Cricket, I don't think we're going to get too far. I've been taking care of myself for too long to be thinking that Prince Charming's going to come along so I can kick back, eat bonbons, read romance novels, and live happily ever after. I think you probably spent too much time writing movies in Hollywood, if that's the way you see things." I drew a shaky breath and took a long sip of wine.

"It looks to me like you do just fine on your own."

"I'm okay. I can mostly pay my bills for a few months, I

have a handful of people I love who genuinely love me, and I'm never bored. How many people can say that?"

"Sounds good to me." Bob looked around at my quiet, carton-filled house. "But don't you think you'll ever get lonely way out here? You might miss having a man around."

"Well, I'm human, so of course I'd like to have a guy around on a regular basis. But by the time you get to be my age most of the good guys are taken. My grandmother used to say, 'It takes a very good man to be better than none.' She was right. If I can't find a good guy, I'm not going to waste my time and energy on a fixer-upper. You know what they say about teaching a pig to sing."

"Huh?"

"You know, 'You can't teach a pig to sing. It wastes your time, and it annoys the pig.' I feel the same way about spending my time with an inappropriate man. I'm sure they're all fine, they just don't have what's right for me. I'm tired of pretending that underneath all the nuttiness, I'm not smart and competent. I just don't feel like putting on the 'Love me, oh, please, love me' song and dance routine anymore."

"Good one about the pig. I should jot that down."

"Feel free."

Thus began months of the strangest dinner conversations I could ever imagine. Topics ranged from the sex life of newts to the menace of buttered toast. We spent several days talking about Bob's bone dust theory (he believed the kind of person you were was determined by the amount of bone dust in your body). I started buying my semi-dry riesling by the case, and developed a taste for very dry martinis. Half of our dinners wound up with me yelling, throwing my hands in the air, and storming out of the kitchen. The other half ended with us laughing so hard tears streamed out of my eyes. What a blast.

Chapter 3
A Measured Life

Why would I even *think* about living by myself by the side of a lake? (Other than financial necessity, of course.) There were few jobs here, which meant few chances to improve my financial circumstances. My sister Angela says the Universe sends us the lessons we need to learn. But what could lakeside solitude possibly teach me?

All I can say is, I was born the oldest daughter (little Mother) in a very large, loud, boisterous Irish-Catholic family. I had to become a responsible, very grown up caretaker at a too-young age. That probably wouldn't be so awful if there were only one or two younger ones to be accountable for, but try to be eleven years old, with a tired, overworked mother and a dad at the office all day, and have six younger siblings to look after. By the time I was twelve, I could do the grocery shopping, cook dinner for nine, get my youngest brother down for his nap, wash laundry, pack lunches, and hem skirts. My baby sister started giving me Mother's Day cards before I hit adolescence. If you ever want a study in discomfort, try this: be a sixteen-year-old adolescent, miserable with blossoming hormones and uncomfortable in your own body, asked how to use a tampon by your thirteen-year-old sister who just made the swim team. I often say I raised my family when I was a teen. As an adult, I never had a strong desire to raise another—one was enough for me. Ever since I've had a choice, I've spent my life looking for peace and quiet.

People who don't come from large families romanticize them. I will say there were definitely fun times, like when we went to the beach every summer, or holidays. But there was always so much kid-clutter, and yelling, and pets, and meals to cook and clothes to wash. It was exhausting. Especially for a thirteen-year-old girl who wanted piano lessons (no money; no room for a piano) and dance lessons (no money) who, instead, got a younger brother or sister every year. The new and improved model, making me ever more obsolete, unnecessary and replaceable. It might be hard to believe, in this day of small families where most children are cherished, glistening works of art and self-confidence, but not so long ago, some people viewed children as commodities, indistinct and interchangeable parts. As a child, I thought caretaking was the only value I had. As a high school senior, I spent many sleepless nights worrying about whether my mother could cope with everything if I went off to college and left her to take care of her children.

No wonder I like solitude now. I've pared my life down to the caretaking basics—no spouses, children or pets, hardly any houseplants. Come the holidays, when I'm invited to someone's house, overflowing with food, loud people, screaming toddlers, and crotch-poking dogs, I still tend to get the heebee jeebies. It's just all too much. My working theory is that you can get Post Traumatic Stress Disorder when you raise a large family, especially if you're too young.

As far as my preoccupation with money—or the lack of it—goes, although it might sound contradictory, one of my favorite memories is of a Christmas when I was eleven or twelve. When I think of abundance, I think of that Christmas. I remember I got up in the middle of the night for some reason. The house was totally dark and quiet, except the living room where the tree twinkled and my mother snoozed on the sofa. She'd been doing guard duty since my youngest brother had a tendency to wake up and rip open all the wrapped presents.

I started up the stairs back to bed, looking at my sleeping Mom, the beautiful tree, and the glittering presents that filled up half of the living room floor. The beauty, the peace, the generosity of those gifts. To this day, when someone says the word *abundance*, the image of that living room on that long-ago Christmas Eve pops into my mind.

As a result of that abundance, though, my parents fought about credit card bills, loudly and often, for months, which probably explains where my carefulness and concern about money started. Few people are as vulnerable and scared as a child whose parents are yelling at each other. The more I write this, the more my solitary, money-preoccupied life on the shores of a lake starts to make sense to me. And my automatic default position of caretaking. If there's a warm body in the vicinity, I'll subconsciously figure out a way to take care of it, whether my solicitude is wanted or not. And, wow, is that a heck of a way to kill a marriage.

All these years later, try as I might, I still haven't totally escaped the instinct to take care of family. Which probably explains how my sociopathic cousin Terri slipped through the cracks.

Chapter 4
A Sociopath Comes to Stay?

"But why does she have to come here?"

Bob's question broke into my thoughts, bringing me back to the present. I looked down at the table, where remnants of my meatloaf dinner lay scattered. The busy leaf-peeping days of October had settled into the quiet, dark nights of late November.

"I told you, Bob, Terri's my cousin," I said, picking up the dropped thread of our conversation. "I've known her all my life, and now she's having some problems with her kids. One son's studying in Denmark, the other wants nothing to do with her."

"Where's her husband?"

"She's divorced, like me. That's why I invited her here. We divorcees have to watch out for each other. Terri's going to drive out from Chicago for a few days. I thought if she could take some long walks and spend some time looking at the water, it might help her get things in perspective. Besides, if she's here, she doesn't have to worry about Thanksgiving without her sons. We'll just go out or something. But I don't want you bugging her."

"I have no idea what you're talking about."

"You certainly do. I don't want any spooky stuff. Vases flying through the air, cold spots in the room, lights turning off and on, that kind of thing."

"Where do you get these ideas? I told you, I'm not one of those immature, thuggish ghosts who have to perform amateurish stunts to get attention," Bob said in an irritated tone. "That's the kind of malarkey you see on your TV shows. How about something with a little more polish, more sophistication? I could mix her a martini in mid-air, or hand her a towel when she steps out of the shower, something like that. Maybe even whisper sweet nothings in her ear as she's drifting off to sleep."

"Don't do anything! She's not going to be able to see you, is she?"

"No. I'm not a peep show, you know. How do you want to handle our daily conversations?"

I gnawed at my lower lip while I thought for a moment. "I guess we could chat for a few minutes at the end of the day in my bedroom. If I put the TV on, Terri won't hear anything." I'd enjoyed our daily dinner conversations over the past few weeks. When I wasn't thoroughly exasperated with him, Bob had the knack of keeping me in stitches. Like the time I'd told him about how the government was arguing with the tourist industry about how long lake trout fishing season should be. After I'd carefully laid out both the government and the tourist industry's positions, Bob pondered for a moment and then asked, "But has anyone ever considered this from the point of view of the trout?"

Or Bob's insistence on creative tax preparations. "They let you take deductions for depleted oil wells," he insisted, "so I deducted all the money I spent putting in a vegetable garden that failed."

"Bob, I'm no tax expert, but I'm pretty sure that's not allowed. You can go to jail for that sort of tax fraud."

"Too late!" Bob said, his tone smug. "Guess I put one over on the tax people!"

"Yeah, sure. All you had to do was die. Great tax strategy, Einstein!"

I'd never met anybody who looked at the world from Bob's stupid, nonsensical point of view. Frankly, it was refreshing. Refreshing, that is, when I wasn't ripping out my hair or yelling in frustration. Amazing how Bob couldn't remember his own name, but he could remember all the details of his tax dodges.

The next day, I met Terri at the gazebo in Southport's central square. Since I live way out in the back of beyond, it's handier to meet people in civilization and then escort them to the boonies. Less chance of Donner-party company that way. Even though the leaves had faded and fallen, it was a lovely drive. The lake shimmered a vibrant blue in the crisp sunshine and now that the trees were bare, you could actually see the houses that were usually hidden by them. An unexpected benefit of winters at the lake.

One of my favorite aspects of late autumn, once the leaves have fallen, is observing my neighbors on the other side of the lake. They are only about three-quarters of a mile away, but the water gives them distance and an interesting perspective. I could make out the houses with a moderate level of particulars: cars driving along the lower lake road, sheets flapping on a clothesline, people moving around in brightly colored coats, the flashing lights of fire engines, etc., but I couldn't see any detail. I could hear the occasional hunter shooting a gun, or an axe cutting wood, but no conversations. It was like having my own personal animated diorama of country life on the shores of a lake.

Terri loved my place. "It's so gorgeous, Roz. I never even heard of Crooked Lake until you invited me here. And Katie has a place just down the road? What a perfect arrangement. You're so lucky . . . I envy you all of this!"

You don't know me very well, so I'll just tell you flat out that few things set my teeth on edge as much as being told I'm lucky. This irritation started when I was in graduate school. I'd been working on my studies and master's thesis sixteen hours a day, living at the library, and only coming up for air to eat, sleep, and take the occasional hour off for an end-of-an-exhausting-day beer with friends. One day I ran into Sheila, a friend of a friend who had wandered through graduate school for three years, changing majors every six months, and spending much of her time in deep conversations about the meaning of life with other academic drifters. I happened to mention that I was on target to finish my MA at the end of the year, and she wistfully observed that I was "so lucky" to be wrapping up on time. Lucky? After a year of doing nothing but work my ass off? I don't think so. And I've reacted to the phrase the same way ever since.

Don't get me wrong. I do think I'm one of the luckiest people I know. I was born in the USA, with good health and a good brain. Those three gifts make me luckier than ninety-five percent of the world's population, and I'm aware of that every day. I do, however, continue to have a major problem with people who confuse long-term, ridiculously hard work with luck.

I got Terri settled into the guest room. Fresh linens, fresh towels, fresh flowers—every amenity I could think of. Mom's pork chops and sauerkraut were waiting in the refrigerator to be heated for dinner, with homemade bread and applesauce. Never let it be said that a Murphy did not go all out for a guest. As my dad once said, "Roz runs the best bed and breakfast in the Finger Lakes."

Terri is about twenty years older than I am. A Brillo-haired blonde, freckle-faced, stocky, and who wears those ergonomic sandals that look as if they'd been cobbled by cavemen. She had a large goiter that stuck out of her neck horizontally.

The goiter surprised me because, as we'd grown up, Terri and her family had been very into appearances. We'd occasionally visit their house in a prosperous Philadelphia suburb, and its many rooms were full of antiques and beautifully upholstered furniture. Terri's dad collected antique cars and guns, and her mom was always talking about their cleaning lady and her membership in the Daughters of the American Revolution. In contrast, my dad was second-generation Irish and an engineer. Although my family was comfortable, we never had the kind of money to splash around that Terri did. Our house growing up was upholstered in kids and their stuff.

After Terri freshened up and unpacked, she came downstairs and we settled in for a drink and a chat. Just as we were working through the traditional topics and getting caught up, Katie called. I put her on speakerphone.

"So how was your trip?" Katie asked Terri.

"A beautiful drive. I can't get over how lovely it is out here. You and Roz are so lucky to live here."

I ground my teeth while I freshened our drinks.

"Have you seen our place yet?" Katie asked. "It's just down the road. Roz, you're going to have to show it to Terri while she's there. In fact, Terri, if you want to stay there for a few days sometime, consider the place your own. We don't have any central heating in the cabin, so you'd want to avoid the coldest part of the winter. Even though there are a couple of oil heaters, they'll only take the edge off the cold. I know it's not much of a time frame, but I wanted to offer it to you, in case you fell in love with the lake like Bill and I have."

"Aren't you the sweetest thing!" Terri cooed. "I may just take you up on your offer. I'll get your email address from Roz and get in touch after the weekend. So Roz tells me your daughter headed off for college a few weeks ago. It's such a tough time, isn't it? I bawled for days after my son went off to Tulsa."

"It sure is a change." Katie's voice echoed tinnily from the speakerphone. "But Amy was so excited and ready to move on to college, we couldn't help but be happy for her. And she loves her classes, so it's all good."

I checked the pork chops and sauerkraut on the stove, and Katie must have heard the pot clang, because the next thing she said was, "Roz, did I catch you two getting ready for dinner?"

"I'm putting the finishing touches on some of Mom's pork chops and sauerkraut. No problem," I said.

"I just heard Bill pull into the garage, so I need to get going anyway. Terri, I'll look for an email from you after your nice long weekend. Have a great Thanksgiving, you two!"

We chorused our farewells, and cut off the cell phone. After I put dinner on the table, Terri and I started eating, and then we moved on to one of the oddest conversations I've ever had in my life. I'd never talked with anyone before who so consistently saw herself as either the heroine, or the victim, of every encounter in her life. She was never just hanging out, never just there.

"Too bad you didn't have a chance to go to Aunt Denise's second wedding," Terri said. "I'm glad I was able to help her. Nothing was ready when I got there so I jumped in to handle things and got the caterers organized, helped her with the flowers, and helped her get dressed."

"No one was there? Where were her kids? She's got four of them."

"Well, the kids were around, but they just weren't focused on Denise. Thank goodness she had me."

I know Denise's children and they are, overall, good sorts. I couldn't see them ignoring their mother when she remarried ten years after their dad's death. Odd. But then again, Terri had been there and I hadn't.

We spent a few minutes chewing over our college years. Terri had gone to an all-female college in the south. Most Friday nights the school would send a bus full of women to a dance or sporting event at the nearby men's college. "Mom would never send me enough money so I could dress as well as my friends," Terri complained, forty years after the fact. "I never had the right clothes or as much spending money as everyone else."

All I could think about while Terri was whining was why couldn't she have gotten a job while she was in college? That would have helped with her expenses. I broached the subject and immediately got shot down. "Oh, I couldn't have done that. Nobody I hung out with worked. Mom should've just sent me more money. She had plenty."

Odd. Most of the people I knew had some kind of job or another while they were in college, including me. I never thought it hurt me to work while I was in school. On the contrary, it always seemed to me that the harder you worked for something, the more you appreciated it when you finally achieved it. As Tommy Paine once said, "It is dearness that gives everything its value."

During our college conversation, I made the mistake of mentioning that I'd had a chunk of my schooling paid for by two scholarships I'd won.

Terri squinted at me. "*Two* scholarships? I had no idea. That's interesting. We never heard in the family that you were smart."

Ouch! Of course they wouldn't have heard. My parents weren't braggarts and certainly would not have called up Terri's parents just to boast about their kids. Was it just me, or was this some kind of passive-aggressive thing? Maybe I was starting to become rusty with my social skills?

"Funny that our paths never crossed when we both worked in Manhattan," Terri continued. "Especially considering we were both doing the same kind of corporate communication work. I had so many problems with it, though. I could hardly move without some kind of sexual harassment situation happening. How about you?" Terri glanced at me, at my could-afford-to-lose-ten-pounds thighs. "Well, maybe you never had that problem."

Sheesh. Definitely passive-aggressive.

"No, I never had that problem because I worked with a bunch of decent people."

Say what you will about accountants and engineers. You might think they're mechanical, they're repressed, or they're not party animals. On the contrary, though, I mostly found them to be hard working, honest, smart, decent sorts. If I can find those qualities in my coworkers, I'm pretty content. Terri worked in a different kind of environment, though. Advertising. I don't think the fact that she relied on flirtation to get her through every business situation helped, though. (Oh, dear. Was that catty?)

After a couple hours of these passive-aggressive, two-track conversations, I literally had a splitting headache. I'd never had a headache like that before. It was as if my mind tried to hear how Terri saw the world and simultaneously translated it into a way of understanding the world that made sense to me. I felt as if I'd been axed right through the middle of my brain.

I decided to go to bed while Terri settled in for some late-night TV. She always brewed a pot of coffee to keep her company while watching, so I showed her where everything was and headed upstairs.

Without thinking, I locked the bedroom door to keep the ghosts out. Yeah, right. Said ghost was comfortably ensconced in my favorite easy chair, so I turned on the TV low to cover our voices. Two martinis sat crowded among the hand lotion and books on my nightstand.

Bob picked up one and handed it to me. "You've earned this."

"You know, I think I have. Is it just me, or is she a tough customer?"

"You're being too kind. She's snooty, pompous, stuck-up. I can think of a million unflattering things to call her."

"Yeah, she is kind of a witch. Kind of a passive-aggressive witch."

"Witch? Well, I pronounce it differently, but I think you've hit the nail on the head."

"Bob, how can this be? Terri's family! How can she be so awful? I grew up thinking that family stuck together and helped each other out. Right now, I can't even imagine how I'm going to put up with her for the next three days. I'm her hostess . . . I can't just boot her out. I need to remember that she's going through a tough time with her son. I've got to try to cut her some slack."

"Cut *her* some slack? If tonight is any indication, I think you should send her son a sympathy bouquet for years of putting up with her. What a nasty piece of work."

"So it wasn't just me? She's really as awful as I think she is?"

"Let's just put it this way. I think the next three days are going to be hellacious for everyone around here. And I don't even have to talk to her."

Bob was right. Again. Those next three days were awful. Maybe I was naïve, but I had been brought up being taught that you give guests your best—your best room, your best food and drink, your best efforts to keep them entertained and happy. And in return, they're thoughtful and kind and on their best behavior. Maybe that's where this all went wrong.

Take, for instance, Thanksgiving dinner. With the recent move and everything else going on, I wasn't up to doing a full-blown classic holiday feast. Besides, it was silly to go to all that work for just two people. Instead, Terri and I had agreed that we'd have dinner at a local restaurant, my treat.

Most of the restaurants in my immediate vicinity are perfectly adequate, but they'll never make it to four stars in the review guides. They offer filling and tasty meals, but certainly not gastronomically inspired ones. Throughout my life, I've wandered in and out of being a food snob, usually depending on my income. Right now, all things considered, filling and tasty worked just fine for me. At least the Country Café served real turkey breast, not turkey log.

Country Café lived up to its name, with lots of farmhouse antiques scattered throughout its three dining rooms. True, there was a little bit of dust in the corners, but the dinginess felt cozy and lived in, more like you were having dinner at Grandma's house than in a restaurant. Toy trains and wooden odds and ends decorated high shelves. Irma showed us to our table by the fireplace.

Terri looked around. "Isn't this special! Do you come here often, Roz?"

"Oh, maybe about once a month. Sometimes I get so tired of my own cooking that I just need a change. Irma's owned this place for decades. When I was here over the summer on one of my house-hunting trips, it was packed with customers. I've heard that people drive out from Buffalo for her homemade marinara sauce."

"Is it any good?"

"I thought it was very good when I had it, but today I'm sticking with the Thanksgiving usual. I haven't had turkey here, but I'm sure it will be delicious."

Terri rubbed a water stain off her butter knife and commented, a little dubiously, "If you say so."

Our meal *was* good. Maybe the turkey tasted a little dry and the mashed potatoes a little leaden, but what would Thanksgiving be without slightly dry turkey and slightly heavy potatoes? Irma brought us, on the house, some pumpkin pie with vanilla ice cream, which made up for a number of gastronomic sins.

While eating, Terri and I chatted about great holiday

meals from our pasts. My mom had been an excellent cook, pulling off holiday meals for twenty without even breathing hard. At least, I thought those meals were effortless; it was only when I started cooking myself that I realized how much planning and organization went into these multi-generation, multi-course family feasts. Turkey *and* ham for Christmas; ham *and* lamb for Easter. When I was in my early twenties, I went into the kitchen one Easter morning and found my mom, all four burners going on the stove, dropping little slips of paper into the empty serving bowls on the counter. On the papers were written words like *peas*, *applesauce*, *olives and celery*, and *potatoes*.

I looked at Mom, puzzled.

"Well," she replied to my unspoken question, "I have to make sure I put the right food into the right dish, or I'll run out of serving bowls." Only then did I start to get a glimmer of how much work these meals were for her.

Terri's memorable family meals were very different from mine. Everyone dressed like a holiday TV commercial. Dishes with French names were served by the housekeeper. People sat on their own chair in their formal, beautifully decorated dining room. (Since there were so many kids in my family, we sat on long benches positioned on either side of the rectangular dining table. These benches made for a lot of fun when too many kids would jump off the bench on one end during dinner. Imagine having two teeter-totters in your dining room during a raucous, crowded holiday dinner and you'll get the gist.)

Overall, Terri and I had a nice time remembering holidays past. When the bill came, I reminded her that this was my treat.

"Thanks, Roz! That meal was so interesting . . . and so cheap! What a find!"

Talk about a backhanded compliment. "You're welcome," I replied.

That night, I debriefed Bob over bedroom martinis while the TV burbled in the background. It felt good to see a friendly face at the end of the day.

"Under other circumstances, this could get kind of romantic here in the bedroom with these martinis and everything," Bob drawled.

"One or two major drawbacks, though," I responded. "Like . . . ummm . . . you have no *body*. Women these days talk about falling in love with unavailable men. You could be the poster child for that. Married, committed to someone else, unable to commit, or . . . a *ghost!* Bob, I'd be a fool to allow even a hint of romance here. I've been called a lot of things in my life, but *fool* is not usually high on that list. Let's get realistic here. This situation is confusing enough as it is, let's not make it any crazier."

Bob threw up his hands. "I surrender, Roz! Jeepers, I was just kidding. You have all the patience of a boiling teakettle these days."

I sighed. "Sorry. Having Terri here has set my teeth on edge. I can't keep my balance with her. Every time I feel like we're starting to understand each other, she pulls the rug out from under me. It blindsides me. Katie was smart to invite Terri to her lake house when she wasn't going to be there to put up with her."

"If it's any consolation, I turned the heater off under her pot of coffee before I came up here."

"You what?"

"Turned off her coffee. You told me not to bug her, but I thought there might be a little leeway in that request now."

"Oh, Bob. How childish." I started to giggle. I couldn't help it. Then Bob joined in, and we laughed uproariously. We couldn't stop. Every time we tried, we'd catch each other's eye and set off again, furiously trying to shush each other.

Inevitably, the knock came at the bedroom door. The

futile turning of the knob. Bob popped out, and I shuffled to the door, wiping tears of laughter from my eyes.

"You lock your bedroom door?" Terri stared at me. "Roz, are you okay? I heard all these noises. Have you been crying?" Terri's gaze darted around the room, settling on the two half-empty martini glasses. "What is going on here? Roz, are those your martinis? Both of them?"

Caught red-handed. What could I say? "I like a little drink before I turn in." I tried to hold in the hiccup, but it burst out.

"Hmm. A little drink. Right." Terri shot me a gimlet eye, checked out the martini glasses again, snorted, and headed back downstairs. I could hear her mutter, "A little drink. Right." Then a few minutes later, "Hey, what happened to the coffee?"

The next morning, after a markedly uncomfortable breakfast, Terri and I decided to head for the Corning Museum of Glass. About an hour away, it's a marvelous place, full of historical pieces of glass, with an area where you can create your own glass masterpiece. For a couple of hours we wandered through the museum, and then we decided to split up for an hour to check out individual interests and visit the gift shop.

I had a great time and then headed back to our rendezvous point. And waited. Tried her cell phone. It was off. And waited. Left another message on her cell phone. After I'd waited for about forty-five minutes, I started to get worried about Terri having a heart attack, or passing out behind a glass sculpture somewhere. After an hour of waiting, I started looking for a location where I could have her paged, to make sure she was still in the museum and okay.

About that time Terri wandered up to me, laden with packages from the gift shop.

"Terri, what happened to you? I was worried!"

"What do you mean, what happened?"

"You're an hour late. I thought you'd had a heart attack or something."

"For pity's sake, Roz! I just needed more time to see everything and get my shopping done. No need to get so dramatic! We still have plenty of time."

I felt like she'd slapped me. No apology, no embarrassment at worrying me, or keeping me cooling my heels for an hour. What kind of person was this? Maybe I was a little oversensitive, but I had been raised to be on time unless some kind of emergency came up. Such a little thing, I guess, but still, to me, kind of shocking.

The drive home was difficult. Ticked, I stayed focused on the interstate while Terri babbled and showed me all the things she'd bought for herself. She'd purchased some lovely items, but since I was driving, I couldn't focus on them. I wanted to tell her how rude and thoughtless she was, but I kept biting my tongue, because she was my guest.

That night, after a rushed dinner, we drove to Geneva for a dance show at the Smith Opera House. It followed the history of popular songs and dances over the past fifty years, from Elvis and Beatles, pop to disco, and Lady Gaga. We enjoyed the performance, and the Smith Opera House alone would have been worth the trip. A refurbished art deco masterpiece, it sits right in the middle of downtown Geneva, home to Hobart and William Smith College, a private institution that now costs more than Harvard, if rumors are true. As always, the drive was Christmas-card lovely: farm houses, barns, cropped fields fallow until spring.

By the time we got home, I was tired. All this socializing, and challenging socializing to boot, had exhausted me. I had started to get out of the habit of people and didn't have a lot of stamina for the delicate social demands of constant civility.

I left Terri to her pot of coffee (of which, it turns out, she only drinks a cup and leaves the rest to go to waste overnight. But she likes to have the full pot there, "just in case." Wastefulness . . . another thing that makes me bonkers.) (At the end of this book I'm going to have to make a list of all the foibles and frailties I've revealed to the world. Then I'll probably take to my bed with a cool cloth on my forehead for the shame of it.)

When I got to my bedroom, Bob didn't appear for our daily debriefing. In his place, he'd left a silent tribute to the awfulness of my day—two very dry martinis on the nightstand. Excellent! I slept like the dead.

Finally, Sunday arrived, Terri's last day at my place. Hurray, hurray, hurray! A leisurely breakfast, an hour with the newspaper, and then she'd be on her way. I made a baked French toast casserole (yum) and served it with fresh grapefruit juice. Only the best for my guests, especially nasty ones when they're on their way *out the door!*

The morning inched along, not as quickly as I would have liked, but it moved. After breakfast, we took our coffee out on the deck overlooking the lake. Although it was chilly, the lake was bouncing and sparkling in the sunshine, little wavelets fripping along. I'm mentally chanting, *one more hour, one more hour*, when Terri brings up the unthinkable: She might like to move to the lake.

What? What! my mind screamed. Yet out of my mouth came the polite hostess words, "Well, that's an interesting thought. How would you go about it?"

Terri launched into an obviously well thought out litany. "I've been thinking of moving out of my place in Chicago, and this area seems to be a lot cheaper. I could rent a room somewhere, and maybe get a job at the glass museum as a guide or something. I'm sure I must know someone who's affiliated with it, and they could put in a good word for me."

I kept my tone civil and refrained from using any of the words bouncing around my brain. "Where would you rent a room? They're pretty inexpensive in Avondale or Southport."

"Oh, no. I'd want to get a place here on the lake." Terri turned from me to study the landscape in front of her.

"Whereabouts on the lake? Lakeside can be pretty pricey."

"I like it best right about here," she said, and smiled with all of the sincerity of Hannibal Lecter.

There it was. The unavoidable hint. I could have a full-time tenant to help with expenses. To rebuild my faltering bank account, waste all my coffee, and make me crazy. Years of social training to support family came screaming into a brick wall. Training: *You have to help family. Family sticks together. Blood is thicker than water.* Brick Wall: *No. Noooooo. Noooooooooooooooooo!*

I turned toward the water, took a sip of coffee, and said, "Hmm."

An image came to me. Of Terri living in my house. Nicely, with all the right words, gradually taking up more and more space, while I got squished into a little corner. My sisters would be gently alienated. I'd become dependent. After years of mild acid persuasion I'd get my mind washed about how her living here had saved me, had kept me from getting nutty living on my own on the shores of my lake. One day, under the influence of the incessant drippy water torture of persuasion, I'd make her the beneficiary of my will. The next week I'd have an unfortunate accident and Terri would get the house of her dreams.

Wow!

I don't usually pay too much attention to messages from my subconscious, but how could I ignore this one screaming up from the depths at me, however crazy and paranoid it might seem? Every fiber of my being told me to stay away from this woman, that she was toxic for me. I might, indeed, be crazy, but my usually quiet instincts were yelling at me that morning. And so, for a change, I listened to them.

"Well, good luck with your hunt for a rental on the lake," I said. "If I hear of anything promising," and I could pretty much guarantee I wouldn't, "I'll pass it along."

Terri gave me a long look. Then she turned and stared, stone faced, at the lake. Check and mate.

Chapter 5
Bob and Time Management

Four days with Terri had fried out my circuits, and it took me a couple of days of eating cheese curls and watching TV to get readjusted after her visit. Let's just gloss over that down time. By Wednesday, I was behind in practically everything. Bills unpaid, no groceries, unwashed laundry, sticky floors, phone calls owed to everyone. Not to mention I was overdue for rebalancing my miniscule retirement portfolio, getting someone to listen to the weird rumble in the car when I started it up, and making my holiday date-nut loaves in time to get them in the mail for various sisterly tree-trimming festivities. Oh, and I had to write a chunky national Community Chest campaign progress report for my biggest client.

It never ceases to amaze me that people think when you live alone you have tons of extra time to do stuff. It's just the opposite. With couples, usually one person takes care of the house, and the other takes care of the car and the yard. Or someone cooks dinner and washes clothes, and someone else pays bills and paints the trim. There's a division of labor. When you live on your own, though, one person does *all* that stuff so, in fact, you have *less* time than most couples. There's no division of labor. You get to do it all yourself. But, on the other hand, I do get to have cereal for dinner when I'm just not in the mood to cook, so I suppose that's one benefit of living alone. And I don't have to negotiate with anyone on how I'm going to spend my money, which is another benefit.

But I digress.

Wednesday morning, my anxiety about how I was going to get all of my work and chores done aggravated me so much I got up at six. Not sure how I'd handle the day, I still realized it was time to get a grip on things. Coffee in hand, I started jotting down a half-hearted to-do list while I stared out the window at the sleeping lake and darkened shore opposite.

Bob popped in. He looked obnoxiously awake and as peppy as he ever looks, which is to say not very.

"What are you doing up at this hour? I'm shocked to see you, since you've spent the past two days lying on the sofa stuffing cheese curls in your mouth."

"Yeah, well, vacation's over. I've got a bunch of things I have to take care of, and I can't afford any more downtime. I need to get going."

"Where?"

I gave Bob the highlights of my list.

"Jeepers, all those jobs will keep you off the streets for a while. What's first?"

"I guess I should start with the Community Chest status report. I can bill for my time on that, and I've got to keep some money coming in. I just have a hard time focusing on writing when the laundry and bills are behind. Especially if my kitchen floor is sticky. But that's the way we're taught to manage time in business school these days. Do the big important things first, no matter how much you don't want to do them, and squeeze in the less important chores around them. I saw a video with a guy who had a bucket, some big rocks, some pebbles, and a lot of sand once that explained the whole thing. If you put in the sand first, the little chores, there's not enough room left for the big rocks, the important chores. So you put in the big rocks first, then the pebbles, and then dump the sand in and it all fits in around the big rocks. You get everything done that way. Or at least that's what the video said."

"You must be out of your mind. I never heard such a cockamamie idea. That's the kind of craziness they teach in business schools these days? No wonder people pay good money to exercise with machines and then pay more money for others to do their chores. You're going about it all wrong. I have my own no-fail formula for getting things done."

"Yeah? What's that?"

"Exactly the opposite of yours. Don't do those reports first. You let those deadlines loom over your head, making you so guilty about ignoring them that you keep yourself busy doing everything else on your list so you don't have time to think about those screwed-up deadlines."

"Oh, for Pete's sake."

"I'm serious. Just jump in on the laundry, make out your grocery list. All the while you'll know you really should be working on those reports and you'll get tons of sublimated energy from your panic in avoiding them."

What the heck, I was so behind in everything at this point, what did one day's difference make? (Actually, in business, and meeting business deadlines, you and I both know one day can mean a *lot*. But it was very early in the morning, and I guess I wasn't thinking clearly with all those cheese curls in my system.)

So I started. First the laundry, because while the laundry was going I could make the grocery list. People with fancy business degrees call it multi-tasking. Around the house, I call it 'being productive.' Shows what a difference an MBA can make.

Sometimes I juggle so many things while I'm multi-tasking that I forget where the whole chain started. Those are the times I find myself striding purposefully into the kitchen and then staring blankly around because I've completely forgotten what I went in there to do. The more I multitask, the more I forget what I'm doing, which probably completely defeats the purpose.

So that morning I got the laundry sorted and started, did an inventory of food in the fridge and cabinets, and used those supplies, plus the Sunday paper's grocery ads, to plan my menus. Then I made out my shopping list. I wish I could say making a grocery list was a simple and straightforward process for me, but it's not. Especially since I'm trying to save money and not waste food. Wouldn't it be wonderful to just sit down and think about what you'd like to eat and then go buy it and cook it? Even better, just go to a restaurant and eat it? Maybe in my next life.

I added all of the ingredients for my holiday date-nut loaves to the grocery list, which was getting pretty substantial. While I organized the shopping list by store layout (dairy, meat, produce—yes, I can see the words *compulsive* and *over organized* hovering in a big balloon over my head), the washer beeped, so I moved that load into the dryer and started another load. Then I tackled the bills.

After twenty minutes, I decided to stop working on the bills and, instead, give the kitchen floor a quick once-over so it could dry while I did the grocery shopping. So far, I was pretty impressed with how much I was getting done, although that Community Chest deadline always lurked in the back of my mind. It felt like a big bubble of pressure in my chest that I kept punching down, like a bowl of rising bread dough.

As I moved productively, some might say frenetically, through my morning, I'd occasionally notice Bob hovering in the background. At first, he wore a cheek-to-cheek smile, observing his theory being put into action. After a few hours, though, I noticed a little crease in his forehead.

"Why don't you sit down and take a break for a few minutes?" he asked at about ten o'clock.

"No, not yet. Once I sit down and relax, I'll lose all of my momentum, and I'll just have to crank it all up again later. It's easier to just keep going. After I do the grocery shopping I'll relax over lunch."

"I suppose that's okay. Look, when I told you my theory for getting things done, I didn't expect that you'd try to do everything in one morning. Usually I'd spread things out over a few days, with lots of naps in between. You'll make yourself sick if you keep going at this pace."

"I might get sick, but at least everything will be clean and tidy when I do. One of my personal mottoes is: If something's worth doing, it's worth overdoing. Okay, I'll see you in an hour or two. I'm going to run to the store while the kitchen floor is drying."

Still moving in high gear, I zipped the ten miles to the grocery store. Running up and down aisles, I filled up the cart. I even broke down and bought myself a TV dinner for lunch, so I wouldn't need to take the time to put something together at home.

Groceries frustrated me. Since I was trying to be thrifty, I'd buy mostly fresh ingredients, like whole carrots, a raw chicken, and hamburger. So that meant that after all that planning and shopping for food, there'd be virtually nothing to just sit and eat. Sure, there were *tons* of food to cook and prepare into meals but, after hours of making lists, planning menus, clipping coupons, shopping, lugging sacks of groceries in from the car, and putting them away, there was nothing to *eat*. Sheesh. But at least I'd thought to pick up that frozen lasagna. God bless TV dinners.

Around two, just as I was lugging the last bag of food into the kitchen, Bob shimmered in.

"Hey, Bob, are you any good at putting groceries away?"

"Probably, but I don't know where anything goes."

"I have a feeling we've had this conversation before. Remind me to draw you a map of my house and put you to work one of these days."

"You don't need anyone else to get work done around here. At the rate you're going, you could build a house in a day," he said in a worried tone.

"I'm starting to wear down. I'm not as young as I used to be. I'll get the refrigerator stuff put away while my lunch is nuking and then take a few minutes. After lunch I'll clean up the rest of this mess."

A plastic tub of hot lasagna in one hand, coffee in the other, I sat at the table and surveyed my domain. If it's always darkest before the dawn, my house looked like a metaphorical four a.m. Bags of canned goods lined the counters; a haphazard pile of bills and paperwork squatted at the far end of the table; furniture was strewn around the living room waiting to be brought back onto the newly washed kitchen floor. Rattan baskets of laundry in various stages of unwash or unfold were everywhere. It was a mini-version of my frosting theory, with four different projects at their messiest, about ten percent away from being done.

A totally maddening situation for this compulsive little overachiever, especially since I was exhausted from going full-throttle since six a.m. I'd be a lot smarter to start just one thing and finish it, but somehow that's never been how my life works. Just as I finished eating the lasagna, the phone rang. And who should it be but Tess, my Ohio client. Of course.

"Hey, Tess, how nice to hear from you. How's everything going?"

"Oh, Roz, crazy as usual. I just got a phone call from the CEOs office. You know that progress report you were going to have for me next Monday?"

"Sure." My stomach started to ache a little.

"Turns out the CEO needs to have it Friday afternoon so he can spend some time with it over the weekend before his meetings on Monday. I want to review it before I hand it in to him. Do you think you could *possibly* have it to me by close-of-business tomorrow?"

Again, the screaming voice from my subconscious. *Tomorrow? Good Lord, that's a twenty-hour project, and Tess wants it in twenty-four hours? With me up since six a.m. and going at warp speed for the past eight hours? And my house a wreck?* Some of those McGregor-blenching words came to mind, but of course, I'd never say them to my biggest client.

"Well, Tess, that is kind of a crunch, but it's partially done *(lie)*, so I'm sure I can pull it together *(lie)*, and email it to you by late tomorrow. Sure, no problem *(lie)*."

"Roz, you're the best. I always know I can count on you. I'll look for the report tomorrow."

I hung up the phone, stunned. Sort of. When you're a glass-half-empty kind of person, there's always a back corner of your brain, like a feral cat, watching out for these SNAFUs. Through sheer necessity, I try to think of these episodes as adventures but honestly, today I was adventured out.

"That Tess doesn't have the best sense of timing in the world," my resident master of understatement said as he shimmered into his usual place by the kitchen cabinets.

"No, it's my fault. I should have known. These kinds of things always happen in business. I could have spent the past eight hours chipping away at that project, but instead I've been wasting my time on chores that could have waited. If I can't pay my bills, it doesn't matter how clean my floor is."

"I think you're being too hard on yourself," Bob protested. "You're allowed to want clean clothes and a washed floor. You didn't fail. Tess moved the goalposts on you."

"Yeah, well, clients move the goalposts on me all the time. I should have predicted Tess would, and started in on that report this morning. As it is, I'll be up most of the night, and I can't even stand to look at this place. It's such a mess."

"I'm sorry you're in this situation. I'd help if I could, but I don't know anything about Community Chests."

"No, Bob, it's my own fault. I know my business, I know how it works. I don't know what got into me this morning that made me screw things up so badly. Must be those cheese curls, huh?" I smiled weakly.

"I think maybe you just wanted a little control over your own life, that's all."

"I should have known better. When you're a freelancer, you have no control. Look, Bob, I'm really going to have to focus on this deadline if I'm going to pull it off, so please just leave me alone for a while."

Bob faded out. I poured myself a big mug of coffee, took a long look at my wreck of a home, and headed upstairs to my computer.

The next eleven hours weren't pretty. I pored over Community Chest campaign reports from the company's thirty offices from Lumpock, California, to little Haverhill, New Hampshire, teasing out successful techniques and results, synthesizing unifying conclusions. By three in the morning, I'd drafted the full report, complete with colored graphs and bulleted summary talking points for the CEO. Too tired to do any more, I dragged myself to bed for a few hours of sleep.

At seven Thursday morning, after a strong shower and a stronger cup of coffee, I started editing and refining the draft, reorganizing for maximum impact and polishing the verbiage. As I said, writing is a solitary craft, just you and the words, sorting, sifting, juggling them for weight and effect. Incredible to think that companies will pay for you to weigh and measure these little assortments of the same twenty-six letters. Phenomenal to think that little collections of these same letters have built empires and brands, and destroyed lives and governments. Usually by the time I start thinking along these lines I know I'm way overtired, and it's time to say goodbye to my project.

After a final read-through, I emailed the report off to Ohio. On time. Chalk up one for the good guys. This is the toughest part of being a writer in a new location. Goal met, deadline achieved, but no celebration. No going out for a drink with the team. No sending out for a late night pizza with the coworkers. No hugs at home from the hubby. Right about now, I'd usually remind myself that every job has its drawbacks. With luck, tomorrow I'd get a complimentary email or phone call from Tess—she was a great client that way, one of the reasons I bent over backwards to keep her happy. Once I'd heard from her, I'd allow myself to sit down, make out my bill, and email it along. Now there's my favorite part of a job.

Even though it was only four-thirty, I decided to have a glass of wine. After a few minutes, I looked up from my winey meditations and there was Bob. Good old Bob. Good old misguided Bob.

"Hey. Great time management theory you've got there, Bob."

He looked a little pink around the edges. Embarrassment, probably. "Now that I think about it, I seem to remember that meeting deadlines was never my strong suit. But I did get a lot of interesting projects done along the way."

"I'll just bet you did. One of these days you'll have to tell me all about them. Right now I'm about ready to call it a day."

"No dinner?"

"Nah. I'll have some cheese and crackers with my wine and head upstairs. It's been a long day."

"Did the report turn out okay?"

"Yeah, I think Tess will be happy with it."

"Mind if I ask a question?"

"Shoot."

"How come you didn't tell Tess that you couldn't meet her new deadline? That her timeframe was unreasonable?"

I thought about Bob's questions for a minute, and then tried to explain my freelance world. "You can't tell bosses they're unreasonable in my business and expect to make a living. What the boss wants is always do-able. It may be borderline impossible, but it's always do-able. Frankly, that's why businesses pay me so well. Because even when their deadlines are crazy, I can still pull a rabbit out of the hat."

"I know you can, but why should you have to?"

"Because even though I'm very good, I'm replaceable. I know that, and they know that. I don't like to think that I'm a professional commodity, but I am. I have to keep meeting these crazy deadlines because I don't want them to start looking around for my replacement."

"Maybe you don't give yourself enough credit. I think you're very talented, and hard working."

Bob's words touched me, but I remained resolute. "I think I'm very hard working and talented, too. But I think there are a lot of very hard working, talented people out there, and we're all fighting for a limited number of jobs. Or then again, maybe I've been a freelance writer too long."

"Could you have pushed the deadline back to Friday morning? Tess would still have had the day to look at it, and you would have been able to get a little more sleep in the process."

"I thought about that. But when I have a client, I try to do more than just get the job done. I want to delight them. If I'd asked for a Friday morning deadline, that might have gotten the job done. But would it have delighted Tess? I don't think so. She likes to start chewing on a project at night. So I lose a few hours of sleep to keep her happy and to make her think I'm amazing. I can live with that."

Tired, I took another sip of wine and studied Bob. He did not look like a happy ghost.

"All these hours take a lot out of you, though, and she might be willing to negotiate timeframes. Maybe you're making things too hard on yourself?"

"Look, Bob." I had to admire the dogged way he pursued this discussion, even though I wished he'd let it drop. "I realized years ago that the only way to guarantee I could make money as a freelancer was to accept the fact that I'd have to be willing to do things others wouldn't, like meet ridiculous deadlines."

Bob's brows drew together. "But you won't always be able to do that, though. At some point you won't be able to work through the night. What then?"

I shrugged. "I'll deal with that when the time comes. By then, who knows? This damned recession might be over and I'll find myself a regular nine-to-five job. Right now I'm just doing whatever I have to do to keep a roof over my head and food on the table."

"Couldn't you write books? That way you'd still be writing, but you wouldn't be killing yourself to meet stupid deadlines."

"Yeah, and that way I wouldn't be able to pay my bills, either. I'd have no deadlines, and I'd have no money. In case you haven't noticed, I like to try to pay my bills. Besides, what would I talk about in a book? My quiet little writer's life here on the lake? Who the heck would pay money to read about that?"

"I would," Bob said softly, "if I had money."

"Yeah, well, you'd be an audience of one, then. I can't take the chance. I don't trust my luck enough to send a book out into the Universe and hope that it will take care of me.

Momma Murphy didn't raise no fools. My job is to take care of things, to pay bills, and you can't pay bills if you're an *artiste*."

For once Bob was mute.

"You know, Bob," I continued, "I'm going to call it a day and head upstairs. I'm too tired to talk about this anymore, so I'll see you in the morning."

Bob sat quietly while I cut a few pieces of cheddar, grabbed half a sleeve of crackers, an apple, and poured myself a refill on the wine. After scrambling through my still-unorganized kitchen cabinets, I dug out a battered old tray covered with pictures of plump teapots. I trudged upstairs and ate dinner while watching a couple of *Frasier* and *Seinfeld* reruns. By seven, I was sound asleep and managed to sleep, unusual for me, for ten straight hours.

By five a.m. Friday I was up, dressed, and ready to head out for a walk. While I'm not big on exercise, I've always liked walking, and my favorite walking takes me up and down hills. Fortunately for me, my lake nestles between two tall hills, so there are lots of hill walks, from bunny hills to coronary tempters. I'll run out of legs before I run out of hills.

The steeper the hill, the more energetic my music has to be to get my butt to the top. Disco works best for me— ABBA, Donna Summer, *Saturday Night Fever*—or rock classics. I make a deal with myself. Anytime I can sweat all the way out to my nipples, I get to have pizza for dinner. It's amazing the bargains a normally lazy person like me has to make with herself to get exercise. Considering how much I dislike working out, I'm always surprised to watch happy, happy ladies in spandex jumping around on television exercise shows.

Three miles and a pound of sweat later (pizza, yay!), I felt more relaxed. A quick shower, fresh clothes, and I was up to dealing with all the house mess left from Wednesday. I folded clothes and put them away. I finally emptied out the bags of canned goods and staples that had decorated my counters for the past two days. I finished paying those bills. In fact, however painful the process, since I'd managed to get three days of work done in one day, I now had a free weekend. Not too shabby, and perfect for getting those Christmas date-nut loaves done.

While I was putting away the groceries, Tess called. She loved my report. I believe the word *perfect* came up once or twice in our conversation. Before anything else, I itemized my bill and emailed it off. Getting clients to pay bills in a timely fashion could be a challenge, so I always submitted my bills while my good work was fresh in their minds. My invoice went out before noon Friday.

I pulled the date-nut loaves out of the oven by three, and decided my ridiculous level of productivity deserved a treat. So, how do you put together a 'treat' when you live miles from town, don't really know too many people, gas is four dollars a gallon and you're trying to live on a budget?

Two thoughts came to mind. I could watch one of my favorite Fred Astaire DVDs, or take this chance to introduce myself to the only people who seemed to live in my neighborhood throughout the winter. Fred beckoned, because I'd found that, the tougher my life got, the more I enjoyed the escapism of an Astaire movie. I totally empathized with the appeal of the light-hearted, carefree characters; mindless plots; beautiful clothes; and upper-crust story lines of his movies to the weary, pummeled-by-reality audiences of the Depression. I've noticed that the heavier my burdens have gotten, the lighter my hobbies have become. As a student, when I hadn't really been expected to support myself, I had plenty of energy to ponder *The Brothers Karamazov* and

Ulysses. Now, later in my life, when my world was full of work and worry, I wanted total escapism and a few laughs in my off hours. *Sullivan's Travels* as lived by a lake woman of a certain age during the Great Recession.

I decided to save Fred for this evening, and cut off a few slices of a fresh date-nut loaf for my elderly neighbors, Mary and Stan. It wasn't too often that I had homemade delicacies to share, so I wanted to take advantage of it. I checked out their small cottage on the spit of land south of me. Smoke drifted out of the chimney, so I knew they were home.

Tiny, and made of bits and pieces, Mary's cottage had been built as a summer cabin decades ago and enlarged haphazardly as need required. The garden had been lovely at its peak, but now everything was dried and brown. Bittersweet grew over the rotted-out hull of an old wooden boat parked permanently in the side yard. Turned out, Mary stored her unused preserving jars in it.

I knocked at the door of their kitchen, a crowded room only eight-by-eight feet with a battered round Formica table taking up far too much space in the middle of it. Startled—there weren't too many drop-in neighbors out in the country—Stan turned from the sink to see me through the door's window. Once I introduced myself, he invited me in for a cup of coffee.

We sat down at the kitchen table to get acquainted. Stan reached into the refrigerator to get some milk, and I noticed it was crammed full.

Seeing my look, he said, "Since I don't drive, sometimes we get stuck here for weeks without getting into Avondale, so I like to be prepared. Mary's kids or my son drive us, and during the winter when the weather's bad, we don't want them to bother. Last year Mary and I went for two months without grocery shopping, and the only thing we ran out of was milk."

Stan said this with a quiet pride that I could respect.

How many people in our take-out society could achieve the same thing, living off their supplies for two months? Heck, there were long periods in my life where I couldn't make it through a morning without buying something to eat or drink.

Stan's physical appearance surprised me. He was still strong and muscular at seventy-five, with a full head of shaggy gray hair, sad, rheumy, green-gray eyes, and he walked in a slumped, tired fashion. I wondered if he was getting enough sleep with all the time he spent caring for Mary. When he smiled, I could see where his front teeth had decayed, leaving very painful-looking stubs. The only other time I'd seen teeth this noticeably decayed was on a vacation in the Appalachians. Using his side teeth, though, Stan was able to chomp through a substantial homemade molasses cookie without any apparent problems.

Stan talked in a halting manner, and I gradually came to realize that today he'd probably be labeled as developmentally challenged. But I noticed how clean and tidy he kept the house, and thought he was doing just fine.

For about fifteen minutes, I talked about some of my corporate moves, and life in Chicago, Connecticut, Manhattan, and Nashville. When Stan found out I'd been raised in New Jersey, he asked if I knew the Macott family. He'd grown up and lived all his life in a small town and had no idea of the vastness of a different state.

In his turn, Stan relayed stories about his early days working in a factory, and then years running a vineyard with his now ex-wife, who ran off soon after their second child was born, leaving him to manage on his own while raising the kids. He talked about pruning the grapevines in the winter and how cold it would get. When he described how he'd cook for his children, I noticed how he would always describe the sustenance the food gave, instead of the taste or pleasure of it.

"Our neighbor," Stan related, "used to give us a fruitcake

every holiday, and I'd always take a piece of it with me when I worked on the pruning. I'd be so tired and cold, but after I ate that fruitcake I could work for another couple of hours before I needed a break."

After chatting for half an hour, Stan brought me into the living room, which was mostly filled with Mary's bed, and the huge TV in front of it. No offense, but Mary looked like an evil witch. At ninety-two, she was skeletal, with wisps of white hair floating around her head and badly arthritic fingers locked and pointed in different, useless directions. Mary waved her hands around like a symphony conductor when she talked, so I couldn't avoid gazing at those fingers.

Over the years, as Mary shrank into her current skeletal state, I think all the goodness leached out of her body, leaving her pointy and nasty at this late stage. After about five minutes, Mary and Stan got onto the topic of my house's previous owner, Harry Berkley. And, in short, what a bastard Berkley had been. How he parked in their parking spot. How he didn't get his holding tank pumped on time, so it would overflow and make a mess. How he threw a dead fish under the tarp of their winterized rowboat and left it there to stink for months.

I must have looked incredulous—and daunted—by this spewing from my two little old neighbors because Mary said, "Stan, get the pictures."

At first, Stan didn't want to, but Mary kept insisting. I thought they might have a couple of fuzzy snapshots to prove what a miscreant Harry Berkley had been. Instead, when Stan finally came out of the bedroom, he was carrying three poster boards mounted with color photos of Berkley's misparked car and his overflowing holding tank. Sheesh, instead of two gentle old folks I might be able to help out once in a while, I'd moved a few houses away from two full-blown paranoid conspiracy freaks.

With very bad teeth and, apparently, very good cameras.

Chapter 6

Solitary Pioneer Fortitude?

Early in December, my sister Katie decided to drive up from New Jersey for a couple of days. The excuse she gave me was that she wanted to pick up some nice wines for the holidays. In reality, I think she wanted to make sure I was doing okay, what with the ghost situation and all. Between Bob, Terri, and my almost–blown Community Chest deadline, I couldn't blame her one bit for her concern. In preparation for her visit, I was making Butter Bombs, Katie's favorite cookies. I think, as long as I don't lose this recipe, I'm guaranteed two or three visits a year from Katie no matter where I'm living. She cheerfully admits she's addicted to them—and they are awfully tasty, although maybe a bit rich for my blood. Full of butter, almonds, and raspberry jam, what's not to like? I've seen Katie gnaw thru frozen Butter Bombs like Popsicles.

Tuesday morning found me in the kitchen, getting ready to bake.

"Hey, Bob," I yelled, "you here?"

"Really. No need to shout." Bob shimmered in. "Just call me. I'll hear you."

"Katie should be here about two. Can we count now as our conversation for the day even though I'm baking cookies?"

"Yeah, sure, I'm pretty easy to please. What is it with all this company? This place is like Grand Central Station.

For someone who thinks she lives alone, you don't spend an awful lot of time by yourself."

"Interesting point. I'm kind of dreading the deep winter months when I get snowed in here for days. I don't want to think about that now, though. It'll be here soon enough." I turned from talking with Bob to preheat the oven and pull out my mixing bowls.

He studied me as I creamed the butter and sugar. "You should move to Hawaii or something. Or maybe a city."

"Yeah, maybe one of these days. For now, though, I'm just going to enjoy Katie's visit. We're going to go to a few wineries tomorrow and do some tastings. Then she'll probably pick up a case or so for the holidays." I reached into the cabinet for the almonds, my mind more on cookies than on the conversation.

Bob said "Tastings sound like a lot of fun. Why don't I tag along? I should learn more about wine while I'm here in the Finger Lakes."

I froze in the middle of crushing the nuts. Chills ran down my spine. How the heck do you corral a snockered ghost? But then again, he might get so drunk he couldn't find his way back to my place. Hmm. I resumed my almond crushing. "No, Bob, I really don't think you want to do that. Why don't you just stay here and I'll fill you in on everything I learn?"

No immediate answer from my spooky friend. Just a look. "I never go anywhere with you," he eventually complained. "I'm always stuck here in the house."

"Well, these days I don't get out a lot either," I retorted. "Anyway, you'll like Katie. She's a lot of fun. I'm glad she's taking a few days off from work. She does financial aid in New Jersey, and it really knocks the stuffing out of her."

"How so? What do you mean, financial aid?"

"You know, when teenagers go to college. The school gives them grants and scholarships, and the state and federal governments sometimes lend or give kids money, and Katie figures out and balances all that money for each kid." I guess paying for college had changed over the years. "Sometimes parents call Katie and ream her out because they think they deserve more money from the school. Or the college administrators ream her out because she's given away too much and then the college doesn't make enough money. It's always sounded like a no-win proposition to me, and I'm surprised she sticks with it. It seems like kind of a soul-sucking way to spend your time." I turned and removed the baked cookie crust from the oven and started mixing the raspberry topping.

"Why does she keep doing it? Sounds like a tough way to make a living."

"She says she helps kids get a chance to attend college. You know, kids who otherwise couldn't afford to attend. It means a lot to her, and it keeps her going." I put the now raspberry-topped crust back into the oven and continued. "Plus, as I've mentioned once or twice, this is a very difficult job market. There aren't a lot of people walking away from jobs these days. I'm so lucky I usually like what I do, with my business writing. Anyway, she doesn't have it easy, so don't bust her chops while she's here, okay?"

Bob drew himself up from his usual slump. "Bust chops? I don't even know what it means to bust someone's chops!"

"I mean, don't give her a hard time. She's got it rough enough."

Bob harrumphed and popped out.

I sighed, cleaned up the baking mess, and set the table. A short while later, a car horn beeped, then the front door opened, and Katie yelled, "I'm heeeeere!"

I ran up the stairs for sister hugs, big old bear hugs that would sustain my cheerful moods for weeks. They were an offspring of Daddy hugs. When we were kids, Dad would take us in his lap and ask us what number hug we wanted, from one to ten. A number four hug was a gentle squeeze; a number ten hug squished your insides out like a rag doll. I usually settled on a number seven hug; my brothers always wanted number ten. I'd put a sister hug at about a number eight—and they were wonderful.

"Fresh Butter Bombs, sweetie . . . still warm from the oven. I'll make some coffee to go with them."

We started toward the kitchen. Since there are so many hills around Crooked Lake, houses often have the entryway on the bedroom floor, and the living room and kitchen are down a flight on lake level.

"This kitchen smells awesome. You are my lake goddess with your warm Butter Bombs! And the place is really coming along!"

"Thanks. Yeah, I'm just about done with the unpacking, except for the dozen or so boxes in the cellar I might never get to. How was the drive? Any more construction on the interstate?"

"Not bad at all. Pop and Milly send their love. Give me a minute to phone Bill to let him know I made it, and I'll be right with you."

Katie walked into the living room while I finished putting out the coffee and Butter Bombs. A minute later, she was back and we sat at the table.

Before Katie even took her first bite, she asked, "So, Roz, what's the story with this ghost thing? Was I right? Were you just a little tired?"

"No, I didn't imagine him. It would have been much more convenient if I had."

"Is he here now?"

I looked around. "I don't see him."

"Can you get him? Ghosts don't scare me at all. We have one at the college, but I've never seen him. Though sometimes I swear I can feel him when I'm working late. A crawly feeling on the back of my neck." Katie finished her first cookie and reached for a second.

"Bob and I are past the crawly stage. Now I'm trying to figure out why he's here so we can finish whatever it is we're supposed to do."

"Can you get him?"

"I'll try." I put down my cookie and said, "Bob? Hey, Bob. Do you want to meet my sister?"

Bob shimmered in, and I focused in his direction.

Katie followed my gaze. "Is he here? Where?"

I gestured toward the counter by the refrigerator.

Katie swiveled in her chair and stared. "Drat. I can't see anything. Can you make him do something, like turn on a light or push the toaster?"

I guess Bob was still ticked off about our last conversation. He stared at me, deadpan. "Please tell your sister I'm not a performing seal. I don't do tricks on command."

I relayed, "Sorry, Katie. Bob says he's not a trained seal and he doesn't perform tricks on command. Frankly, he seems kind of cranky right now, so I don't think you're missing anything."

Katie turned back to look at me, pursing her lips like she was evaluating the ripeness of a melon. "So he's standing right there, Roz, but he can't do anything to prove it, even something really, really easy. Sure, no problem. I'll just take your word for it that he's here. Kind of like when my daughter was young and she had an invisible friend for a few months." She shook her head slightly and changed the subject. "Do you have any milk for the coffee?"

Thank goodness for those Butter Bombs. They took most of the awkward edge off our chat. Besides, Katie adored lake life, so there was lots to catch up on, including my wacko neighbors.

After a pleasant dinner, we sat down to watch the latest Netflix installment of *The Tudors.* We'd watched Henry VIII plow through his first four wives on Katie's previous visits to Nashville and were bound and determined to see how he handled wives five and six. We called these visits Hankfest and usually wore sparkly tiaras while watching, but I'd lost the tiaras in the move. Besides, the glitter on them could get kind of distracting when you were watching the bitter, gory ends of some of Henry's enemies. Talk about nutcases. Wife five's ending was not a pretty one.

The next morning, after a late and lazy breakfast, we hit the Crooked Lake wine trail. This route wound itself around the lake and led to many family-run vineyards. One winery boasted a large zinc bar from France; others showed more Swiss and German influences.

Since it was midweek in early winter, there was not a lot of traffic at the wineries and the pourers were happy to spend a little extra time with us. We pulled into the Royal Egret winery on the lake's east side just behind a mini-van of seniors from Rochester. Egret was ready with three different pourers. I grabbed Katie's arm and made sure we wound up at the station of the cute pourer I'd noticed on my last visit. He was still looking good, and filling out his well-worn jeans in all the right places. A bit more tan, maybe, and the Selleck/Firth resemblance came through stronger than ever. He hoisted a case of wine off the floor as if it weighed no more than a carton of eggs. There must be some awfully hard muscles hiding under that soft flannel shirt. Hmm.

I looked around the room, but didn't see Pat from my previous visit. Since this was Katie's first time here, I decided I'd let our new pourer go through his whole spiel without telling him I'd been here before.

"Good morning, ladies, I'm David. It'll be two dollars each for your tasting. Here's a listing of our wines. Just pick out the five you'd like to try this morning and I'll be happy to answer any questions you might have." David collected our fees.

"I like whites, and my sister prefers reds," I started. "Maybe you could give us some recommendations?"

"Happy to. Well, first off, tastings will usually start with whites and work toward the heavier reds. You probably know the Finger Lakes are most famous for their whites. One of our area whites actually made *Wine Spectator's* Top 100 list of best wines in the world a couple of years ago, and the wines have only gotten better since then.

"Since our climate resembles Germany's, we do very well with the kinds of wines that are grown there, like rieslings and gewürztraminers. Right now, Finger Lakes rieslings are taking double golds in different international wine competitions, even beating out German wines. You might want to try a dry and a semi-dry riesling, our leading wines in the Finger Lakes area." As he spoke, David began lifting various bottles that we could sample from the storage area below the bar.

"What's the difference between dry and semi-dry?" Katie asked.

"Have you ever heard of *terroir*?" he continued. "That's a broad term for growing conditions. The minerals and vegetation in the soil, the water, the hours of sunlight a day, things like that. Our dry riesling is grown on a thin layer of soil that's over a thick layer of shale, so the grapes pick up a lot of flinty, mineral taste from their growing conditions. Now, you take those same grapes and grow them in a different area, one where the soil is warm and full of decayed vegetation, and that wine develops a sweeter, more tropical fruit flavor. That's our semi-dry riesling. You almost can't go wrong with any kind of riesling from a quality grower here on Crooked Lake."

He was right. When I sipped the dry riesling, I could taste hints of minerals, of rock. The semi-dry was a little sweeter, a little more fruity. The gewürztraminer was delicious as well, in a spicier way, but it's hard to describe a good wine; it's as hard as describing a good kiss.

Katie asked, "So what would you serve with these rieslings?"

"Rieslings and gewürz are great with Asian or Chinese food, as long as it's not too hot or spicy. Or fried chicken, sweet roast ham, or turkey. They're pretty versatile. You can even try a riesling with your sushi!"

Katie and I smiled at each other. Sounded just about right for the holiday turkey.

"What about the reds?" Katie asked.

David answered thoughtfully. "Twenty years ago we didn't do a lot of bragging about our Finger Lake reds. California pretty much had a lock on them. We're definitely a cooler climate than California, and many reds like long, sunny growing seasons.

"Lately we've been picking some grapes the second week in November instead of in late September or early October," David continued. "We're essentially stretching out the growing season. This is helping us improve the qualities of our reds, and some, like cabernet franc and lemberger, are doing really well. In fact, we're one of the few places in the country that grows lemberger, so you really are drinking a local wine when you try it."

Katie glanced at me with a grimace. "Lemberger? Isn't that a stinky cheese? What an awful name for a wine!"

David chimed in smoothly, "I've heard that lemberger grapes and limburger cheese actually came from the same area in Europe. That's why their names are so similar. Some people call lemberger wine 'blau Frankish,' but we mostly use the term lemberger here in the Finger Lakes. It's a pretty hearty vinifera here, and the wine it makes is definitely different. We're still learning our way around it. If lemberger wine were a woman, I'd say she was complicated, challenging, and maybe a little crabby at times. To my mind, a lot more interesting than the mellow California reds."

"Gee, Roz, you should buy some of that lemberger wine—it sounds just like you," Katie added, smiling mischievously.

"All right now, Katie, don't get carried away," I said, a little brusque.

David studied Katie, then turned to me. "Even if you hadn't mentioned it, I could tell you two were sisters. You sound just like me and my sister."

After rinsing our glasses to clean out the whites and dumping the water into the slosh jar, David poured a blend of cabernet franc and pinot noir.

Even though I'm not very good with reds, I could tell that this varietal wasn't as acidic or raw as most reds tend to taste to me. After we finished our tablespoons of the blend, David grabbed another bottle and poured a small bit of a darker red in our glasses, the lemberger.

"Most Finger Lakes wineries blend their lemberger with other varietals, like cab franc or pinot noir. This year, we've created a pure lemberger wine. You'll notice it's got a nice edge to it, earthy and chewy. It would go perfectly with a beef stew with all those root vegetables to pick up the earthy flavors. Or with some kind of beef and mushroom dish."

The lemberger seemed strong to me, but I could see how it would taste great with a good stew. Katie started avidly completing her order form for her holiday wines. David recorked bottles, put them away, and wiped down the wooden bar while she debated. As he worked, I leaned toward him and confessed my inability to appreciate reds.

"I don't really know how to explain it," I said. "But reds somehow taste raw or incomplete to me. When I drink them with food I'm okay. I like them then, but they're hard for me to taste on their own."

"I've heard that before from other customers." David stashed his damp cloth under the bar and picked up the bottle of lemberger we'd sampled earlier. "I grew the grapes that made this wine, though, so I'm particularly fond of it," he added with pride.

I must have looked puzzled, because he continued, "I grow on the western side of the lake and sold my whole crop to Royal Egret. I only help out in the salesroom when they're short-staffed."

"Whereabouts on the west side?"

Turns out David's vineyards are only a mile or so up the hill from me. "I walk up that way once in a while," I said. "Maybe we'll run into each other one of these days."

I opted to buy a bottle of David's lemberger. Drinking wine made from grapes grown within walking distance of my house was exciting.

For our final Hankfest festivities that evening, I splurged on a bottle of reserve gewürztraminer that tasted like rose-infused, spicy gold. Katie spent a bit more time with David, working through her holiday menus and wine choices. She finally settled on two bottles each of the cabernet franc-pinot noir blend, lemberger, dry and semi-dry rieslings, gewürz, a bottle of bubbly, and a bottle of the superb reserve gewürz. Not a bad morning's work!

While David helped Katie, I browsed through the gift shop. Wine-themed tee shirts and jewelry, recipe books using wines and pairing them with foods, books about the wine industry, crystal wine glasses, cheeses made with local wines, wine-filled chocolates. Wine is one aspect of the Finger Lakes I love! Maybe it could even make up for the winter isolation and the lack of coffeehouse civilization.

David carried Katie's case of wine to the car, and we said our thanks and goodbyes. As we got settled into the car and started heading down the driveway, Katie turned to me and said bluntly, "Well, you played *that* all wrong!"

"What?" I stared at her, shocked.

"You heard me. A good-looking man with no wedding ring and you didn't even flirt with him a little bit. Would it have killed you? He was interested in you, Roz, especially when he found out you lived just down the hill. You could have been a little warmer toward him."

"Give me a break, Katie."

"No, I will not give you a break! You and Matt divorced a long time ago, and it's time you found someone else. You've been on your own way too long, and we all worry about you getting older with no one around. It would be good for you to meet someone. And now all this craziness about a ghost. What is going on with you?" She concentrated on a turn in the road for a moment, but then jumped right back into her lecture. "I'm worried about you, Rosie. We all are. Now here's this nice guy, David. You thought he was cute, didn't you?"

I pictured those dark eyes and too-long hair in my mind. Really, not bad at all. "Yeah, he was okay."

"You'd better start taking some nice long walks up to his vineyards pretty soon. Bring one of your date-nut loaves."

"Fine, fine! If I promise to do it, will you get off my back so we can enjoy the rest of the day?"

"I won't say another word, but believe me I'll be asking about how your walks are coming for the next few weeks."

Now grumpy, I settled into my seat, and we headed off to the next winery, which was located inside one of the pre-Civil War mansions that dotted the area. Katie picked up a couple more bottles of riesling "just in case," but I had other things on my mind. Turns out, the Brebeck winery boasts more than quality wines; it also has ghosts—a husband and wife who had died in a freak storm around the time of the Civil War. Now, according to the pourer, they slam doors and tear the covers off the beds of unsuspecting sleepers in the oldest part of the house, which had been turned into a bed and breakfast. I wondered if Bob knew the Brebecks. Maybe I should bring him over sometime for a play date.

After Brebeck's Winery, Katie treated me to lunch at the local hot spot—The Speratazzatura. Another classical white mansion, with porticos and columns, the Spera Mansion was built at the head of Crooked Lake in the 1830s and enlarged over the generations. During the winter, with the leaves down, you could see it from almost any vantage point on the western side of the lake.

The owners had renovated the restaurant and bed and breakfast back to its original 1830s grandeur. Now the building showcased gleaming wooden floors, a stately curved staircase, and rooms furnished with burgundy and dark green velvet-upholstered antiques. Fine china and crystal graced the tables, sitting atop gleaming white linens. A lovely place, but a little over my current budget, so this was my first visit. I got a kick out of the antique Rolls-Royce sitting in the parking lot. According to our seating hostess, the Spera Mansion hosted a good number of wedding receptions.

Since it was a chilly day, I opted for vegetable soup and a turkey and brie-stuffed croissant. Katie went for her favorite: grilled sea scallops. We sat by the crackling fire and gazed, mesmerized, at the lake outside our window. Beautiful scenery, great wines, the occasional luxurious meal—really, sometimes I wondered why I worried so much about living here on my own.

Katie, of course, knew the answer to that one, and it involved a good-looking grape grower with dark eyes and too-long hair.

It is true what they say about no free lunches. That tasty turkey and brie croissant cost me one stiff lecture on the topic of getting out more. But it was worth the price.

On the way home, we stopped in town so Katie could pick up a few local specialties before heading back to New

Jersey the next day: Mennonite-cured bacon, genuine maple syrup, a bushel of apples for holiday pies and crisps, a few chunks of cheddar. Katie had all the appropriate souvenirs of a visit to western New York.

Finally, by four p.m., we were back at my place, tired but happy. Katie checked in with Bill, and I told her I was going upstairs for a short rest before setting the table for dinner.

"Going to chat with Bob, huh?" she asked.

I sighed and headed up the stairs. Sure enough, there he was, comfortably stretched out in my bedroom easy chair.

"So, how was your day?"

"Lots of fun, and I think I might have met a couple of friends of yours."

"Huh?"

"Marcus and Felicity Brebeck, over at Brebeck Wineries. They're ghosts. Do you know them?"

"Never heard of them, but I can look them up in the directory later. You met them?"

"What directory?"

"*The* directory. Our listing. You know, like a telephone book. It lists all the ghosts in the area, so I can contact them. Our organization gets some things right once in a while."

"Amazing. No, I didn't meet them, and that's fine with me if I don't. Do you want to meet them? Would I have to drive you or would you meet them somewhere on your astral plane? I still haven't worked out all the logistics of this situation. It feels kind of like parallel universes."

"I have no idea what those are. Yes, I could probably find the Brebecks on my own, but it might be more fun to take a jaunt in an automobile. That way I could sample their wines, too."

"I did buy a few wines; Katie bought a lot. I'll open the reserve gewürz for us tonight, while we're watching the end of *The Tudors*. I can save some for you if you like."

"Sounds good, thanks. What else did you do today?"

Keeping my voice low, I told Bob about our lovely lunch and shopping. I even mentioned David and the lemberger, and my future mandated walks to the vineyard.

"That Katie can be kind of bossy sometimes," he observed in a mild voice while pouring himself a second martini.

"No, she loves me, and I guess she's worried about me being by myself up here. It makes a lot of sense to get to know more of my neighbors. And if those neighbors happen to be cute and within walking distance, so much the better."

I glanced at the dark outside my window for a moment, then pushed myself off the bed and headed downstairs to set the table. Katie was in the guest bedroom getting organized for tomorrow's drive. Since the slow cooker soup didn't need a lot of fine-tuning, I made up a loaf of garlic bread, and we sat down to an early dinner.

Even though we both knew the ending to the tale of Henry VIII, we enjoyed the final episodes. With a couple of glasses of reserve gewürz Katie and I saluted monstrous Hank into his extremely toasty afterlife.

As I headed off to bed with Bob's glass of gewürz, Katie observed, "More wine, Roz? It was delicious, but don't you think two is enough?"

"It's not for me. I promised Bob I'd let him try it."

Now there was no denying the concerned look on Katie's face. "For Bob, huh?"

"Yeah. He's looking forward to it."

Katie shook her head, but didn't say any more about it.

When we got up the next morning, there were light flurries of snow. Kamikaze snowflakes dive-bombed the deck on the north side of the house; on the south side, flakes drifted down half-heartedly, as if making up their minds en route. Occasional wind gusts would catch the flakes and toss them upwards. A light layer of snow rested neatly on top of the deck railing. The whole world looked as if it had been lightly frosted by a master baker. When the sun rose over the bluff, the view exploded into shards of color and sparkle.

Katie and I stood speechless in front of the kitchen's picture window, sipping coffee and trying to absorb the spectacular view through our pores so we would always carry it within us. "Roz, I can see I'm leaving you in good hands with all this beauty around you."

"Who needs people when you have all this for company?"

"Nevertheless, I want to hear about a few hill walks in the next few days. Promise?"

"Yes, I promise, I promise. Sheesh!"

"I'm going to pull things together and hit the road." Katie walked over and placed her empty mug in the sink. "Don't bother with breakfast. I'll get something when I gas up at the Kwik-Fill."

A quick flurry of loading up the car, including date-nut loaves for Katie's family and Pop and Milly, promises to see each other for Christmas in a few weeks, and she was gone. The house felt extra empty without her.

I trudged back to the kitchen and mapped out my day over my second cup of coffee. Now that my Ohio client's Community Chest campaign was well underway, I needed to focus on the wrap up for my Arizona client.

The next two days were a blur of report summary spreadsheets and long-distance phone interviews that resulted in three versions of a congratulatory letter to be sent from the CEO. I finished the letters early Saturday morning and emailed them off, then cleaned up the mess around the computer. Goopy half-drunk cups of coffee, bits of paper with ideas and phrases scribbled on them, marked-up early drafts. At least I hadn't worked through the night the way I had with Ohio's report.

Chapter 7
Christmas Cookie Walks

After a check-in phone call to my sister Angela in Mississippi, in which she assiduously avoided the 'g' word (I could see the sister grapevine was in top form), I checked the clock. Only nine a.m. I still had time to drive into town for the Christmas cookie walk I'd read about in the local paper.

Pretty cookies are one of my favorite treats. I rarely left New Jersey after a visit to Pop and Milly without a pound of assorted Italian bakery cookies stashed in the car somewhere. They froze beautifully and, with care, I could stretch them out for a couple of weeks.

Set up to benefit the local hospice, apparently this cookie walk had been a tradition for the past few years. Even though I wasn't sure how the whole process worked, I figured if I got there early enough, I'd have time to ask a few questions.

Every space in the church parking lot was filled. People packed into the vestibule, and fellow cookie-lovers were already lining up outside the church door when I arrived. I'd lived in this area for weeks, and I'd never seen so many people in one place before. Taking a spot at the back of the line, I listened as a woman up front explained the purchase procedure.

"We've set up two sizes of empty boxes on the side of the room—two pound and four pound. Inside each box is a plastic glove, and we ask that you wear it when picking your selections. Fill as many boxes as you want. Cookies are eight dollars a pound."

"Hey, Roz!" I turned around in surprise and Bev, my wine road-trip friend, gave me a hug.

"What are you doing here?"

"I come every year. They have a great assortment of cookies and this way I don't have to spend all my spare time baking for the kids. I dropped some cookies off last night."

"What kind did you make? I'll be on the look out," I said.

"A few dozen springerlies. They turned out well this year. I think you'll like them. I made both lemon and anise flavors."

"Wow, Bev, springerlies, huh? I've never had any luck with them. Mine always have the form and texture of hockey pucks. I'll look forward to trying yours." I would have chatted more, but the crowd was restless.

People weaved back and forth like racehorses getting ready to charge out of the gate. Two women behind me reminisced about great cookies from previous years, and I felt my excitement level start to rise. Bev and I picked up empty boxes, snapped on our plastic gloves, and were nudged forward as the doors to the auditorium slowly creaked open. We headed into Cookieland.

Long tables were set up like a huge maze, and the crowd started moving through it, happy rats all. Platters of homemade cookies covered every inch of the tabletops. Husbands dutifully held boxes while wives filled them to the brim. Three-dimensional cookies—you could assemble a little Christmas village! Springerlies—pressed cookies from generations-old molds of bells and holly leaves. Multicolored butter cookies, stuffed with chocolate or raspberry fillings. Dainty spritzes. Every cookie a little gem, a treasured family recipe. I paused, stunned by the variety, and almost got run over by the cookie-starved hoards of townspeople. Bev gestured toward the platter of her springerlies at the end of the row, waved, and started maneuvering through the crowd toward the chocolate cookie section.

I slowly made my way through the Cookieland maze, selecting the prettiest, most buttery offerings. As hundreds of townsfolk made their choices, empty platters were whisked away to the kitchen. By the time I made it to the end of the maze, the first few tables were almost empty, even though there were still masses of people crowding through the doors. I could see Bev Miano still at the far end of the room and next to her, the pourer from Royal Egret, Pat. They talked away, ignoring the crowd milling about them. I waved and moved to the check-out line.

Several of the people in line carried four and five boxes of cookies, and I had visions of some very happy college students at home for the holidays. I guesstimated every cookie would be sold by eleven a.m. What a great idea for a fundraiser! Plus, I was set for the holidays and beyond.

As a pre-emptive atonement for all the cookies I could see in my future, I decided to take a decent walk after I got home with my loot. Before leaving, I packed up a sampling of my cookie treasures and popped on the iPod.

Of course I headed up the hill toward David's place. I had to have my story in place when those sisterly phone calls started coming through. By this time the sun had melted off the frosting glaze of snow we'd had that morning and after two miles of hills, it was starting to feel very warm for December.

The smell of a wood fire gave away the house's location before I could even see it. Many houses around the lake heated with wood stoves. As a city dweller, the first few weeks I'd lived here, the smell of burning had always thrown me off balance when I was driving down the road. I'd frantically check my dashboard to see if the car was overheating. I'd mentioned it to Bev on one of our jaunts, and she got a good laugh out of it. Over time, as I'd settled in, I became more accustomed to the smell of burning in the car.

A pick-up truck was in the driveway, so I marched up to the door, cookies in hand. Maybe a wife would answer— no wedding ring was no guarantee of no wife these days. But what the heck, I was just being neighborly. I rang the doorbell and took a few deep breaths to settle down my heart rate. After a minute, a very puzzled David opened the door.

"Good morning!" I said, a little too loudly. "I was out for a walk and I thought I'd bring you some Christmas cookies." David continued to look a little confused by this sweaty stranger who showed up on his doorstep waving a bag of cookies. I felt a bead of sweat form on my upper lip. "I'm Roz. My sister Katie and I met you at the winery Wednesday when we were there for a tasting?"

"Oh, oh, of course! I'm so sorry, I was in the middle of paying bills so my mind was a thousand miles away. Come in and have a cup of coffee. It's great to get a visitor out here."

If David did have a wife, she had a real fondness for wood paneling. You talk about rustic. The house was basically one big room with a fireplace on one end and kitchen counters on the other. In the middle, a floor-to-ceiling window overlooked acres of vineyards running downhill toward Crooked Lake.

I moved toward the window, mesmerized by the sight. "I thought I had the best view of the lake, but I think there might be some serious competition here."

"I've come to the conclusion that Crooked Lake is like a photogenic model. She has no bad angles. How do you like your coffee?"

"Extra light, no sugar. Where are those lemberger vines you were talking about?"

David gestured toward the far corner of his window. "They're way down toward the water."

After craning my neck to see the lemberger vines, I turned around and shook my bag. "Here, you've got to check out these cookies. I just got them this morning at the Christmas cookie walk in town." I started telling David about my experiences that morning, and my yapping got us through those first early awkward moments of conversation.

"I don't think I've ever met anyone who was so passionate about cookies before," David said at the end of my speech. I think he was trying not to laugh.

"Yeah, well, everybody needs a few hobbies," I replied jauntily. "How about you? What do you do for fun when you're not growing grapes or running tastings?"

"The usual out here. I like hunting and fishing when I can find the time. Summers and autumns are some of my busiest times, though, with the grapes and helping out at the winery, so sometimes it's hardly worth the money for me to buy hunting or fishing licenses. About the only time it slows down is over the next couple of months, so I should be able to catch up on my reading and some football. That's what I was trying to do this morning." David gestured over to the paper-strewn cocktail table in front of the fireplace. "Get caught up on some of the bills that have piled up over the past few months during harvest."

I recognized that clutter—a checkbook, bank statements, a ledger, a pile of bills, and a calculator. A clutter that was near and dear to my heart.

"I just moved here a few weeks ago so I'm still transitioning my bills from Nashville. There was one morning a few weeks ago where I did nothing but talk with different insurance companies. It's such a pain getting everything moved around."

"My wife and I moved here from Rochester about eight years ago, but I still remember how crazy it was to get everything relocated. I'd been in Information Technology at Xerox, but we wanted to raise our kids outside of the city."

"Oh, so you have children? That's wonderful!" I scanned the cottage, puzzled. No family pictures decorated the shelves and I didn't see any evidence of the toys, clothing or sporting gear that I associated with children.

David's face turned gray, and he clenched his teeth. "No, it didn't work out the way we planned. When Bethie didn't get pregnant, we went in for some tests and they found ovarian cancer."

"Oh, David, I don't even know what to say. I'm so, so sorry." My heart ached for the man. He must have lived through some miserable times. How awful.

"Me, too."

David moved uncomfortably in his chair, and reached into the bag for a cookie. "I don't normally eat a lot of sweets, but I think I'll make an exception for these. Can I warm up that coffee for you?"

"Sure, just a little. I'm going to have to head back in a few minutes."

Coffee warmed, cookies in hand, the lake shimmering down the hill—this felt comfortable. Comfortable enough that I decided to risk a confession. "Hey, David, can I tell you why I came here today?"

"I thought you were just being neighborly and Christmas-y."

"Yeah, I was. But it was a little more than that."

"Please, do tell." Again, I could see the hint of a smile on his face. If all else failed, at least I was somewhat amusing.

"You met Katie, my sister."

"Nice lady."

"Yeah, sure, but she also has a whim of iron. In the family, we refer to her as the iron fist in a velvet glove. Nice as all get-out, but somehow she manages to get her way with things."

"Gotcha. My sister Annie's like that, too."

"After Katie and I left the winery, I got a couple of very pointed lectures on meeting new people and getting out more. So I am going to count you as one of my new people, and tell Katie about it."

By this time, David was openly chuckling. "I'll make a deal with you. My sister is always on my case about the same things, so I think we can kill two birds with one stone here. How about I stop by your house for coffee next week, and we can both make our sisters very, very happy?"

Good show! Happy siblings! One of my constant goals! After working out a few details, I headed down the hill, ABBA's *The Winner Takes It All* warbling in my iPod.

As I walked, mental inventories ran through my head: Hunting (blech), fishing (blech), IT background (interesting), sense of humor (very nice), reader (hurray!), football (okay), makes very good coffee (gold star), deceased wife (awful, but shows ability to commit). A mixed bag.

Now, how would that inventory look on his end? My going to his house (outgoing? or maybe creepy or aggressive?); brought cookies (generous, likes holidays); way too passionate about cookies (nutcase), cares about sister's feelings (fond of family or co-dependent). Definitely another mixed bag. Heavy sigh.

After a quick shower, I searched for Bob in the kitchen while I was making a sandwich. No sign of him. "Hey, Bob," I said, as I started picking through my cookies for a smidge of dessert. "I've got some great cookies here. You might like one." Still no Bob. Very odd. A little off-putting, really.

With no Bob to regale with stories of my morning, I felt somewhat lost. He'd always been there when I called. Now what the heck was I supposed to do with myself for the rest of the afternoon? Strange to think that in the weeks I'd lived by the lake this was the first time I'd felt totally alone. I guess I'd been kidding myself all the while about my solitary pioneer fortitude. There'd always been a cushiony spirit at hand whenever I'd wanted company. Now the house felt empty, and I didn't want to be there anymore.

When I'm looking for solace, the first place I go is the town library. Probably not too many people say that these days but, to me, libraries are miracles. Just think, all the free reading you can handle. People buzzing around, using computers, making cocoa, chatting with the checkout lady, rummaging through shelves of the collected knowledge, thoughts, and dreams of the ages. All the resources of the world right at your fingertips.

My local library was a hoot. Only one room, although it was good sized. A librarian who knew everyone in town and didn't believe in hushed voices so, by osmosis, I was getting to know everyone in town. The library offered a great place to hang out, especially when you were restless and discombobulated, as I was this afternoon. Once there, I spent a few minutes visiting with the librarian. Spent a while thumbing through the new magazines (my favorite magazine cover headline: "20 Ways to be More Original." Yeah, right). Spent a while with a cup of cocoa and my latest paperback.

After a couple of hours, I felt more settled and headed home. This time, when I yelled for Bob, he popped in. "I'm glad to see you. I tried to get you a while ago and you weren't around."

Bob looked frazzled. "I got another assignment. Usually they don't double-book, but this was kind of an emergency."

An emergency that required deft martini skills and vague answers? That must have been one heck of an interesting emergency.

"Do you want to talk about it?"

"Maybe later when I figure out what's going on. So anyway, if I'm hard to get once in a while, you'll know why. What did you want to tell me?"

"I was going to show you these gorgeous Christmas cookies I got in town this morning. Look." I opened the box and Bob peered in.

His silent eyeball roll told me he was underwhelmed.

"Well, *I* think they're pretty," I grumbled, and took a couple more. Thank goodness Christmas came but once a year. At this rate, the cookies weren't going to last too long, and I'd be doing a lot of uphill walking to compensate for them.

"I took some to David, you know, that grape grower I was telling you about. He thought they were good."

"Bully for him."

"What is up with you today? That other assignment must have been tough."

"Can we just give it a rest, please? I'm not used to dealing with two assignments. As you might remember, juggling priorities is not my strong suit."

"True. Too true." I thought about the debacle of Tess's report a few weeks ago, and shook my head. Then I turned to Bob and asked, "So, with this second assignment, how are we going to handle my Christmas trip to New Jersey? I thought you were looking forward to going with me."

"I was, but now I'll have to research my options. Maybe I can get a substitute for Lola."

"Here we go again. Substitute ghosts, aptitude tests, the directory. You just crack me up, Bob. I had no idea ghosts had to work with such a bureaucracy. Just so you know, I was going to do a day trip to Manhattan with my niece, Amy. You might enjoy Manhattan."

"I'm fairly sure I know the city. I might be able to remember a little more about my body days if I went there."

"The city always looks so lovely for the holidays. That's my favorite time of year in Manhattan. I worked there for years, so I got to know the different seasons. Did you know, at Christmas, all of the lights on the Empire State Building are red and green? I think, for Hanukkah, they're all silver and blue. I used to love coming out of my office at night and seeing those lights."

"Another place you've worked. You were all over, weren't you?"

"Sure feels like it. Manhattan, Chicago, Connecticut, New Jersey, Nashville . . . I figured once that I'd moved seven times in twelve years, usually for business. The tough thing was that I never really set down roots, never really felt like I belonged in a community. All that moving was tough, but then the economy took care of my little problem."

"At least you live in a pretty area now." Bob looked at the lake.

When I glanced that way, I saw the shadows cast on the far bluff by passing clouds. It had been years since I'd noticed that clouds could throw shadows.

"It is gorgeous," I admitted. "But we'll see how I feel about it after a long, snowed-in winter. Let's face it. The person you marry is not always the most handsome guy you've ever met. There's got to be a lot more under the surface before you commit. That's how I feel about staying here for good. Sure, the landscape is lovely . . ." Reluctantly, I looked away from the window. ". . . but how much more is there under the surface? I've always been a city girl, and I like coffee shops and theaters and symphonies and shopping. So far, I've found great wineries, a charming library, and a couple of nice restaurants, but I don't know yet if that will be enough. Only time will tell."

"True enough. So you might as well just relax and enjoy what you've got while you've got it."

"That's what my sister Angela always says. She says we have to be happy where we are because happiness attracts more happiness. She's way out there with all of her vibrational beliefs. I don't understand half of what she tells me. But she really believes it, so that's good enough for me."

"You've found lots of good stuff here . . . wineries, cookies, a few friends."

"Okay, okay, I get your drift. I'll work on my Pollyanna skills." I felt like this conversation would never end.

"Not Pollyanna." Bob paused for a second, as if searching for the right words. "Just try seeing the glass half-full once in a while."

"Fine. You can stop preaching now. Instead of my moods bobbing up and down all the time, you want me to concentrate on staying up. Fine. I think I need another cookie." I rummaged through the bakery box, and then resolutely snapped down the lid and started looking for tape to seal it for a while. This cookie thing was getting out of control. Frustrated, I turned to Bob. "Do you think if you were given another assignment your boss thinks maybe we're wrapping up? You know, with our working together?"

"Do you feel like things are getting better for you?"

"I don't know. I saw Pat and Bev at the Cookie Walk today, so I'm getting to know a few more people, which is good. I'm getting to know the area a bit better, which is good, too. I feel like I'm collecting the building blocks for being happier, but I haven't started making anything out of them, if that makes any sense."

"Sure it makes sense." Bob observed in a reassuring tone. "It sounds to me, though, that it's still early days for us. I feel like I'll probably be around for a while yet. Why do you ask?"

"You know me, I'm always living in my head, trying to figure stuff out. I was just wondering."

Then the oddest thing happened. We fell silent for a few minutes. No laughing, no banter, no nonsense, no frustrations. Just quiet. Enjoying the sparkles on the lake, the lapping of the waves, the late afternoon sun slanting through the kitchen windows. The peace. We gave each other little half-smiles and Bob patted at his smoking jacket. He reached in, pulled out the rye, silently offered me the flask, but I declined. He took a healthy swallow and put it away. "Let me know about your plans for Christmas and I'll start making arrangements on my end. I'm going to toddle off. I'll talk with you tomorrow."

"Have a good night."

"You, too."

Chapter 8

Bob Goes Christmas Shopping . . . sigh . . .

"I just don't have a good feeling about this, Bob. Why on earth would you want to come Christmas shopping with me? Going to the mall at this time of year is like visiting an insane asylum."

"How am I ever going to help you if I don't know what you have to deal with? What your world is like? I've never been outside this house with you. Not to the wineries, not to Mary and Stan's, not to David's house, not anywhere." If middle-aged male ghosts could pout, I'd say Bob was pouting. But, of course, that's ridiculous. "I promise," Bob continued, "you'll hardly know I'm there."

Famous last words. By now, you'd think I'd recognize them when I heard them, wouldn't you?

I couldn't get rid of Bob tonight. He'd been following me around since dinner, when I'd made the mistake of mentioning my shopping plans for the next day. Bob acted like I'd been keeping him bound and gagged in a cellar all these weeks, the way he was carrying on about going to the mall.

I tried to ignore him while I took an inventory of socks and underwear with the thought of buying new ones tomorrow after I'd finished my Christmas shopping. Despite my frugality, I loved buying and wrapping presents. A throwback to the Christmases of my childhood, I guess. I'd already bought Pop's gift—since he was always chilly these days, I got him a lovely lightweight plaid woolen shirt that was on sale at Pendleton. Katie's husband, Bill, would be easy—a good bottle of single malt Irish whiskey. Some gourmet chocolates for Katie, a couple of CDs for my stepmother, and I'd be almost finished. I wasn't sure what to do about my niece Amy, though. Should I buy a gift for her if I wasn't going to buy and ship gifts to all my nieces and nephews? All fifteen of them? I've just never been very good with the politics of gift-giving.

Bob's pestering distracted me from my counting. Exasperated, I said, "I don't even know why you'd want to go. It's going to be so crowded and crazy. I wouldn't be shopping now except that I need to get some presents if I'm driving to New Jersey in a few days." He wouldn't give up. He stared at me balefully from my easy chair while he upended another martini. I promptly forgot how many underpants I owned and started recounting the dratted things. Bob kept staring.

"Oh, all right!" I threw up my hands, dropping all of the underpants. "You can come, you pain in the butt, but don't say I didn't warn you. I'm not happy about being out in public. Too much can go wrong, and I don't want any problems." Bob sprang from the chair, started singing *We're in the Money* (I have no idea why), and began a happy tiptoe dance that vaguely reminded me of the frolicking hippos in Disney's *Fantasia*. I sighed, picked up the underpants, and said, "We'll need to get going by nine."

Since I lived so far out in the country, Cummins Mall was about one-and-a-half hours away. It was no spur-of-the-moment indulgence to go there. It was a full-day trip, mapped out and organized to get the maximum from a tank of gas.

Bob finished his exuberant dance and bowed. "No problem, I'll be here with bells on," he said.

And he was. The next morning, Bob showed up, resplendent in a well-cut suit with a tattersall vest. His mustache gleamed with wax. His shoes glistened from coats of polish, and he even wore a hat. A fedora? I think that's what it's called. Even with his bit of a spare tire, he could have stepped in for the second-level leading man in a Fred Astaire movie. Probably the orchestra leader who was always scheming to win Ginger away from Fred. I couldn't help it. I gave a wolf whistle as I walked slowly around him. Maybe it was the light, but I could have sworn I saw the tips of his ears turn pink.

"If you're finished ogling me," Bob harrumphed, "I thought you wanted to be on the road by nine."

"I certainly do, but you've taken my breath away, you look so . . . what's the word I want? Debonair. Definitely, debonair. I feel positively underdressed by comparison."

Let's face it: blue jeans and a leather jacket, no matter how spiffy, can't hold a candle to a tailored suit. But if I was casually dressed, wait until Bob saw some of the other shoppers in their pajama bottoms, flip-flops, and bed heads. America, land of Slob-ortunity.

Five minutes later, lists in hand, we were on the road. Bob rode shotgun, nattering away about the scenery, cows, smells, clouds, countryside, Mennonite buggies, migrating geese, pretty much anything that caught his attention. Maybe he really had been cooped up for too long. Traffic was light while we were in the countryside but it picked up as soon as we hit some small towns. Bob studied shop windows and pedestrians, strip malls and SUVs.

"You didn't tell me that America was at war," he observed thoughtfully.

"Huh?"

"There are so many tanks on the road."

"Those aren't tanks. They're the kind of cars a lot of

people drive these days, especially when they have kids and have to haul a lot of people and stuff around."

"They're huge."

"Yup."

We finally pulled into the Cummins Mall area, which was packed with cars and shoppers.

"This place is for shopping?" Bob asked incredulously. "It looks like a walled city in Europe."

"Americans do a *lot* of shopping these days. From what I understand, the US economy mostly depends on Americans spending money and shopping."

"Amazing."

"So, Bob, first I want to go to the bookstore and get Milly's CDs. I usually let myself browse there for a while since I hardly ever get to a bookstore. Are you going to be okay with that? If we get separated, let's just meet back here at the car at four."

"Roz, I told you I'll be fine, I promise. Don't worry about it."

I love our vanishing bookstores, with their built-in coffee shops and half-price racks. After picking up two CDs I knew Milly wanted, I wandered into the book section. I passed by the coffee shop, and there sat Bob, at a table with an elderly woman who seemed to be muttering to herself. Her numerous, slightly tattered, shopping bags surrounded them. Bob waved as I walked by.

One of the big display racks caught my eye. A picture book of English Royal jewelry. Ooh! I grabbed a copy and found the nearest easy chair. Thumbing through a book with chapters entitled "Diamonds," "Emeralds," "Rubies," and "Pearls with Diamonds" was kind of fun. After a few minutes, I noticed Bob perched in the easy chair next to mine.

"What're you reading?" he asked.

I felt in my pocket for my cell phone. I figured I could use it when I talked to Bob so people wouldn't think I was nuts. Then I remembered I'd left it on my nightstand in my hurry to leave that morning. Of course. I glanced around to make sure I had no witnesses as I started talking to thin air. "I like jewelry, and rumor has it that the Queen loans brides in her family a tiara for their wedding. I just wanted to see her tiaras before the next royal wedding."

Unfortunately, the book had no chapter entitled, "Tiaras," so I had to look them up individually from the index. "This one's my favorite, but it might be too fancy for a wedding." I showed Bob a picture of the Cambridge Lover's Knot Tiara, with dangling pearls hung in the middle of diamond arches. "When I was a girl, my mother had this record of Strauss waltzes. I loved that record, and I'd spend hours studying the album cover. It showed an elegant couple dressed for a ball. He wore a tux, and the lady held a glass of champagne and wore her dark hair piled high on her head, with a delicate little diamond and dangling pear-shaped pearl tiara. Here I was, a chunky kid in suburban New Jersey surrounded by clutter, laundry, screaming kids, and yapping pets, but that picture gave me a glimpse of a life of grace and elegance that I've searched for ever since. I'd give a week's paycheck to find that album cover again."

A passing salesman gave me a strange look, so I shut both the book and my mouth, and moved on to the mystery section, where I picked out a couple of books for the quiet days between Christmas and New Years. Funny how you'll scrimp and scrimp in some areas of your life (like heating and food for me) yet spend money with an open fist in others (like books, bottles of wine, and the occasional nice restaurant meal).

Bob and I headed toward the check out. I withstood the loathed ten-minute sales pitch from the cashier: Would you like to become a member? Would you like to upgrade your membership? Would you like to purchase? Would you like to donate? It's getting harder and harder just to pay for a purchase and leave a store unscathed.

After that minor skirmish, it was time for lunch, a splurge at Chen's Palace. Bob did a double-take at the terra cotta funeral statues of medieval Chinese warriors. After we were seated at a circular booth against the wall, I held my menu over my mouth so I could explain to Bob that a farmer found those statues in a field in China about forty years ago. I couldn't remember how old the originals were, but I think they've found about 6000 of them so far. I swear, one of these days I'm going to get over to China so I can see them in person.

"That's kind of strange, having burial statues in a restaurant. It's like eating in a funeral home," Bob said.

"It's not that bad. The statues add a lot of atmosphere, don't you think? Oh, I just love the food here." I ordered an appetizer and an entrée—sheer luxury—and settled in my comfortable seat. The waiter seemed a little disconcerted when I held on to my menu, but it was either duck under the table to talk with Bob or keep the menu in front of my face, so the menu won.

I have to admit, though, that so far Bob was not a bad traveling companion. For the most part, he seemed happy to look at things and periodically mutter to himself. Or shake his head. Especially with the way people were dressed, like wearing flip-flops in December. The worst part seemed to be when shoppers unknowingly walked through a piece of him. They'd get a funny look on their faces, as if part of their body had been dumped in an ice bath. Bob didn't appear particularly happy when it happened either. "It feels like when you've been pushed by a wave in the ocean. You keep standing, but you feel pushed around, somehow," is how he described it in an unhappy voice.

The waiter came over, introduced himself, and gave the customary spiel about the sauces. As the waiter wrapped up, another voice interjected, "Roz? Is that you?"

I looked over, and there was David following the hostess past my booth.

"David! Wow, hi! What are you doing here?" Now this was a pleasant surprise. Complicated, but pleasant.

"Decided to stop by for lunch on my way home from Rochester. You?"

"Christmas shopping."

"How's it going?"

"Pretty good so far, but I really just got started."

"Mind if I join you for lunch?"

Bob made a face, but I said, "Of course not. Please do."

I put down the menu and started scooting toward a more central seat in the booth. David sat at the far end of the circular booth and began moving toward me. He bumped into Bob, got the customary strange look on his face, and backed up a bit.

"So, have you ordered?" he asked, as he picked up the menu I'd been holding.

"Yup. Spinach with garlic, and house combo lo mein."

"Sounds good." David reviewed his choices for a minute. "The food here is something, isn't it? One of my favorite restaurants. Too bad it's so far from the lake." David motioned our waiter over and ordered a bowl of beef and broccoli. Afterward, looking around, he observed, "These terra cotta warriors are interesting, aren't they?"

"That's what I thought, too." I cut my eyes over to Bob as I said it. He was too busy examining David to pay any attention to me. David looked good, I might add, in his blue jeans and well-worn Irish fisherman's sweater, topped off today with a tweed jacket.

"I've always wanted to go to China," I continued, just making conversation.

"How come?" David turned, and eyed me curiously.

"I'm not really sure what started it," I answered, nudging my silverware as I thought. "I know I loved all the Clavell books about the Orient, especially *Noble House*. And these days you can't pick up a newspaper or watch a news show without someone talking about how China is whupping America's butt in some way or another." I paused, then continued in a rush, "Sometimes I wonder if America isn't like England was late in the reign of Victoria. Sure, today the sun never sets on our business empire, but there are a couple of big looming countries that might be able to clean our clocks in a few years unless we keep our wits about us. So, I've just been curious." My spurt of talking dribbled to a close. "I'd like to see China for myself instead of always hearing about it second-hand."

"Interesting." David looked at me again, but I got the feeling he was really seeing me for the first time. "And here I thought cookies and wines were your favorite pastimes."

I grinned. "I *love* cookies and wines, but they'll only get you so far, don't you think? How about you? Are you interested in China?"

"Not particularly, but I love the food."

"You'll get no argument from me on that one." I took a sip of my ice water and glanced at Bob. His attention had drifted and now he was studying our fellow diners. Relieved, I turned back to David. "So what were you in Rochester for?"

"Boring legal stuff. As I said Saturday, this is the time of year that I get caught up on everything I don't have time for when I'm busy with the grapes. I had to sign off on my will. Pretty cheery, huh?"

"Not very cheery, but I'm impressed. I don't know lots of people who take care of that kind of thing." I admire conscientious people. It may be unfashionable, but I always have. "I try to update my will every ten years or so, mostly so I don't leave my sisters with a mess if anything happens to me. I always get depressed while I'm working on it, but then I feel very grown up and responsible when I can put it behind me for another decade." Trying to remember David's lunch order, I asked, "Are you sure you don't want a glass of wine with lunch? I always need one after I've been working on my will."

"Nah, I'm fine," he answered in a matter-of-fact voice. "It's all just part of owning my own business, the vineyard. Doesn't bother me at all. I'm glad you mentioned the Christmas shopping, though. I should pick up a few things while I'm here and save myself a trip later."

"Good idea. They've got some great stores here. I especially like the Godiva chocolate shop."

The waiter appeared with our lunches, so we broke off talking about the mall stores and focused on our food. We shared my delicious garlicky greens. Bob had been quiet while David and I talked, but he started getting fidgety while we ate. I gave him the stink eye, which quieted him for a second, but then his hand flicked out and David's knife fell to the floor.

While David bent over to pick it up, I muttered between clenched teeth, "Cut it out, Bob!"

David's head popped up. "Huh?"

"Oh, nothing, I just got something caught in my throat."

Bob flung his head back on the seat cushion and pretended to snore from boredom. His body gradually slipped under the table, and I noticed him wandering out of the restaurant. Fine! Good riddance! I knew it had been a bad idea bringing him.

Conversing with David got easier now that I didn't have Bob's head turning back and forth between us like a spectator at a tennis match.

"So, what are your plans for Christmas?" I asked David.

He swallowed the mouthful of food he'd been chewing and said, "I haven't really given it much thought, but I'll probably go down to my sister's place in Ithaca. Her two kids will be home from college, so it should be a lot of fun."

"Yeah, I'm going to my sister's, too. I'm heading to New Jersey to spend time with Katie, the sister you met, her husband and daughter, and my dad and his wife. It'll be good to reconnect after spending the last couple of months moving in and getting settled."

"You never told me why you left . . . where was it? Nashville?" David asked while our waiter cleared the empty dishes.

I refilled our cups of green tea. "Ugh. Depressing story." I didn't like thinking about those depressing years of my life.

As if sensing my reluctance, David added, "You don't have to tell me if you don't want to."

"It's just I hate telling stories about myself where I look like such an idiot. I mean, talk about making mistakes. I feel like I've made every one in the book. Divorced, overreached myself financially by buying a second home as an investment, then lost my job when my employer shut down its American branch in Nashville. Now I've got all my savings locked into a lake house, and I won't see a penny unless I sell it, and nobody's buying houses these days. Sheesh, talk about the stereotype for the Great Recession." I took a breath after my confession, then continued. "So now you know why I carry on so much about cookies and wines. The rest is too painful to think about."

"You're not alone," David said, pushing his teacup in absent-minded circles. "Millions of people are in the same boat with unemployment and stagnant home sales. Hell, I'm one grape harvest away from being there myself, and don't think worrying about that doesn't keep me awake nights."

"It's such a brutal economy. My sister tells me I have to keep thinking about the good things in my life, like my freelance writing, and the fact that I have a little savings to keep me for a while. And I live in a beautiful place, and have family who love me. Those are genuine blessings but, like you said, they're tough to remember at two in the morning." I drank the last of my tea and pushed my cup away.

"Actually," David added, "for me, it's one in the morning. I must go to bed earlier than you because I have to be up early for the vineyard."

"Got ya." I smiled. Even though I was sure it went against all the dating rulebooks, it felt good to talk honestly with someone, and get honesty back.

Our bills came, and David swooped both of them up.

"David, really, you don't have to do that."

"It's my pleasure. You can pay me back by showing me where this Godiva store is. I bet my sister would like some fancy chocolates when I go to see her for Christmas."

David settled the check, I gathered my shopping bags, and we squirmed out of the booth. David offered to carry my bags, and I happily passed them over to him. A gentleman. How nice to run across a member of that vanishing breed!

We wandered out of the restaurant and through the crowded mall. Christmas decorations hung everywhere, and a cheerful, festive mood filled the air. Once we made it to the chocolatier, David made his selection fairly quickly, and then headed off to the department store to finish his shopping. We'd agreed he'd stop by my place the following morning for coffee.

I continued to study the chocolate selections. About fifteen minutes later, I settled up and headed for the department store to browse for a little something for my niece. I'd decided to compromise and get her a smallish gift, not one that was so big I'd feel bad not buying presents for all my other nieces and nephews. The politics of gift-giving are exhausting.

But what to get? I pushed my way through the department store crowds. Finally I wandered into the linen section, and

there was Bob, stretched out on one of the showcase beds.
I sat down next to him and pretended to reorganize my
shopping bags.

"Hey, Bob, let's get going."

"Huh?"

Bob was not one of those snap-awake kinds of ghosts.
He woke up slowly, looking disoriented. "This was the only
place I could think of to keep people from walking through
me. I was starting to get a little nauseated with so many
people just bashing through me."

"I tried to tell you it would be crowded."

"Yes, you did, but it was still worth it to come. Are you
finished? Are we going home now?"

"Just about. I saw a pretty pair of earrings downstairs
that I think Amy would like, so I'll pick them up on the way
out."

I re-gathered my ever-heavier shopping bags and purse,
along with Bob, and walked over to the downstairs escalator.
He gestured for me to go ahead of him and squeezed onto
the next step down. People packed on behind us. The whole
store was mobbed.

And there, lurking at the bottom of the escalators, were
the dreaded perfume sprayers, squirting atomizers of scent at
the unwary. By the time I got to the bottom of the escalator,
the pretty young thing bellowed "Marabec 12?" and spritzed
in my direction before I could yell "No!" I ducked out of the
spray's path unharmed, but it caught Bob square in the eyes.
He screamed like a banshee.

Things got awkward at the base of the escalator. I tried
to step away from both the squirt girl and Bob, who was
yelling, stumbling around, and rubbing his face like a dying
tenor at the opera or Hamlet chewing through the scenery
in his death act. Of course, nobody else saw Bob, so I must
have looked like I was stumbling about aimlessly as I tried

to avoid him, and all hell broke loose when I wheeled around and hit those display shelves of crystal, and they fell crashing to the floor.

Sheesh.

Thank goodness no one got hurt. Thank goodness it was cheap glass, not real crystal. Thank goodness I was merely solicitously escorted out the door instead of being forced to pay for everything. And, I'm ashamed to say, I let them usher me out with hardly a backward glance at Bob, who was still flailing around, bellowing like a bull in the middle of a Christmas-spangled china shop.

I'd had enough. This was worse than shopping with crabby two-year-old twins.

After being politely but firmly pushed out of the store, I collapsed on a bench outside the mall door and waited for Bob. After about ten minutes he wandered out, saw me, and sat down. I couldn't wait until we got to the car and blurted out "What the hell, Bob! Are you kidding me? It was like the final act of *Tosca* in there!"

I didn't care if people thought I was nuts. I was getting used to it.

"It stung!"

"You're ectoplasm, for Pete's sake! That spray should have gone right through you. What was all the drama? Do you know how badly people could have gotten hurt with all your carrying on? With that broken glass all over the place?"

"She surprised me! You try getting a face full of chemicals and see how much you like it!"

I was tired and crowded and sick of lugging around shopping bags. "Let's just get out of here," I muttered and started toward the car. Bob trailed after me, neither one of us particularly happy. And I never did get those earrings for my niece.

It took twenty minutes of jockeying to get the car out of the heavy traffic of the busy mall parking lot. Lots of traffic for the first hour home, so I focused on my driving. By the time we hit the open countryside closer to the lake, I was feeling better and said to the mute figure at my side, "So, are we okay?"

After a pause, he answered, "Yes, sure, and I'm sorry about all the hubbub at the store."

"I'm sorry I was snappish, too," I admitted. "The older I get, the less I like dealing with mobs of people, and it makes me cranky. I'm sorry I yelled at you." I negotiated a four-way stop, then continued. "But I've been thinking, Bob. What are we doing here? I don't feel like we're making any progress with your assignment. Have you even figured out what your job is yet?"

"As a matter of fact, my mission has gotten clearer. I caught my boss by the water cooler yesterday and bent his ears for a few minutes. I'm supposed to help you decide whether you want to stay at the lake or not."

Now that was one bizarre assignment. "Why on earth would anyone care whether I live on the lake or leave it? What difference could it possibly make to anyone except me and maybe a few people in my family?"

"I think it's got something to do with whether or not you do something while you live here." Bob shrugged his shoulders in puzzlement. "And before you ask, no, I don't have any idea what the doing something involves. Frankly, I'm surprised my boss told me as much as he did. He's famous for being close-mouthed."

This was ridiculous. I burst out, "Do something? Do something? What the heck does that mean? That could be anything! Bake a cake or have a baby! I don't do much of anything that people can see. I don't save lives or teach children or build homes. I write speeches and articles for executives, and develop charitable campaigns." I calmed down a bit as I started to think this through. "Maybe I'm supposed to develop something for one of my clients?"

"I honestly have no idea. I don't even know if I have anything at all to do with this something you're supposed to do," Bob pointed out. "I'm just supposed to help you decide whether you stay at the lake or move somewhere else."

"Don't you think that's kind of a weird assignment?"

"I've had odder ones. When I was talking to my boss, he reminded me about the time I had to help Charlie decide whether to buy a television or not. That was decades ago, when televisions were a big deal and very expensive."

Maybe Bob was trying to be helpful, but his example just got me more confused. "How long did you spend on that project?"

"Months."

"Did Charlie buy the television?"

"Eventually, yes."

"What happened to him and his TV?"

"Sorry. That part I don't remember."

"Of course not," I said sarcastically. Living with this ghost made me nuts sometimes.

By the time we pulled into the driveway, it was dark. I schlepped all the bags into the house, piled the presents into a bedroom corner for wrapping, then headed downstairs for a well-earned glass of wine.

Bob waved and said, "See you tomorrow," then shimmered out.

I turned on the radio to catch up with the news, took out a container of frozen homemade soup to nuke for dinner, and started putting together a dinner-sized salad. An exhausting day, but mostly productive and kind of fun—if you didn't count all the broken glass.

Chapter 9
Road Trip!

The next morning found me up bright and early. Lots to do. As we'd arranged at our first meeting, David would be coming over for coffee at ten, so I wanted to bake a cinnamon streusel coffeecake for us. The Christmas cookies, unfortunately, were gone. Shocker. Then I needed to wrap the Christmas gifts I'd bought yesterday, and I needed to get organized to head off to New Jersey the following day. Hard to know what to pack. The weather in the Finger Lakes had been so warm lately, weird and almost spring-like. I knew that couldn't last too long. And I wanted to check in with my clients to wish them a happy holiday, make sure they got my presents, and remind them I'd be out of pocket for a week. I'd be monitoring email, but still, a reminder wouldn't hurt.

I bustled around, got the coffeecake into the oven and a pot of coffee started. Then I sat down to make lists. One of my lists included—don't laugh—stick figures, one for each day of the week I'd be in New Jersey. I'd draw various mix and match outfits on each stick figure according to the day's planned activities.

These diagrams made it made it easy for me to pack. I guess I needed some kind of visualization to figure out which clothes to pack without bringing my whole closet. Silly, but it worked. Though I pitied the poor person who tried to figure out my packing list.

Promptly at ten, the doorbell rang. I ran up the stairs to answer it. The house smelled wonderful from the coffee and cinnamon cake and David had a nice smile on. Life was good. I gave him an informal tour as we walked down to the kitchen. In the guest room, I mentioned my little episode with the glassware at the department store.

David stopped looking around the room and focused on me. "As long as no one was hurt, that's the important thing," he said. "But you sure had an odd afternoon, Roz."

"Oh, that kind of thing always happens to me," I said, trying to be casual. We walked into my bedroom and I continued. "I've noticed it all my life. Weird stuff just always seems to happen to me. I went to the opera one time, Mozart's *Cosi Fan Tutti*, and the lead soprano had a sore throat so she couldn't sing. But her substitute was in a wheelchair with a broken ankle, so even though the substitute could sing, she couldn't walk and do the acting. So the soprano with the sore throat acted out the role while the substitute soprano sang the part seated in her wheelchair at the side of the stage. It worked, but it was so bizarre the *New York Times* had an article about it the next day. And I was there."

"I'm not a big opera fan," David said. I think he was more interested in my old-fashioned radiators than my opera story, but I continued talking while we went downstairs and into the living room.

"Another time I went to a concert in Nashville conducted by Kenneth Schermerhorn. The fire alarm went off in the middle of it, and the audience was all in a dither because we didn't know what was going on. Maestro Schermerhorn calmly stopped the orchestra in the middle of the music, walked offstage to ask Security what was happening, came back, told us the fire alarm was malfunctioning and we could ignore it, went back to the podium and just started up the orchestra right where he'd left off. It was amazing. But I told John the Third, my date, that this kind of thing was always happening to me. It's why I developed another one of my mottoes—It's always an adventure in Roz-ville. For someone who lives on her own, somehow the oddest things are always happening to me. It keeps my life pretty darn interesting most of the time."

David finished running his hand along the top of my antique fireplace mantelpiece. I couldn't tell whether he was checking for dust or enjoying the smooth surface. I got my answer when he said, "This mantel is beautiful, Roz. You don't see workmanship like this much anymore. It's quarter-sawn red oak, too, which is virtually impossible to find these days." He looked around. "Where do you keep your wood?"

"I don't have any yet," I confessed. "The realtor suggested I get the chimney cleaned before I tried to light a fire and I haven't gotten around to it yet."

"Cleaning is a good idea. We get too many creosote fires out here. Just let me know when you want some wood and I'll bring it over." He paused and glanced at me. "By the way, do you know how to build a fire?" My deer-in-the-headlights look probably answered the question because he laughed and added, "I'll show you how."

"Well thanks," I replied, breathing a sigh of relief.

"Anyway," David continued, picking up the thread of my story as we entered the kitchen, "It sounds as if you do have an interesting life. Not exactly the peaceful, quiet life I might imagine judging by externals."

"You have *no* idea. I think the quietest life can be phenomenally rich and complex, but it seems to be very hard to explain that to most people.

I cut the cake while David poured the coffee. We sat down and I said, "Before you came, I was starting to get myself organized for my Christmas trip to my sister's house. I'll be heading out tomorrow and getting back right after Christmas. I was making out my list of clothes to pack, but this warm weather makes it hard to know what to bring."

"From my point of view," David said, taking a good-sized forkful of cake, "this warm weather is a lot more serious than trying to figure out what to wear."

"What do you mean?"

"I'm worried about my vines. Over the past few months the weather would typically have been cooling off gradually, so my vines would have slowly become hardened off and used to the cold. If the temperature drops drastically now, it could kill off any buds because they wouldn't be accustomed to the cold. A quick temperature drop could be fatal to my harvest for next year, so I'm hoping the temperatures start to drop slowly."

I didn't know a thing about growing grapes, but I didn't want to see anybody hurt by the weather. I said, "Well, in that case I'll start hoping for cooler weather too. These warmer temperatures really are sort of freaky. I think it's the kind of weather where you can get the flu. But I didn't realize how serious the situation would be from your point of view. I'm sorry. I hope things get better."

"That's how it goes for farmers. If it's not one thing, it's another. If you can't deal with the fluctuations in the weather, especially around here, you shouldn't be in the grape-growing business."

Every time I talked with David, his common sense impressed me. It made a good counterpoint to my drama queen tendencies. He said, "To change the topic to something more pleasant, though, I like your house. Especially the way you're right on top of the water. I bet you'll love it in the summer, what with fishing, boating and swimming. I think you'll have a lot of fun here."

"Yeah, I guess. We'll see," I said in a noncommittal voice. Since I wasn't a big nature girl, I had my doubts.

"Have you gotten to know your neighbors? Is anyone here this time of year?"

That got me started on Mary and Stan. Then we went on to local politics and the extended fishing season question. Before I knew it, it was almost noon. David noticed the time flying right about the same time I did.

"Noon? I'd better get going. I've got tons to do today. And I've got to let you get to your packing. How about I call you when you're back after Christmas?"

"I'd like that. Have a good time with your family. I hope your sister likes her chocolates."

"You, too. Have a good Christmas. I'll see you afterward."

We gave each other a neighborly Christmas hug, and David was out the door. Still awash in happy holiday feelings, I wrapped up a few pieces of coffeecake to take to Mary and Stan. Wackadoos they might be, but it was still the holidays, and I was feeling optimistic.

I sat and visited with Stan for a few minutes over a cup of coffee and he seemed happy to get the coffeecake. Mary was napping so we didn't get to visit, but Stan said he'd pass along my holiday wishes. I asked him if he'd keep an eye on my place while I was away and call the police if he saw anyone walking out with a TV. No problem.

Finally, about two in the afternoon, after my very social morning, I called my clients to wish them a happy holiday and remind them I'd be away, paid a few bills, did a small load of laundry, and finished making my lists. I wrapped the Christmas presents and started packing. At five I pulled another container of homemade soup from the freezer (it was really good soup but, frankly, I was starting to get thoroughly sick of it), added some cheese and crackers, sat down at the table and called Bob. He shimmered into the chair on my left.

"So, you all set to head to New Jersey tomorrow?" I asked. "Do you have your substitute spook in place for Lola?"

"I pulled in a few favors, so I can leave whenever you're ready."

"Do you have to pack?"

"Nope. I can dress as we go along. As long as I know what I should be wearing, I can make it happen."

"You mean, if I asked you to wear something different from that smoking jacket right now, you could?"

"Sure. What do you want me to put on?"

"Oh, I don't know. How about a scuba outfit? Or a cowboy suit? Or you could be a clown?"

Bob gave me one of his patented deadpan looks. "Don't push your luck. Here, I'll put on the outfit I'm going to wear when we motor down to your sister's place tomorrow." Bob's smoking jacket began to waver, like a pot of water shimmers when it starts to come to a boil. Segments of clothes shifted and wriggled, and the next thing I knew, I was eating dinner with a Ricky-Ricardo-motors-to-California look-alike. The slacks, the hat, the tailored jacket—all I needed was a chorus of ba-ba-loo.

"That is totally cool, Bob! How neat to be able to wear anything you want. Sure cuts down on luggage complications, doesn't it?"

Bob reached into his jacket, pulled out the omnipresent rye, and took a slug. "Makes life a lot easier."

"I guess you don't really need to pack, then. Except for my Christmas present, of course."

Bob got a wary look in his eyes. "Christmas present?"

"You've been living with me for weeks now. Yeah, I'd say a Christmas present is in order." Actually, I was just razzing him. How could a ghost give me a present? If he didn't have money, how could he get one without stealing it? And I didn't want any stolen presents, thank you very much. But it was kind of fun to let him stew and sweat once in a while. Made for a nice change of pace.

"So how is this holiday going to work?" Bob asked.

I started outlining my carefully mapped itinerary. "I'll spend the nights at Katie and Bill's place. Pop and Milly live a mile down the road from them, but since Dad's almost ninety, having people stay at their house is a little too much for them. I'll spend most of the day with Dad, though, and then spend the night at Katie's house. We'll bring Pop and Milly over to Katie's for a quiet Christmas dinner. Then the day after Christmas I'll take my niece Amy into Manhattan for the day. I know she's been wanting to see the Egyptian wing at the Metropolitan Museum, so we'll probably spend most of the day there. Then come back here."

Bob looked intrigued. "Sounds like fun. I'm looking forward to getting into Manhattan again. It'll be interesting to see if it's changed much."

I crunched into a cracker, swallowed, and said, "I'm sure it's changed a lot. It's changed a lot since I used to go there as a teenager with my mom. Have you remembered when you were there last?"

"I can't be sure, but I think I was there during World War II. And I think I lived in Manhattan before that, in the nineteen-twenties and thirties."

"So that's what, eighty, ninety years ago? Oh, yeah, you're going to see lots of changes. Be prepared," I cautioned.

"Oh, I'm not worried," Bob replied, nonchalant as always.

"No, you never are, are you?" Which probably explained why I was seeing more and more gray hairs lately. "What happens if we get separated and you get lost? Can you find my sister's place in New Jersey? Or would you come all the way back here?"

"Good question," Bob replied. "I have no idea. My hunch, though, is that since I'm your ghost, I'd find you wherever you were. Just don't run off to China or anything. That might be stretching it."

I'd never really understood the rules behind this haunting situation. Frankly, I had a sneaking suspicion Bob made them up as we went along.

Friday morning found me up at seven to put the finishing touches on my packing. I come from a family of hit-the-road-at-crack-of-dawn sorts, but that's not my style anymore. These days, my only goal when I drive somewhere is to get to my destination on the outside of a body bag. If it takes me half an hour longer to get somewhere because I take a few coffee breaks on the road, that's fine with me. This attitude makes my family nuts. For decades, after our welcome home hugs, my father's first question when we'd walk in the door would be "So how long did your drive take?" The second question would be "How was your mileage?" Only to be expected, I guess, when you come from three generations of engineers.

Bob and I got started about nine, and I opted to drive the longer southern route to New Jersey, south along Route 15, and then east along 80. The northern route, through Binghamton, was shorter, but it had a lot more traffic. Big semi-truck traffic, and I drive a very squash-able VW. The southern route was gorgeous, offering wide-open highway through magnificent mountains. I never could resist the lure of the open road.

"I'm glad we're doing this drive," Bob said. "I think I spent most of my life in cities, and I'm not sure I've ever been out here before. This countryside is amazing."

"I love driving trips and train trips," I confided as we navigated the mountain highways. "I was thinking the other day about my favorite moments in my life. I decided that one of the things that makes me happiest is standing on a dark, chilly railroad platform, very early in the morning, with a cup of hot coffee in one hand and an unknown adventure waiting ahead of me. I love passing through a place in a car or a train, instead of just flying over it in a plane.

"I used to have a job where I did a lot of traveling for a small start-up charitable organization," I continued. "I'd fly into a new area, rent a car, and then spend the week driving to meetings in lots of small towns and suburbs. It was great, seeing so much of the country up close and personal. One thing that cracked me up would be that, no matter where I was renting a car—Ohio, California or Texas—the radio station in it would always be tuned to a country-western station. Always."

"If it was such a great job, how come you're not doing it anymore?" Bob asked.

"Well, for one thing, since it was a very small charity, it had no benefits, and it didn't pay much. And, as much as I liked the traveling, it wore me out being away from home so much. I got divorced somewhere in the middle of that job, and I felt like I'd lost my roots. I felt untethered to anybody, and I hate that feeling. Like I was wandering the universe without a home base. I remember I'd call my sister Angela every night from the road so someone would always know that I existed and where I was. For a few years, my divorce really messed me up. I think I've got my balance back now, but it was actually a long, hard struggle. But let's not talk about that now. I've got a fresh cup of coffee, an open road, and beautiful scenery. Let's just enjoy this while we can."

After a few more hours, I pulled into one of those huge trucker stations where you can buy a hot meal or take a shower. Bob wandered around while I used the bathroom (as they say, you don't buy coffee, you rent it), and I found him over by the trucker accessories.

Bob asked, "How'd you like a GPS system for your Christmas present? What is a GPS system, by the way?"

I gave a quick glance around. "No, thanks. I'm good. I'm going to get a sandwich. You want anything?"

"No, thanks. Everything's jake."

One ham and cheese on rye later, we were back on the road. By three p.m., I was navigating the local roads I'd learned to drive on. It's always so strange to go back to your hometown. I passed by the place where my sister totaled our VW Beetle when she went toe-to-toe with a deer. A few miles further, I came to the part of the road where the police caught my twelve-year-old brother doing twenty miles per hour in his homemade go-cart in the dead of night, and escorted him home. I'm amazed parents don't automatically get issued gray hair when they take their newborns home from the hospital.

Katie and Bill had a roomy, newer colonial about a mile down the road from Pop and Milly's older, more child-worn home. When I pulled into Katie's driveway, she was waiting for me. "Roz, you made it!" she yelled.

"A little butt-sore, but all in one piece. Hey, sis."

Many hearty sister-hugs later, Katie helped me get my bags into the house. After taking everything upstairs to the guest bedroom, Katie looked around. "So, is he here?"

Bob waved from the chair. "Give her my regards."

I answered, "Yeah. He sends you his regards."

"Great, just great. He still can't push over a salt-cellar, though, can he?"

"I guess not. He can be awfully stubborn sometimes."

Katie sighed. "Fine. Whatever. I'll be downstairs while you settle in. You want some tea?"

"That'd be great. I'll be down in a few minutes."

Oh, it felt good to be back. True, Katie and Bill had a couple of big crotch-poking dogs, but I could deal with that for a few days. After unpacking my valise, putting the bags of gifts in the corner, and getting out the oversized jug of maple syrup and Butter Bombs I'd brought as hostess gifts, I headed to the kitchen.

Katie slid me a cup of Irish Breakfast tea. "So, you're still wandering around with Bob, huh?"

"Yeah, he wanted to meet the family and come into Manhattan when I take Amy in. He says he used to live in Manhattan back in the 1920s and 1930s."

There was just no disguising the worried look in Katie's eyes. She resolutely changed the topic, though. "So, other than Bob, is everything else going okay? How's work?"

"Not bad. Both Community Chest campaigns went pretty well, which is a miracle in this economy, and both Tess and Amanda want to compete for the America Wins! Community Chest awards this spring. And they're competing in different categories, so I don't have any conflict-of-interest worries. I'll have lots of work helping to put their entries together for the next few months, which is great. So financially I should be okay for a little bit. Treading water, but that's what a lot of people are doing these days."

"Did you and David ever get together for coffee, the way you were telling me?"

"Yup, he came over yesterday, and we spent a couple of hours talking. You were right, Katie. He is a nice guy."

Katie looked totally smug. Talk about the cat who swallowed the canary. "Yeah, I thought he seemed nice. What about after the holidays?"

"He said he'd call. Sheesh. Will you wipe that grin off your face?"

Katie laughed out loud at the crabby tone of my comment. "It's just good to know you have a real person keeping an eye on you. I don't know if Bob would be much use if your heating went out, for instance. This way you could call David."

"Actually, I'd probably call a plumber. But I know what you mean." I shuddered to think of Bob trying to deal with a real-life emergency. Bob and a gimpy distributor cap. Bob and a leaky ice dam. Bob and a burst hot water tank. For that matter, Bob and a burst appendix. Yikes! The mind boggled.

"I've got a little bit of good news about Bob."

"No kidding. Tell me. I could really use some good news about Bob."

"He found out what his assignment is with me. He's supposed to help me figure out whether I should live at the lake or not."

"With all the lake real estate in the tank, I don't see how that's really a decision right now, is it? Could you even sell your place if you wanted to?"

"I don't know. I don't think a lot of people are buying lake houses these days, especially in the dead of winter, but I haven't really looked into it. I'd be happy to stay at the lake. It's gorgeous. If only I could find the kinds of things I like. People, music, classes, bookstores, and coffeehouses. But I don't know if I'll find them. It's pretty isolated."

"You have to give things a little time, Roz. You just moved there. Frankly, I think Bob's assignment is pretty stupid. I don't want to get your visit off to a bad start but you know me, I say what's on my mind."

Sigh. I sure did. And she sure did. "I know, Katie, and I halfway agree with you, but I don't have a whole lot of control over the situation. Besides, I like having Bob around most of the time. He can be a pain in the butt, but he's also a lot of fun once in a while. So, in the big scheme of things, it's not a big deal."

"Couldn't you exorcise him or something?"

"He's a ghost, Katie, not a devil."

"Get the house blessed, then. Doesn't that get rid of ghosts?"

"I have no idea. I know in Charleston they paint their ceilings, doors, and window frames this shade of blue—I think it's called Haint Blue—and that's supposed to keep out ghosts."

"Try that, then."

"Katie, I thought you were okay with ghosts. Why are you starting to get so bent out of shape about this now? I've actually gotten used to it, and I'm pretty comfortable having Bob around now."

"*That's* why I'm so upset! The more comfortable you are with a ghost, the less you're going to be going out and spending time with real people. You're going to become a nutty recluse, and I love having my big sister around, and I don't want you to go crazy!"

I could see poor Katie was getting genuinely upset, so I went over and put my arms around her. "Oh, sweetie, you're getting all worked up over nothing. I'll be fine."

"Sure, that's what you say, Roz, but, trust me, this is a really bizarre situation you're dealing with. I want to support you, I always do, but this is getting kind of crazy. My big sister, who I've always loved and respected, is starting to lose it."

"Katie, look, I promise I won't talk about Bob anymore. Would that help?"

"Not talking about it is not the same as fixing it."

"I know, but I don't know what else to do."

Katie wiped her eyes.

"Look, let's just drop it for now, okay? I'll just concentrate on having a good time with you and the family and enjoying the holidays. Can I give you a hand with dinner?"

Katie blew her nose and got up from the table. I could see she was trying to get her balance back. What a sweetheart she was. My rock. "Why don't you set the table," Katie said. "All four of us will be here for dinner. Bill should be home from work soon, and Amy will be back from her friend's. You know where everything is."

I did know where everything was. That was one of the true joys of spending time with people I knew and loved. I remembered, for instance, being with Katie twenty-some-odd years ago when she had bought the good china I was setting on the table.

"Hey, Katie, you remember when we bought this china in Flemington?"

"Oh, my gosh, what on earth made you think of that? That was so long ago." Katie walked into the dining room and picked up a plate, looking at it with fresh eyes. "I've always loved this pattern. Twenty years, and I'm still not tired of it."

"I remember how much fun we had shopping that day. Now me, it took me forever to find wedding china I liked. I loved flowers, like you have, but I wanted a white background, and every floral pattern I saw had bugs or birds or bees on it and I just didn't want china with livestock all over it."

Katie laughed and looked as though something clicked into place in her mind as she did so. "You know, Roz, I've just decided I'm not going to worry about you and Bob any more. Livestock! You've always been a nutcase, and you've done fine. You're just running true to form with having a ghost, and I'm not going to waste any more energy worrying about it. You're my brilliant, nutty older sister, and I wouldn't change a thing about you. I'm delighted you and David are getting to know each other but, hey, whatever happens, happens."

"I love this new mellow, Katie! How about I open some wine and we drink to that, sis? I promise, if I think things are ever spinning out of control, I'll let you know."

"*Que sera, sera*. Whatever will be, will be. Bill's going to be here any minute, so let's get this wine open."

By the time Bill walked in fifteen minutes later, Katie and I were starting to feel much better. Bill oversees the grounds-keeping for several public golf courses. Although he's in management now, he still had the muscles and stamina of someone who'd spent decades working on the greens. Strong like bull.

When Katie started getting serious about Bill, I'd been surprised to learn how much work goes into keeping those golf courses green and attractive. Bill sat through forty hours a year of classes on garden pests, fertilizers, soil types and remediation, and ground cover mowing techniques. Here I'd thought golf courses were natural green grass that you kept mowed; just shows how ignorant I can be. In many ways Katie and Bill were perfectly matched—both very practical and down-to-earth people. Their infrequent fights were spectacular, like grand Italian opera. Even though I could butt heads with either or both of them once in a while, I loved them both dearly.

After friendly hello hugs and kisses, Bill checked out our riesling and opted for a beer instead. "So how was the drive, Roz? You come the southern route?"

"Yeah. I know it takes a little longer, but I like the scenery. I'm hoping it stays clear after Christmas. I don't like the idea of driving those hills in snow."

Katie piped in, "You know you can stay as long as you want here, Roz. Don't rush home on our account."

"Thanks, sweetie. I'll watch the weather and play it by ear, but if it's possible I'd like to try to get home a couple of days after Christmas."

What I couldn't admit to Katie, who was not a reader, was that I had a private annual tradition called Couch Potato Days during the week between Christmas and New Years. It usually involved spending four or five days stretched out on the sofa, eating little but the holiday treats I'd accumulated (good chocolates, Christmas cookies, Texas red grapefruits, annual cashews from my friend Susie, artisan bread, a nice chunk of Brie or Stilton, stuffed green olives as big as plums), with my nose buried in a book. After a day or two of intensive reading, I'd come up for air, book drunk and disoriented after spending hours in Clavell's Hong Kong, Austen's England, medieval France, or Hogwarts. I'd stay in the real world only long enough to make a few phone calls to reassure people I was still alive, replenish my stash of finger foods, pick out another reading adventure, and then submerge. Antisocial? Probably. Glorious? Definitely!

After another few days of intensive reading, my deep cravings would be satisfied, and I could come up for air on New Year's Eve and hang out with friends like a normal person. And, of course, on New Year's Day I'd wake up like most Americans, full of resolutions and eating only diet food. The yin and yang of Couch Potato Days and New Year's austerity might not work for everybody, but it worked for me. Although I'm embarrassed to admit I've had the same New Year's resolution for about eight years now, and I still haven't been able to do it.

You know those movies where the heroine is lying down reading in bed in her satin pajamas and lipstick, and the next shot you see of her shows her asleep with the book upside-down on her generous chest? *That* has been my New Year's resolution for years—to fall asleep in bed with a book upside-down on my chest. I just can't do it. I'm such a control freak that, even though I read in bed all the time, I *always* have to get up to pee last thing before I try to go to sleep. *Always*. Which means I'll never fall asleep with a book on my chest. It's just one of the many Catch-22s I've managed to build into my life just to keep things interesting. I told Katie that if she ever found me dead with a book upside-down on my chest she should know I went out perfectly happy. Katie just sighed and shook her head.

Anyway, where was I? Oh, yes, Bill and Christmas plans. After a few minutes with our drinks, Amy walked in.

Nineteen years old, very smart, with the Murphy green eyes and her dad's straight brown hair. Amy wore it long, and this week the fringes were dyed a dark navy blue. Katie had long ago decided she'd need to pick her battles with her adolescent daughter, and she'd opted not to waste energies on skirmishes over hair, an endlessly renewable resource.

I gave Amy, who was also my godchild, a very enthusiastic hug. I had a soft spot in my heart for her. She was a bookish, school-loving child in a decidedly non-bookish, non-academic family. In many senses, though totally beloved, she was an alien baby in her parents' very practical household. That's where aunts and uncles came in handy once in a while to help bridge the gap between such different species. I've had my share of unhappy phone calls from both Katie and Amy over the years, and yet we'd all made it through in one piece.

Amy was following a medieval studies program at school and totally loved it. With a little encouragement, she opened up about her classes and her plans for a junior year in Cork, Ireland. Her parents weren't enthusiastic about their only child wandering so far from home, but they were doing their best to be supportive.

Katie brought in a salad and the turkey tetrazzini casserole that smelled so good, and we settled in to enjoy. Is it just in large families, or do all families have a couple of minutes of total silence when the food hits everyone's plates? I personally think of that quiet as the Murphy minute, where everyone's focused on the food. Eventually, Amy and I started working through our New York City plans for Friday, two days away. Our main focus would be the Metropolitan Museum. Amy didn't know it, but her godmother would also be treating her to a fancy tea at the Palm Court in the venerable Plaza Hotel. What can I say? I've always been one for the occasional grand gesture.

Katie brought out a plate of her killer brownies for dessert, which she ignored so she could dive into her Butter Bombs. The rest of us made a nice dent in them, though, and then I got up to load the dishwasher and set the kitchen to rights. After another hour of chatting, I headed upstairs. It had been a long drive, and I wanted to get over to Dad's right after breakfast tomorrow.

Chapter 10
Double-Dutch Holidays

After fifteen years of marriage, Pop and Milly were still on their honeymoon, so we kids gave them lots of space and privacy. No drop ins. Mom passed away twenty years ago, so it was good to see Dad getting on with his life. Although Mom and Milly were both New York City girls, with strong attitudes and accents to match, physically they couldn't have been more different. After giving birth to many children, Mom had put on a few pounds. She had also stopped worrying about the small stuff and was easy-going and inexhaustibly kind. Milly, an only child with no children of her own, was full of nervous energy. But she and Pop seemed happy together, and that was all that mattered.

I wish I could write a merry section on my visits with Dad and Milly over the next few days, but I can't. Every life has challenging, even miserable, things in it. Right up at the top of any list of tough things to deal with is watching a parent age badly. Dad was almost ninety, and his lungs were shot from his seventy-year-long, two-packs-a-day habit (although he insisted it was from the asbestos he had worked with in his youth). A glistening plastic umbilical cord now tethered him to a wheezing oxygen pump the size of a small filing cabinet.

Whenever I came to visit, I stepped into a brisk minuet of unbreakable schedules and routines. Baths on Wednesday and Sunday mornings; daily naps from ten-thirty to eleven-thirty and two to four; inviolate mealtimes, television programs, and baseball games.

As a girl, I had played Double Dutch jump rope. Two friends would spin two long ropes between them, with the ropes alternately hitting the ground. The trick to Double Dutch was timing your entry into the ropes, and then being nimble enough to keep jumping. That's how it felt going to visit Dad: like jumping into an intricate game of Double Dutch, participating in the game without messing up any of its iron-clad timing.

I did my best. In honor of my visit, Pop switched his daily cribbage card games with my stepmother to Scrabble, which I loved. And at which he cheerfully cheated, since he knew I'd never call him on it, despite my loud protestations. (*Tunafins? Denfog?* I don't *think* so, Dad!) Dad had fought cancer a couple of times over the past decade, and his body was getting tired. If we'd wanted to, we could have read the writing on the wall, but we all had our backs resolutely turned to it. These were Dad's choices, and we'd support him whatever he wanted to do.

It was a grim and beautiful time. My visits with Dad always were. Milly would usually leave for a few hours when Dad's children stayed with him. She needed a break after her days of careful caretaking, and she knew he'd be in good hands.

I only saw Bob a couple of times when I was at Dad's. He sat in on a Scrabble game, and he was there once during lunch. Like many men, I don't think he was comfortable with the atmosphere and paraphernalia of frailty, aging, and death.

After a long day with Dad, I cleaned up the dinner Milly had prepared for us and wrapped up for the mile walk back to Katie's house. Even though it was dark, there were sidewalks and streetlamps throughout the route, and I looked forward to some fresh air after the hot, very-lived-in, boiled-potato-and-overcooked-broccoli-scented air at Dad's.

Heartsick, I trudged to Katie's house. As tough as it had been to see Dad with his challenges, it was just as tough to imagine myself in his shoes, decades in the future. Only there wouldn't be a devoted spouse dedicating his life to making my last years comfortable, as Milly did for Pop. And there wouldn't be children showing up on my doorstep offering me free passes to cheat at Scrabble. Awful to think about it, but maybe my best-case scenario would be to keel over with a heart attack like my mom. Now if I could just time the heart attack for about age 80.

Shaking off my grim mood, I looked around at the comfortable suburb I'd grown up in. It was very prosperous now, a bedroom community for Manhattan. When my parents had moved in decades ago, it had been a small Italian farm town. Now elaborate Christmas lights and decorations dressed up virtually every Cape Cod and colonial home. The pizzeria had become an upper-class Italian restaurant; the Dairy Queen had morphed into a jewelers.

As I looked around, I noticed Bob floating along beside me, keeping step without moving a muscle. For once, he didn't seem goofy.

"Tough day today," he said.

"It's not easy for me to see Dad like that. I'm used to him ruling my world. Seeing him hobbling away to pee every forty-five minutes or cheating at Scrabble is so different from the pigheaded and loud father I've known all my life. No matter how wrong he'd been about something, he'd always been loud about it. But I need to focus on the good side. He's still living in his own home, and he's surrounded by people who love him who are going out of their way to help take care of him. How many of us are going to have that as we get older? And by us, of course, I mean me." I kicked a small rock out of my way on the sidewalk.

Bob didn't answer for a while, he just floated along next to me. "I think I died pretty quickly, when I was relatively young, maybe in my fifties. So I didn't have to go through everything your dad is dealing with."

"Was it bad? The dying, I mean."

"No. Not at all. You close your eyes in one life, and you open your eyes in the next. Not a big deal at all, at least for me. The only problem is, when you open your eyes in the next life, you have no clue what's going on or what you're supposed to do. It can take years to figure that out. I've heard rumors that they're working on an orientation program for new arrivals, which would be very useful, but it's not a very efficiently run operation. I'm about the least efficient person I know, and even I can see that."

"But Bob," I protested, "people have been dying for millennia; you would think the other side would be a lot more pulled together by this time. What's the hold up? How come it's not better organized? Do you know how they decide who's going to be a ghost, and who's going somewhere else?"

"Don't ask me. I'm just a low-level peon. I wander in, get my assignment, and wander out until it's done. Unless they start messing around with all this double-booking nonsense, which gets everyone confused. Your questions are way above my pay grade."

We strolled along in the darkness a little further, and I nodded at the dog-walker who passed me. The dog snarled at Bob, who recoiled. After we were out of hearing distance, I continued our conversation.

"But think about it, Bob. You've got all these dead geniuses up there—DaVinci, Einstein, Washington, Jefferson, Henry Ford, and all these engineers and management consultants— you'd think they'd be able to pull the after-life together."

"All I can say is, look at Congress on this side. Smart

people, every one of them, but they can't get anything done when they have to work with each other."

"A hit! A very palpable hit! Good point, Robert!"

"Besides, we've got all the doubles to deal with, which messes up our numbers like crazy."

"Doubles?"

"Sure. Let's say I married twice, and I loved both wives. Each wife could get a ghost of me. So I'd be doubled. And sometimes it happens even if you're not married but you're in love. Not to mention the children, brothers and sisters, and so on. Then there's ghosts assigned to people, and ghosts assigned to places. Believe me, it can get pretty messy."

"Wow. So there could be many Henry VIIIs up there? What a logistical nightmare. No wonder it's so chaotic."

"All I can say is, enjoy over here while you can. If you think *this* world is nutty, wait until you get to the other side. It makes this one look like a cakewalk."

By this point we were walking into Katie's driveway. I opened the kitchen door. Katie and Bill were in the living room watching TV. "I'm having a glass of wine," I said as I poked my head around the corner. "Can I pour some for anyone else?" Bill shook his head, and Katie got up to join me in the kitchen.

"How's Dad?"

"He's good enough to cheat like crazy at Scrabble, but it's hard to see him like this. You're such a good daughter, Katie, to be here for him and Milly. I don't know what we kids would do without you."

"I'm lucky I can get the time off from the school to give them a hand. Seniority comes in handy once in a while."

"If things get too intense you know you can always call on me to help. It's only a six-hour drive if the weather cooperates, so I can drive down for a while."

"I know, sweetie. So far we're okay, though. Milly's dealing with most of Dad's care. Anyway, let's talk about something more cheerful. Are you all ready for Christmas tomorrow?"

"Sure. I'll put my presents under the tree tonight. What time can I bring Pop and Milly over tomorrow?"

"I'll have dinner on the table at two, so why don't you drive them over here at one. Take my car, it's bigger, so Dad has more space to deal with his portable oxygen tank."

"Is there anything I can do to help you with dinner before I leave in the morning? Peel potatoes? Scrape carrots?"

"No, Bill's going to help me, so there's no problem. We won't open gifts until Pop and Milly get here, so you can sleep in a little if you want."

"That's okay, I'd rather spend the time with Dad."

"Not exactly a relaxing visit for you. Lots of schedules."

"Hey, that's real life these days. Trying to get six people from four households into one place at one time requires some juggling. I'm just glad I'm here. I don't know how many more Christmases we have with Dad."

"Yeah."

"Enough of this. I need some good, mindless TV for a few hours. What's on?"

Katie and I wandered into the living room and settled in. Fortunately, there was no shortage of mindless TV shows to choose from, so we turned off our brains for a couple of hours.

Once again, there was no Bob around as I settled into bed, and off into a deep sleep populated only by a constant wheezing from the oxygen machine in my dreams.

I woke with a jolt. Predawn gray had started to lighten the room. Startled, I fumbled for my glasses to see what had scared me awake. No dog in the room. No college student tiptoeing by my door to her bed. What the heck?

Then I turned and saw Bob sitting in the chair by my head. Staring at me.

"For Pete's sake, Bob! Is something wrong? You scared the snot out of me waking me up like that!"

"It's Christmas."

"Yeah. So?"

"It's been years since I had a Christmas. It's exciting."

"It'll still be exciting after a couple more hours sleep."

"No, this is the best time. Early, before everything gets crowded and ripped up. Come on, get up and let's turn the tree lights on."

I flopped back down on my pillow. "Oh, for Pete's sake, Bob. I could have slept in a little bit more."

"Please? How often do I ask for anything? This can be your Christmas present for me."

Ouch. He had me there. I hadn't really gotten him anything for Christmas.

"Fine," I grumbled as I struggled out of my cozy warm bed and into my arctic robe and slippers.

We tiptoed down the hallway past Katie and Bill's bedroom, and down the carpeted stairs. Katie's dog, Texas, looked up from his bed at the bottom of the stairs, gave us a half-hearted "Woof?" and then, being a very intelligent animal, went back to sleep.

I turned on all the Christmas tree lights for Bob, then headed for the kitchen to crank up the coffeemaker. While the coffee brewed, I watched Bob through the pass-through between the kitchen and the living room. He was one happy spook, sitting on the sofa gazing at the tree's twinkling lights and shimmering tinsel. I walked in with my coffee, and sat down on the adjacent loveseat.

"It's beautiful, isn't it? See those cookies hanging on the tree? They're made out of salt and flour. Amy and I made them when she was just a kid. Somewhere in there is her Martian cookie; mine were a little more traditional."

"I used to have nice Christmases," Bob mused. "Especially when the kids were young."

"So you had children, Bob. That's great! You remembered!"

"Two boys, I think. I was never assigned back to them, so I guess they did okay. But then again, you almost never get assigned to family when there's a project to do. Like a surgeon, you don't operate on your own family. And I must have been married, but that's still kind of blank."

I heard footsteps on the stairs and turned around. Katie.

"I heard voices. You okay, Roz?"

"Oh, sure, just spending a little quiet time looking at your lovely decorations. It reminds me of Mom's house when we were kids. Want some coffee?"

"In a minute. Is Bob here?"

"Who do you think made me come down to look at the lights? Believe me, it wasn't my idea."

"It is nice, isn't it?" Katie came down the rest of the stairs, sat beside me on the loveseat, hugged me, and said, "Merry Christmas, Roz."

"Same to you, sweetheart."

Then Katie said, "Merry Christmas, Bob."

Bob started, then said, "Tell Katie Merry Christmas," which I did. Then I had a brilliant idea.

"Hey, Bob, you know how I got up really early to look at the lights with you as your Christmas present?"

"Yeah?" Bob turned to me, puzzled.

"I would like to ask you for a special Christmas present right now."

"What?" Bob asked.

My eyes darted around the objects on Katie's coffee table in front of us, and I grabbed Katie's hand.

"For my Christmas present, could you knock over this angel-shaped candlestick so Katie knows you're real?"

Katie stared at me and Bob stared at me, then stammered, "But it's against the rules!"

"Rules, schmools, Bob. It's Christmas, and I gave you a present!"

"Blackmail! Pure and simple, blackmail! You set me up!"

I chuckled. "Now, Bob, what's a little blackmail among friends? Please?"

Katie stared at the candlestick. Bob stared at me, looking crabby. But eventually his hand reached out, gently picked up the candlestick, and even more gently laid it flat on the table.

"Oh, my gosh." Katie's breath hitched. "Oh, Roz, he's really here."

"I *told* you I wasn't crazy!" I said in a voice louder than I'd intended. I couldn't help it. "I told you!" I repeated, more quietly the second time.

"Wow." was the extent of Katie's contribution. "Oh, Roz. Wow . . ."

For a minute we just looked at each other as the news sank in. Then Katie got up and shuffled off, muttering, "I need coffee."

I trailed into the kitchen after her. "So, what do you think?"

"I don't know what I think, Roz," Katie responded. "I'm going to need some time to figure all this out."

"Yeah, tell me about it."

I refilled my mug and went back to the living room. Katie stayed in the kitchen, procrastinating and puttering. Eventually she poked her head through the pass through and said, "Hey, Roz, with everything going on the past few days, I forgot to tell you. Terri called last week."

"What? Why?" I still didn't want anything to do with the woman. Even the sound of her name made me uptight.

"Remember how I offered to loan her our cottage? Back when she was visiting with you over Thanksgiving?"

"Of course I remember." I'd thought the offer was very generous at the time. Now I just thought it was stupid.

"She wanted to take me up on it. She's going to be there at Easter."

I didn't like this. Not one bit. "Easter?" I said, my voice squeaking. "Are you and Bill going to be there?"

"No, just Terri."

Bob looked up from the sofa. I'd never seen a look of horror on a ghost's face before. "We don't have to see her, do we?" he asked.

"I have no idea," I muttered. Then louder, I said, "Katie, I don't want anything to do with her!"

"I know you didn't enjoy her visit very much," Katie said, walking in with her mug. "But we have months until Easter. A lot can change."

"Hmmphh." I was not convinced.

"Besides, she sent you a Christmas present. I mentioned that you'd be here, and it arrived a couple of days later. I put it with the others under the tree."

Even though I was skeptical, I dug through the gifts until I found it. A long narrow box, the shape you might put a bracelet or a bookmark in.

"Are you going to open it now?" Katie asked.

"No, I'll wait until we're all opening gifts this afternoon. It's got an unusual shape, though. You think it's a bracelet?"

"After all you told us about her visit, I have no idea. Should be interesting, though."

The rummaging and conversation woke Amy and Bill, so soon we were all involved in Christmas hugs and kisses, and breakfasting on our traditional Christmas bacon, egg, and cheese casserole. As tasty as it was, I still hustled through it so I could be with Pop and Milly. I decided to bring their presents with me so they'd have a few treats to open in their own home on Christmas morning.

Katie's SUV (or gas pig, as she called it) started right up. I'd driven a subcompact for so long steering Katie's car felt like piloting an ocean liner. Fortunately, it was only a short drive to Pop's house. What a change from Katie's vibrant, twinkly living room to Dad's subdued, oxygen-wheezing one. From color to black and white, like a reverse *Wizard of Oz.*

Pop and Milly sat at the kitchen table, drinking coffee and dawdling over their breakfasts. I cut a piece of the date-nut loaf that had been sitting in their freezer since I'd sent it down with Katie weeks ago. It added a festive touch to their usual meal. Thank goodness I'd brought their presents along with me this morning. Since they'd decided not to exchange gifts this year, there wasn't a single gift-wrapped item in the house. What's Christmas morning without a surprise or two? Faugh!

Milly liked her CDs, and ran to put one on. Dad fumbled in his pocket for the pocketknife he'd carried all his life. Slowly he opened a blade worn thin with honing over the years, and meticulously cut through all the tape on his gift. Then he folded the wrapping paper neatly before even opening the box. He seemed tickled with his plaid woolen shirt. He'd be even more delighted when he'd open a few matching turtlenecks from Katie later today. A new winter wardrobe. Great!

"Now, Roz, you remember I told you not to buy us any more presents. There isn't a single thing we need, and we can't afford to buy presents for all of you kids any more. You don't need to buy for us."

"Pop, it's not a matter of need to buy. I wanted to get you a little something for the holiday, and I don't care whether you get me anything or not." It was true. I actually didn't care, which is pretty amazing for a materialistic little Taurus like me. "I'm just glad you like your shirt." Judging by the way he patted the shirt back in the box, and refolded the tissue paper just so, I'd say it was a success. And, judging by the way Milly spent the morning singing along with her CDs, I'd say they were a success too.

After a bit we settled into some three-handed Scrabble. Dad's holiday spirits buoyed him to even higher levels of Scrabble chicanery (*Loyalshoe? Barkboat?*), but I let him have them all and he mopped the floor with me. Merry Christmas to all.

We made it over to Katie's by one and visited for a bit, snacking on Bill's antipasto and enjoying some of the Finger Lake wines Katie had bought weeks ago. Dinner began promptly at two and, as we slowly moved into the dining room, I saw Bob settle into the easy chair Dad had just vacated. "Are you going to take notes?" I muttered to him as I passed by on my way to the table. He just gave me a cheerful smile, and winked.

"So, Aunt Roz, what time are we leaving tomorrow?" Amy asked as we sat down.

"The bus runs in front of the house about ten after the hour, and you could flag it down," Katie offered while passing the potatoes. "It will only run at seven-ten, eight-ten and nine-ten, though. They've cut back on bus services since the trains were expanded."

Like most bedroom communities, bus and rail were the public transportation arteries into the beating heart that was Manhattan. Most residents knew the commuter schedules by heart, the way a beach resident knows the tides.

"Why don't we shoot for the eight-ten?" I decided. "That'll get us into the city nine-fifteenish and we'll have forty-five minutes to grab our bagels and coffee and get up to the museum for ten o'clock. We'll spend a few hours there and then window-shop our way down Fifth Avenue. Who knows? We might even run into some fabulous Christmas sales."

Amy beamed, and I understood. There's nothing more fun than Manhattan during the holidays, especially when it's on sale.

"What time do you think you'll be home tomorrow?" Katie asked. "Should we hold dinner for you or will you eat in the city?"

"Don't worry about dinner. We'll be fine. If we're hungry when we get home, we can make a sandwich." As I remembered, the Plaza's cream tea would keep us full for days.

Dinner slowly wound down and Bill got up to help Dad into the living room. I had a feeling a nap was in Dad's immediate future, regardless of the excitement of opening presents. Amy, as youngest, got the job of handing out all the presents from under the tree. I helped clear the table and then stayed in the kitchen loading the dishwasher while Katie packed away leftovers and set out the desserts.

Katie loves making desserts. This year there were three: cherry cheesecake, a banana cake with gobs of glossy white frosting, and a carrot cake. I already mentally incorporated some of the leftovers into my Couch Potato festivities in a few days.

By the time we joined everyone in the living room, a small mountain of gifts bearing my name sat on one end table. A beautiful bright pink down vest from Katie and Bill, perfect for keeping out the winter chill in my under-heated home, and books, a shirt, and a tote bag from Amy. I thought of the meager, though cute, pair of earrings I'd finally found for her and felt like a schmuck. I never seem to get the gift balance right at Christmas, damn it. Well, maybe I could make it up to her tomorrow in Manhattan.

I saved Terri's box until last, and held it up. "Any guesses on what Terri sent me?"

"A bracelet?" Milly asked.

"A bookmark?" Amy guessed.

"A ruler?" Bill contributed.

"A martini stirrer?" Bob chipped in.

Dad snored.

I opened the gift card, which I read aloud. "Happy Holidays, with thoughts of your warm hospitality at Thanksgiving."

"Warm hospitality?" Bill asked. "I change my guess. I think it's a fire starter."

I slowly unwrapped the paper, opened the box and pulled out—a knife. A *knife!* Oh, my God, she really did want to kill me! A neon message straight from Terri's subconscious.

The room fell silent. The ripping of wrapping papers stopped.

"Oh, my . . ." Katie said. "I never heard of giving someone a knife at Christmas. But wait a minute. Maybe it's a letter opener. You know, for your desk."

"I don't know. It sure looks like a knife."

It had a jet-black handle, and a long, wickedly-sharp thin blade. "Whatever it is, it totally creeps me out. Maybe I should just throw it out. Or toss it way out into the middle of the lake. That would get rid of it," I said.

"Don't throw it in the lake," Katie said. "It'll put bad cooties into the water, and you don't want to do that. Just put it away for a while. Maybe you'll figure out what it is in a few months, and then you can use it."

"Sure, I'll start opening bills or slicing carrots and with all the bad mojo in it I'll cut off a finger. I think I'm getting a little nauseated from this thing."

"Well, don't throw it out," Milly said, practical as always.

"Oh, Roz, you're being such a drama queen about this." Katie reached over and grabbed Terri's gift and shoved it in the box. "Just put it away for now. Forget about it. Maybe it was her idea of a joke. Don't let it ruin your Christmas."

Just then Pop snorted awake, which broke the weird, subdued mood that had settled on us when I'd opened the knife. (All rational arguments to the contrary, in my heart, I *knew* it was a knife.) Katie packed it up and buried it deep in my pile of presents.

"Hey, Dad," Katie said. "Why don't you open your presents and then we'll have some dessert."

"Sure," Pop agreed. "Just let me get out my pocketknife so I can cut the tape." Pop looked surprised as we all broke into jittery laughter. As I predicted, he definitely liked his turtlenecks from Katie and Bill, and the decorative deck of playing cards from Amy.

Once more we headed into the dining room, and I tried to shake off the dark mood that was dogging my holiday. Seeing my frail dad with his oxygen and walker always made me sad. And now that lethal black knife. That knife felt like a very thinly disguised statement of intent from my overbearing cousin. I wanted to get rid of it, and I didn't want to ever let her under my roof again!

I stuck with coffee for dessert. Somewhere along the way I'd lost my appetite. Besides, now there'd be more leftovers for Couch Potato Days. Around six, Bill drove an exhausted Pop and Milly home. They were laden with gifts and enough holiday treats to last for days.

We were all tired and sprawled around the much-emptier-looking living room.

Amy got up and put on her heavy sweater. "Mom, I'm going over to see Hannah. I'll be back in a few hours."

"Sure, sweetie. Say hi to her parents for me."

Then it was just Katie and me, sitting in the same seats

we'd been in twelve hours ago, only a lot fatter now and a lot more tired.

"Roz, are you and Amy okay these days?"

I paused, a little surprised by Katie's question. "Yeah, I thought we were. Why do you ask?"

"The gifts."

I interrupted her. "I blew it, Katie. I had no idea Amy was going to get me so many nice presents, and I only got her those earrings. I feel like a schmuck. I always have such a hard time finding the right balance with gifts. I'll make it up to her tomorrow, I promise. I'm going to treat her to cream tea at the Plaza."

"She'll love that, Roz. Don't worry, Amy wasn't upset. I think she was just a little confused by the discrepancy."

"I don't blame her. She was very thoughtful, and I'm looking forward to dipping into those books she picked out for me. They look interesting." I paused for a moment, and chose my words carefully. "So, should we talk about the elephant in the room?"

"Would Bob appreciate being called an elephant?"

"He'd probably be furious, but you know what I mean."

"Is he here now?"

I glanced around. "I don't know where he is. He's been in and out all day. I'll catch up with him later on. You're dodging the question, Katie. What do you think?"

Without hesitation she blurted out, "Frankly, I think the only thing worse than you having an imaginary ghost is you having a real one. Interacting with him is just going to suck off energy you could be putting into relationships with real people, like David. I wish you could get rid of Bob so you could get on with your real life."

"Gee, Katie, why don't you tell me what you *really* think?" I said sarcastically, but changed my tone when I saw the combative look she shot me. "I will get rid of him as soon as I figure out what this thing is I'm supposed to do, and I can just do it."

"What do you think it could be?"

"The best I can figure is to help one of my clients do something with their corporate charities. They make an enormous difference in their communities, and when I work with them, I indirectly improve the lives of thousands of people. So I think the doing something has to do with my work. United Way, Community Chest, and the Red Cross don't get tons of publicity a lot of times, but they make huge improvements. And the more money I can help my corporate clients raise for these organizations, the more good they can do."

"So that's how you think about your work? Kind of abstract, isn't it?"

"I don't think so at all. Did you ever hear the story about the three stonecutters?" I asked. Katie shook her head. "There was this philosopher walking through a stone yard and he passes a stonecutter. 'What are you making?' he asks. 'Are you stupid, man?' the stonecutter responds. 'I'm carving a brick.' The philosopher keeps walking and meets a second stonecutter. 'What are you making?' he asks again. The second worker answers, 'I'm carving a brick. I think my boss is going to use it in a church somewhere.' The philosopher keeps walking and meets a third stonecutter. 'What are you making?' the philosopher asks again. 'I am the luckiest man alive,' responds the third stonecutter. 'This stone I'm carving will be part of the greatest cathedral ever raised to glorify God. And my contribution will be a part of it.' Every stonecutter told the truth, but only one of them got immense satisfaction from his work. That's how I feel when I work for my clients. Ultimately, my writing helps lead to happier lives for thousands of people. It might be a weird way to look at things, but it helps keep me going."

"I don't think it's so weird," Katie said. "It's kind of similar to the way I feel about the financial aid office at the college. There's tons of process work, just getting files from one side of your desk to the other. Students dropping classes, transferring, taking an online class. Pretty much every time they make a change it affects their financial aid, and you have to redo everything. If I thought about it all the time, how I've had to readjust one student's aid *eight* times, I'd go nuts. I can't dwell on all that process work. I have to think about the one kid in one hundred who will have a better life because he or she got a degree. Most days that's the only thing that keeps me going. Except lately . . ." Katie drifted off, looking thoughtful.

"Except lately what?" I asked.

"Well. . ." Katie paused, as though reluctant to even admit it to herself. "Lately I've been wondering if we're doing some of these kids any favors with the way we load them up with loans."

"I'm totally lost, Katie. What are you talking about?"

"Let's say you're a student who's going to be a pharmacist. I have no problem approving a $20,000 loan for your tuition every year because I know you'll be making $80,000 or $90,000 a year soon after you graduate. So you won't have any problem paying off a big school loan. But what about the kids who want to be social workers or grade school teachers? They'll be lucky if they'll make $40,000 a year, so letting them graduate with a $100,000 debt is going to have a huge impact on their futures, on their ability to buy a house or save for their own children's education. The college is so willing to pile loans on these kids to make sure they get their pound of flesh. Oh, I don't know."

"But it's the kid's choice, isn't it? They could go to a community college, right? And they've got their parents to advise them, don't they? Katie, you're not responsible for their decisions," I said, trying to make her feel better.

"How many good decisions did you make when you were eighteen, Roz? And the parents? Most of them are clueless about money. They just want to keep little Susie happy today, and the heck with ten years from now. No wonder we're in a recession."

"I'm so sorry, sweetie. You really do have a lot on your plate." I sighed. "It always seems to come back to money, doesn't it?"

"Yeah, well, I'm not sure how much longer I'll be able to justify doing financial aid to myself. But I guess, for now, it's a living. But anyway, Rosie, we got off your elephant in the room and on to a sacred cow."

"Good one. But back to Bob . . ."

"Let's just keep Bob between you and me for now, Roz. I don't see how it can do any good to spread the word. They'd put both of us away."

"So I shouldn't tell Amy?"

"Good God, no."

"That'll be a bit of a challenge when we're traveling with him tomorrow, but I'll do my best. I'll try to set up some ground rules when I talk to him tonight."

"So that's how you do it? You talk to him at night?"

"Usually we talk over dinner, but we're supposed to get together once a day."

"Sounds like most marriages."

"But no sex."

"As I said, sounds like most marriages," Katie repeated with a smile. "Too bad Bob can't do something useful, like make predictions or pick lottery numbers."

"Yeah, that's what I thought at first. He's a good talker, though. We talk about the screwiest things. He cracks me up all the time. And he makes a wicked martini. Maybe he'll make one for you one of these days."

Katie stared at me. "Better be careful, Roz."

"Careful about what?"

"Don't get too fond of Bob. It's very easy to fall for someone who keeps you amused. Companionship and laughter, that describes just about every good marriage I know these days."

"I still like a little sex in there, sis."

"We all do. But it gets less important as you get older. Don't get me wrong. Sex is still wonderful, but I think it drops way down on the list in most relationships. If you've got laughter and companionship with Bob, you've got more than a lot of people I know."

I got up, bent over, and gave Katie a kiss on the forehead. "Sweetie, I'm worn out. I hear what you're saying, but I know myself. It takes me forever to get into a relationship, but when I finally get there, I'm very physical about it. I'm not worried about Bob, and neither should you be. Tell Amy I'll see her in the morning. And thanks for a fabulous Christmas. Today was beautiful, Katie."

I headed upstairs, washed, and got into bed with one of Amy's gift books. I flipped the radio on low and whispered, "Bob? Hey, Bob?"

No answer. Strange. I thought he was supposed to be covered for his other assignment. I tried again. "Bob?"

This time I heard a soft moan that raised the hairs on the back of my neck. "Bob?" A soft cough made me scrunch to the far side of the bed and peer over the edge. There was Bob, in a rumpled suit, with a paper crown jammed on his head. He lay flat on the floor on his stomach.

"Bob? What the . . .? What's wrong with you?" I whispered.

"Here kitty, kitty, kitty," Bob mumbled.

Oh my God. Drunk as a lord. I knew it was just a matter of time with all the rye and martinis, but why now? Why at my sister's house? Why on the holiday?

I leaned over the edge of the bed, holding the mattress, until I could get my mouth close to the wrinkled crown. "Bob!" I yelled.

Bob's head reared up, and he flipped onto his back and moaned.

"What the hell are you doing?" I hissed.

"Here kitty, kitty. Oh, it's Rosie!" Bob slurped.

"Yes, it's Rosie. You're drunk, Bob!"

A beatific smile spread over his face. "Yessssss . . . drunk . . . nice . . . kitty, kitty." His eyes drifted closed.

"Bob!" I yelled again.

His eyelids popped open, but there was no one at home.

"Don't forget we're going to New York tomorrow."

"Shure, shuuure, shuurrre," blended into gentle snores as his eyelids drifted shut again.

"Nuts," I muttered. Nothing much I could do, though. I didn't happen to have any ghost coffee on hand, and I wouldn't know how to make it if I did. Oh, tomorrow was going to be buckets of fun: Manhattan crowds and a hungover ghost. Did it get any better than this?

Chapter 11
Tilt!

I was cruel, I admit it. Come seven a.m., I stepped out of the pounding shower, wrapped myself snugly in a towel while the water still ran and yelled, "*Bob!*"

A pale shadow wavered in at the edge of the bathroom. It trembled visibly, but I was relentless. "Bob! You ready to go?"

A quiet moan. A little more half-hearted materializing. I could almost make him out, and it wasn't pretty. Bob sat on the closed toilet in his wrinkled suit, hunched over with his head in his hands. "For the love of God, please stop yelling," he whispered. "Every inch of me hurts."

I turned off the shower and spoke in a lower voice. "Yeah, so? You knew we were going to Manhattan today. Why'd you have to get blitzed last night? You see this, Bob?" I rubbed my forefinger and thumb together. "It's the world's smallest violin. I have no sympathy for you whatsoever. You'd better go drink some coffee or something, because Amy and I are getting on the bus in an hour, with you or without you."

Bob wavered out with a shaky moan. I continued resolutely to get dressed. The poor schlub sure looked miserable, though.

Amy, by contrast, shone with happy youth and energy. Had I ever been that young? Such infectious energy was hard to resist in such a good young woman. We giggled over a light breakfast and grabbed water and heavy sweaters for the day. It still hadn't gotten cold, and I worried about David for a few milliseconds, wondering how his grapes were doing.

By eight o'clock we were out of the house and ready to flag down the bus. At five after, Bob wavered into view. Every inch of him was crinkled, but at least he'd tried to dress up a bit. A nice suit and tie, although wrinkled and bedraggled, huge wrap-around sunglasses and . . . a sombrero? "Oh, for Pete's sake," I muttered to Bob while Amy watched for the bus.

"The light, my God, the light . . ." Bob whimpered in response, shading his eyes with shaking hands.

Traffic was thin heading into the city this Friday after Christmas. Many businesses closed, so the regular commuters snoozed at home, snug in their beds. A handful of energetic bargain hunters chatted in the middle of the bus, comparing notes on various sales.

Amy wanted to sit up front, close to the driver, so she could watch all the traffic and scenery. Bob drifted toward the rear of the bus and I saw him snoozing in the back row with the sombrero tipped over his face.

We pulled into Port Authority, my transit point during years of commuting. I'd been away for a long time, and it had certainly buffed up in my absence. The skeleton was familiar, but the old girl had had several face-lifts. Little shops selling Indian turquoise jewelry and books had been replaced with overpriced French bistros and cell phone kiosks. The poor lost homeless souls of the nineteen-eighties-era Port Authority had been moved along, who knows where. Now the ladies' rooms actually smelled of bleach, and the stalls weren't furnished with paper bags holding a life's grubby possessions. This being New York, though, I'd still tucked an extra twenty-dollar-bill in my bra just in case of purse-snatching. Old habits die hard.

Amy and I got in line at the bakery so I could get my fix: a buttered poppy seed bagel and coffee extra light, no sugar. God help the poor tourist who didn't know exactly what she wanted by the time she made it to the head of the line. The servers at the bakery handled hundreds of customers an hour, and there could be a very fine line between efficient service and rudeness.

After a few minutes worshipping at the altar of bagel, Amy and I moved along, walking through a cleaned up and Disney-fied Forty-second Street. Others might carp at the loss of the authentic drug and alcohol culture of the nineteen-eighties, but not me. I preferred feeling a bit safer and cleaner walking through the midtown area.

We headed toward Madison Avenue, where we'd catch a bus north and walk over to the museum. Bob drifted alongside. At one point, Amy paused to examine a shop window while Bob and I continued on a few feet.

"Hey, Bob," I whispered. "You're tilted."

"Huh?"

"Did you know you're leaning over when you float? You're tilted."

"I don't feel any different."

"Maybe it's your hangover?"

"No idea." Bob sounded awfully crabby. Functional, but crabby.

Amy rejoined me. "Did you see anything interesting, sweetie?" I asked.

"Not really. Those sweaters caught my eye, though. They had some nice colors."

"I'm sure you'll see a lot more when we walk down Fifth Avenue this afternoon. We'll have to check out the sales at Saks."

We continued walking through Times Square. As gray and utilitarian as it appeared this morning, a week from now this place would be ankle deep in trash after the New Year's Eve countdown. I loved Manhattan, but I didn't mind watching that madhouse from the comfort of my sofa. My ex and I had done a New Year's Eve at Times Square once, and once was enough. A place so crowded your arms were jammed into your sides by drunks all around you, and you couldn't lift your hand to your nose to push up your glasses. No, thanks.

We continued past Madison so I could show Amy a little bit of Grand Central Station. Once there, we explored the underground terminal. Lots of boutique shops were tucked into the arches of the original structure: florists, bakeries, cafes, wine shops, even a bookshop where Amy and I paused to browse for a minute. Then back to Madison and on to the bus, which we took north for forty blocks, passing by all the designer boutiques with the skeletal mannequins in their windows.

Amy was not very interested in the designer names, but she loved the energy of the city. All youth, all potential. Manhattan throbs with possibilities, definitely one of the most exciting cities on the planet. I've often wondered if the tap water there is laced with caffeine instead of fluoride, the place is so full of buzzing intensity. I love Manhattan but, like the New Year's Eve's festivities, I prefer to take it in bite-sized doses, usually from a distance.

At Seventy-ninth Street we got off the bus and walked west to the Met. Bob still tipped, but now he was pointing toward southern Manhattan, almost as if he were a needle in a compass that kept fixing on some unknown true north. We didn't get a chance to chat since I was focused on Amy and making this a fun day for her.

You've seen pictures of the Metropolitan Museum, so you know what an amazing building it is. Huge, statuesque, traditional: a comfortable and comforting reminder of a more gracious age. Amy and I checked our bags and wraps, picked up maps of the enormous building, and headed toward the Egyptian wing.

We wandered though the Egyptian wing, lingering for a moment at the reflecting pool and creeping through the diminutive temple installed there. Brilliant light flooded through the wall of windows, casting an almost Egyptian glare on the artifacts. I stopped dead at the mummy in the next room, and looked around for Bob. He was floating by the windows, still tipped toward mid-Manhattan. He'd lost the sombrero, thank goodness. Amy wandered ahead, and I motioned him over.

"Is the mummy's ghost still here?" I muttered.

"No, his spirit is long gone. Nothing there but dust and bones."

"Still," I said, "it doesn't seem very respectful to keep him on display here. I don't think I'd like to be a peep show for eternity."

"Wouldn't bother me," Bob replied in a matter-of-fact voice. "Why would it matter if his spirit's moved on? His remains are just a thing, like everything else. But now there is something interesting going on over there." Bob gestured to a beautiful pair of gem-encrusted royal earrings in a display case over by the corner of the room.

"What's happening there?" I asked.

"I guess you can't see him. The artist who created those earrings is over there, just hanging around."

"You mean from Egypt? Why is his spirit here, but the mummy's isn't? That's weird."

"I'll find out." Bob drifted over to the case, and I had the strange experience of watching him converse with empty air. Now I knew how odd I might be looking to other people. It certainly felt bizarre, I'll grant you that.

I wandered back to the stone bench by the reflecting pool, keeping one eye on Amy and the other on Bob. Bob chatted away amiably (he could speak Egyptian? I had no idea) and at one point seemed to drink something. Amy browsed through the exhibit cases.

After a few minutes, Bob drifted to my bench. I pulled out my museum map and unfolded it in front of my face, so I could talk.

"Can you speak Egyptian, Bob? I'm impressed!"

"Don't be. I have some kind of universal translator gizmo. That's another thing they managed to get right." Bob settled on the bench. "Interesting guy. He pretty much lived for women and booze when he was alive. Creating those earrings was the finest thing he ever did in what some might think of as a wasted life, so he opted to stay with them for eternity. He's been all over the world. I don't think he imagined he'd be holed up in a museum at this point, but he doesn't seem unhappy. He's got plenty of home-brewed beer, which is excellent, by the way, and he seems to be enjoying himself. We'll probably meet a few others like him if we see more of the museum. Artists are kind of a nutty group. More into their creations than they are involved in their real lives."

"Aunt Roz?" I jerked back to reality.

"Oh, Amy, sweetie, sorry, I was daydreaming."

"I've been calling you forever. Are you tired, or can we see some more?"

"I'm not tired at all, and I'm thoroughly enjoying seeing this place again. Absolutely. Let's keep going."

We kept wandering through the exhibition rooms. The artwork was magnificent, of course, but I'd always been more drawn to the room recreations: a dusky Venetian bedroom from the 1600s; a small, dark living room from a colonist's house in the New World. Sure enough, Bob did locate a few more artists who had decided to stay with their handicrafts: an armorer from Tudor England; a painter from Medici Italy; a humble, tubercular woodworker who carved decorative panels in Switzerland; and a man who did mosaics in Pompeii.

Bob relayed their stories to me as I walked with Amy. I had to be careful to edit myself as we chatted about the displays. Once, I slipped. I mentioned that the Swiss woodworker was tubercular and Amy looked at me, clearly puzzled.

"How on earth do you know he was tubercular, Aunt Roz? It doesn't say anything about that on the write-up."

"Oh, I guess I must have read it somewhere," I said. "You know me. My nose is always in a book."

"Yeah, I guess," Amy responded dubiously.

After a couple of hours of close calls, I needed a break, so we made our way to the cafeteria and had salads. By two, I'd had enough history. Amy could have wandered the museum for days, but I wanted to get her over to the Plaza by four for our cream tea treat. And we had a little matter of shopping to do first.

We stepped out of the silent, reverential museum and into the raucous bazaar that was Fifth Avenue. Taxis beeped, traffic lights flickered, pedestrians pushed through each other. Carts of treats populated every corner; hot dogs, caramelized nuts, gloves, genuine (?) pashmina scarves, tangerines. We pushed through bustling mobs down Fifth, pausing at festive windows, and even went into the holiday-dressed Saks to check the sales. Who could resist cashmere sweaters at thirty-percent off? I noticed Amy eying a sea-foam green turtleneck and suggested she try it on. The color made her skin look like fresh cream, so I insisted on buying it for her. It felt very good to fix the insensitive gaffe I'd made with presents on Christmas Day. I wouldn't knowingly hurt this child for the world.

Cashmere sweater and museum souvenirs in hand, we strolled toward the Plaza through the darkening afternoon. All around us, stores flipped on their holiday lights. The Channel Gardens at Rockefeller Center glistened with white-lit angels, and holidaying tourists packed the ice. It would be good to sit down, stop carrying our parcels, and refresh with a hot cup of tea. And some snacks, of course.

I love grand dame hotels and resorts, the ones that combine history and panache, like the Plaza or the Parker House in Boston, or Starved Rock Lodge in Illinois. Originally built in the early twentieth-century, the Plaza maintains the grandeur of its earliest vision. High ceilings, beautifully decorated, columns inside and out, solicitous workers, gold gilding, and plaster rosettes evoke days of style and wealth. Since I was not one of the Plaza's wealthier clients, my splurge this afternoon with Amy would require payback in the form of eating franks and beans for a month, but you know what? It was totally worth it. Once in a while you have to build a memory, and that day was becoming one for the books.

While Amy and I rubbernecked our surroundings and waited for our tea (and mini-sandwiches, scones, jam, and cookies), Bob wandered the room. The Egyptian beer had helped with his hangover, so he'd lost the sunglasses and some of the wrinkles in his suit. In fact, in his tailored clothing, he looked more at home in the splendor of the Palm Court than Amy and I did. Unfortunately, Bob's leaning was worse than ever; he was tipped almost at a forty-five degree angle now, and seemed to be constantly pointed south. I almost started worrying about this anomaly, but then our tea came, and I got distracted. Funny how some of the most memorable moments of my life involve beverages.

Amy and I sipped and talked about the city and the museum, sweaters, school and, unfortunately, the tubercular Swiss woodworker.

"That's just so strange that you knew about his tuberculosis, Aunt Roz. Especially since the sign said the woodworker was anonymous. You'd think the museum would update their signage if more information was uncovered." Amy stared at me while I squirmed uncomfortably in my seat, avoiding her eyes. Drat these smart kids anyway! And me with a glass head, no good at lying.

"It's a long story, sweetie. You'll have to ask your mom."

"My mom? Why on earth would she know anything about a Swiss woodworker?"

I broke into a light sweat. "I'm sorry, Amy." I wriggled in my chair. "Please, sweetie, can you just talk to your mom and let's change the subject, okay?"

One of many things that Amy inherited from my sister was her stare. It nailed me to the wall like a collector's pin through a bug. "Okay, sure, Aunt Roz."

I sighed with relief and took a big mouthful of tea. I looked around the room at my fellow diners—elegant and polished, just nibbling at the goodies on their plates. That must be how they stayed so skeletal. One woman wore ropes of gorgeous pearls, and I pointed her out to Amy.

After spending a rare, civilized hour lingering and chatting over our tea, I settled the bill, and we walked into the New York night. The city certainly was not dark, with all the car headlights, brightly decorated store fronts, and street lamps, yet the texture of light was very different than daylight, creating a chewy atmosphere, with secrets tucked around every corner. There was a palpable feeling in the dark of time to get home and close the doors behind you. I'd wandered carefree all day. Now I felt a little bit like scurrying.

Bob drifted in front of us as we walked briskly south on Fifth. The further south we walked, the worse his tilt got until, at Forty-fifth Street, he practically floated horizontally. At Forty-fourth Street, he started zooming west, shrieking loudly. Amy, who was talking about her upcoming college courses, kept walking while I stopped dead in my tracks to watch a yelling Bob being carried off into the night. It was as if he had a loop at the top of his head and someone had grabbed it and yanked, hard.

"Amy, let's cut down Forty-fourth here." I tried to keep my tone normal.

"But I thought you wanted to stay on the main streets after dark," she protested.

"Ummmm, yeah, I did say that, but let's take a detour here."

Amy glanced down the side street. It looked empty and dark, the kind of place I usually tried to avoid. "Are you sure?" she asked.

Bob's shrieks echoed down the empty street. "Yeah," I replied. "It's kind of an emergency." I grabbed Amy's arm and started jogging west. Halfway down the street the shrieking stopped, which made me drag Amy along even faster. I braked abruptly when we hit the entrances to the Algonquin and Royalton Hotels. Not a sound.

I must have looked worried and tense, because Amy said, "Aunt Roz, you're scaring me."

"I'm sorry, sweetheart, but . . . ." I paused, trying to hear Bob's voice. "Let's go in here." I pushed through the doorway of the Algonquin Hotel . . .

. . . And into a parlor from the nineteen-twenties. Potted palms decorated a comfortable living room full of easy chairs and small casual tables. It took my mind a minute to realize that this was a painstaking recreation of the old Algonquin. All the people wore modern clothing. The hotel had just done a detailed remodel of how the lobby had looked almost one hundred years ago. There was Bob, sprawled on one of the loveseats, pale as a—*hmm*—ghost, and throwing back rye like it was the day before Prohibition.

"Roz, Roz." Amy tugged on my arm, looking very worried.

"Amy, I'm in trouble here and I need your help. Can you help me, sweetheart, and not ask any questions? I promise I'll explain everything later." Oh, her mother would kill me.

Amy looked around, clearly confused, but then seemed to get a hold of herself. She reached down and briefly squeezed my hand. "Sure, Roz."

"Follow me." I indicated to the young blond hostess where I'd like to sit, and we trailed behind her through the obstacle course of closely placed wing chairs and occasional tables, trying not to bump into people's pre-dinner cocktails. When we reached Bob's loveseat, I sat next to him and motioned Amy into the wingchair on the other side of him.

"Amy, lean over a bit and pretend we're having a quiet conversation."

I bent toward Amy and said, "Bob!"

Amy's head snapped back, and her eyes widened, but after a second she ducked back in, willing to continue our charade.

Even for a ghost, Bob looked pale. His swooping through the air screaming had not been the best prescription for curing a fading hangover. "What happened, Bob?" I asked. "One minute you were in front of us, the next you were flying down the street like a bat out of hell."

He hunched forward, holding his hand to his head. "I don't know what happened. It was like something yanked me out of the dark. When I stopped screaming, I was sitting here, with a headache like you wouldn't believe."

I sat up and looked around. Such a domestic and cozy place. It was hard to imagine why Bob had been pulled here so violently. The hostess, seeing me look up, came over to take our order for drinks. This was certainly turning into a liquidy afternoon, and I thanked goodness for the newly clean bathrooms at Port Authority. Otherwise it would be a very long bus ride back to New Jersey.

I leaned back into our tripartite huddle. "Do you have any idea what brought you here, Bob? Will you be able to come back to New Jersey with us?"

"Give me a few minutes." Bob wiped his forehead with a shaky hand.

Amy stared at me with big round eyes, but didn't say a word.

I reached over and grabbed her hand. "Amy, I know this is going to be a tough one for you, and your mom's going to be furious with me for telling you, but I have a ghost. His name is Bob, and he's right here, but he's not feeling well."

I didn't think Amy's eyes could open any wider, but they did. "A ghost? Here?" she whispered.

"Yeah, and I'm a little worried about him. I think he might be sick."

Amy didn't say anything for a very long minute. Then, being the Taurus daughter of a very practical Taurus mom, she said, "Can we get him a ghost doctor?"

I stared at her, nonplussed. "I have no idea. I'll ask." I turned to Bob. "Can you call for a ghost doctor or something? You know, to help?"

Bob rubbed his face with both hands, and sat a little straighter in the loveseat. "I'm feeling better already. I just need a little time for everything to settle down. I'll probably be fine in half an hour or so. Just have your drinks and I might be ready to go when you are." Bob unscrewed the top of his omnipresent flask of rye.

"Is more booze the best thing to do here, considering the circumstances?" I muttered.

Bob thought for a moment and, for the first time since I'd known him, put the flask away untasted. "Probably best if I keep my wits about me tonight."

I turned back to Amy. I was starting to feel like a simultaneous interpreter at the United Nations. "Bob thinks he'll be fine in a little bit. Let's just relax for a few minutes and see how it goes."

"Okay."

After her initial shock, Amy seemed to be taking the news rather matter-of-factly. Maybe too matter-of-factly? I felt a little disconcerted. "Amy, honey, do you have any questions about Bob or, um, this whole situation?"

Amy thought for a minute. "How long have you had a ghost?"

"Since I moved to the lake house, a few months."

"Is he the one who told you about the woodworker?"

"Um . . . yeah. Bob talked to the woodworker's ghost while we were at the museum."

"Uh . . . neat."

Neat?

"You don't seem to be too surprised, sweetheart." I was kind of worried at her non-reaction. "Are you okay with everything?"

Amy looked thoughtful again. "Yeah, I guess so."

Now I was disconcerted. My ghost was a non-event.

Bob looked at me and said in a dry tone, "I feel vaguely insulted. Have I let the child down?"

Amy saw my puzzled look and continued. "It's really not a big deal, Roz. I mean, think about it. I've grown up surrounded by stories of wizards, vampires, werewolves, goblins, trolls, fairies—you name it. A ghost is really not a very big deal."

Jeepers. Well, okay then. Not a very big deal.

Our drinks arrived, and I'm not sure I've ever been happier to see a glass of wine. Amy even seemed happy to see her ginger ale. I took a good-sized gulp.

Bob looked around. "You know, this place does seem awfully familiar. I feel like I used to spend a lot of time here."

I looked around the cocktail parlor. "It's a really nice place. Cozy. I like the palm trees."

Bob flipped a hand. "No, not them. Off in the dining room. There used to be lots of people, all talking for hours on end. It feels like home."

"Interesting. Are those memories what pulled you here, do you think?"

"Those memories? Maybe. Otherwise I have no idea why I'd be slammed through space to come here." Bob drifted up, and started floating through the hotel's ground floor rooms, poking his head into different corners. While he did the grand tour, Amy and I finished our drinks. I checked my watch.

"Sweetie, we're going to have to hustle to make that last bus." If we missed the seven p.m. bus, we'd have to hike down to the train station, and it had been a long day. My feet were tired. I'd already walked four or five miles. In heels, no less.

I withdrew a twenty for the drinks (ouch!), gave Bob the high sign, gathered up Amy and my bags, and headed for the door. We trotted to Port Authority, had just enough time to duck into the ladies room, and got on the bus with seconds to spare. Even though the bus was full, we found two aisle seats, but not in the same row. Probably just as well. I could use a few minutes alone with my thoughts. No sign of Bob, but I was okay with that, now that I knew he was feeling better. I had a gut feeling he'd show up sooner or later.

The bus chittered through the Lincoln Tunnel, with the subterranean lights flickering through the windows, bars of black and white flashing over the passengers' faces. Using the overhead spotlight, my seatmate rustled through the sports section of the *Times*. Amy pulled a book out of her backpack and was deep in it in minutes. A girl after my own heart.

Lots to think about. Bagels, books, tubercular woodworkers, mummies, the Algonquin, scones . . . I drifted off. The next thing I knew, Amy was shaking my shoulder. "Here's our stop, Roz." I was completely disoriented but managed to get off the bus with all my packages.

As Amy and I walked up the driveway, we saw Bill in the garage, wrestling with a broken starter motor. I waved and said, "Hi," while Amy paused to fill him in on her day.

I headed into the house. Katie looked up from the loveseat in the living room. "Hey, Roz, how did it go? Did you and Amy have fun in the city?"

"I don't know if *fun* would exactly be the operative word," I replied. "Interesting, maybe, or challenging, but I'm not sure about fun."

"Dare I ask?" Katie questioned with a small smile.

"Why don't we wait until Amy gets in from talking with Bill, because she's part of the story."

Katie's lips tightened and thinned. "I thought I asked you not to say anything to Amy about Bob."

"You did, but the situation was kind of out of my hands there for a while." I tried to find just the right word to describe my afternoon. "Bob got snatched."

"Snatched?" Katie repeated in disbelief.

"Yeah, he got dragged across town by this big, invisible hook or something. He was screaming his head off, so I got worried and we chased after him down Forty-fourth to the Algonquin."

"I thought you were going to stay on the main roads after dark."

"I was, but—"

Katie interrupted. "Roz, you know I love you, but this makes me crazy. I entrusted you with my only child, and you go running down deserted side streets with her after dark? Are you *nuts*?"

"But Bob—"

"Damn it, Roz," Katie pounded the arm of her chair, "I'm sick of Bob! As far as I'm concerned, he could have been lying there bleeding, and I wouldn't care. Your priority was taking care of my daughter. *Nothing* else matters! I have a very high tolerance for your nuttiness, Roz, but *not* when it comes to endangering my kid." She pounded the chair again.

"Katie, calm down. I don't think we were ever in danger. It was just a little dark."

"Oh, grow up, Roz! Where the hell do you think the muggers and rapists hang out? In broad daylight?" Katie was on a roll. Her anger upset me, but I've also learned from experience that it wouldn't be a Murphy holiday without a huge fight, or hysterical tears at some point.

Just then, Amy pirouetted in wearing her new sweater, sucking in her cheeks and mimicking a runway model.

Katie stood up suddenly and hugged her. "Sounds like you and Roz had quite the day today."

"Mom, it was great. We did so much and went so many places. The city was gorgeous with all the Christmas decorations."

"And you're okay?" Katie pushed Amy out of their hug and stared intently into her eyes.

"Sure, I'm fine. Why wouldn't I be?"

"Sounds like you heard about Bob."

"Yeah?"

"And?"

"And what, Mom?" Amy shrugged. "Like I told Roz, ghosts are no big deal. I read about them all the time."

Katie brushed back Amy's hair and gave her another hug. "Go show that lovely sweater to your father. It's gorgeous. In fact, I might just have to borrow it one of these days. . ."

"Mo-om!"

"Go on, show your father." Katie pushed Amy toward the garage and turned back to me.

"Roz, I love you very much, but I'm really upset about this. If I say any more right now, I'm sure I'll regret it. So I'm going to drop it." She paused briefly. "Are you hungry? Can I heat up any dinner for you?"

"No, I've had plenty today." I collected my shopping bags from the floor. "I'll just go upstairs and start packing for the morning. I want to say goodbye to Pop and Milly before I head back, so I'll probably leave pretty early, maybe about eight."

"That's fine. We can have breakfast together before you go."

I started up the stairs. "If I don't see you before I turn in, have a good night, Katie."

"You too, Roz." Katie turned and went into the kitchen.

I could hear her running water into the kettle to make tea. That was her tried-and-true method for dealing with stress.

Once upstairs, I slumped on the bed. How could one well-meaning, fairly intelligent person keep screwing things up so often? This was another reason to stay at the lake; fewer people living within screwing-up proximity.

I slowly started organizing the masses of stuff I'd managed to accumulate during my short visit. I shoehorned my lovely Christmas presents and laundry into my suitcases. After a few minutes Katie, holding two mugs of chamomile tea in her hands, knocked softly at the door with her foot and pushed it open.

"I'm sorry I bit your head off, Roz. I get unglued whenever I think about my daughter being in danger."

"I understand, Katie," I said, reaching for a mug. "All I can say is that I know Manhattan pretty well, and I would never have put Amy into a dangerous situation. The street was empty and dark, but I didn't see anyone or anything there that made me worry. I've spent enough years working in Manhattan to trust my gut. I had to think on the spot. But I'm very sorry I upset you."

Katie sat on the bed. "I'm sorry, too, Roz. I know I can over-react. It's just been so hard for me, with Amy going to college this year. I know I get overemotional about her, and I know she was safe with you today. It's awfully hard for me to let go."

"Yeah, I know, sweetie."

We were quiet for a couple of minutes, while I kept putting things into my suitcase.

"So, what the heck happened with Bob today?" Katie asked.

"Strangest thing. As soon as we got off the bus in Manhattan, he was pointing toward midtown. Literally, his whole body was leaning. Wherever we went in Manhattan, he'd point toward Forty-fourth Street like he was the needle on a compass. And then, by the time we actually got to Forty-fourth Street, he was almost horizontal, and it was like he was pulled over there. He wasn't happy about it, I can tell you. He was pretty sick by the time we caught up with him at the Algonquin."

"That old hotel?"

"Yeah. Amy and I found him in the lobby, sick as a dog. That's when I told Amy about him, when I was trying to figure out how to handle the whole situation. She doesn't seem to be the least bit freaked out about it, though. Must take after her mother."

Katie smiled. "She can be a tough little thing."

"After a while, Bob seemed to be feeling much better, and Amy and I had to run to catch the last bus. I didn't want to hike all the way downtown for the train."

"So did Bob make it back with you?"

"No. But since he's my ghost he said he'd be able to find me wherever I went, so I'm not too worried. He was exploring the hotel, so maybe he'll find out something about his past."

"It's always an adventure in Roz-ville, isn't it."

"Amazing, huh?"

"So you decided to stick to your original schedule and head back tomorrow? I can't persuade you to stay a few more days?"

"Thanks so much for the offer, sweetie, but I should get back. You've given me a wonderful holiday, and I loved spending today with Amy, but it's time. Looks like there's bad weather coming in a few days, and I don't want to be driving in those mountains when it does. But if anything happens and you and Milly need a hand with Pop, just call me, and I'll come right back, no matter what."

"I know, Roz." Katie got up. "I'll let you pack then, and I'll see you in the morning."

Big sister hugs, and Katie went down the hallway toward her bedroom. Amy stopped by for a few minutes to thank me for her fun day in the city. I finished packing, got ready for bed, and settled in with the rest of Delafield. Still no sign of Bob . . . still not worried.

The next morning, Bill took my bags to my car before he left for work. Katie, Amy, and I ate a quick meal of cereal and coffee, then Katie loaded me down with a shopping bag full of leftovers and baked goods. *Score!* I felt a great Couch Potato holiday on the way!

It was hard leaving Katie and Amy, but I since I talked with Katie several times every week, I could handle it. Besides, I'd be back in a couple of months. I'd determined to see Pop more often these days.

After leaving Katie's, I gassed up the car and headed to Pop's for a cup of coffee for the road. As much as I know Pop loves me, in his own way, I could tell he wanted to put the holidays behind him and settle back into his regular routine. I chatted about my day in the city with Amy, but I could see the weariness in Pop's eyes. When I caught him surreptitiously checking his watch to see if it was time for his nap, I knew I had to leave. Hugs and kisses to Pop and Milly and, as always, I saved my tears for Dad and our lost opportunities for the car.

I drove home through a cloudy and quiet day. The closer I got to Crooked Lake, the more the clouds scudded in from the west, bringing ugly weather with them. I'd feel better when I could watch it from my living room window.

After hours on the road I stopped in at the Southport supermarket for some bread, eggs and milk, and headed off into the hills around my lake. As I pulled into the driveway, I congratulated myself on another family holiday survived, mostly with grace.

Chapter 12
Moonlight Becomes You

The next day, Sunday, I did manage to have one lovely Couch Potato Day before all hell broke loose. The weather had turned bitterly cold, and more and more clouds blew in from the west, making a perfect gray day to huddle guilt-free on the couch with a book and a blanket. The fridge was full of Katie's takeaways, so I didn't need to waste a minute worrying about cooking. As far as I could tell, there was no Bob lurking in the house. He must still be hanging around in Manhattan somewhere, maybe exploring his roots. I was beginning to look forward to his return. There would be some wild stories, to be sure.

For one precious day, my only problem was deciding what to read. I had a stock list of writers that had made the cut for CP Days: Stephanie Barron and her Jane Austen mystery series; Louise Penny and the Three Pines novels; Elizabeth George and her Lyndley stories; Laurie King and Holmes; Cara Black in Paris and anything by Tracy Chevalier or Deanna Raybourn. If these writers had a new book, it was automatically CP Day-eligible.

I settled into the latest Raybourn, with the exploits of Lady Julia and Brisbane in India, and the hours passed. At three I slid off the sofa and went out for a short walk before it got dark, just to get my blood pumping again. Even through my sweaty walk, I could feel the temperature dropping—a lot. I wondered how David's grapes would be doing and how, in fact, David was doing. How was Christmas with his sister's family? Maybe I should invite him over to dinner? That would be fine as long as I didn't have to waste time cooking during Couch Potato Days. After all, priorities are priorities, and I only indulge in CP Days once a year.

It had been a long, quiet day. I loved these days but, after my people-full Christmas week, I needed to get used to the quiet again. I gave Angela a call when I got in from my walk. We spent an hour on the phone, not unusual, getting caught up on our respective holidays. She'd had both of her children at home, so she was over the moon with happiness. You see in the news all the time how screwed up families are these days. Both of my sisters had raised healthy, happy, smart, productive kids, and their achievements always impressed me. What an amazing feat to lie down at the end of your life and feel that you've added a few assets to mankind.

But there are lots of ways to bring good into the world and, in all honesty, I wouldn't diminish my own contribution. Helping corporations raise money to feed the hungry, house the homeless, and build community centers to keep kids off the streets deserved a little credit, too. I could sleep at night feeling that, in my own small way, I made a difference. I was carving a stone for the cathedral of mankind.

Well, most nights I could sleep. That one I couldn't. Maybe there had been too many transitions lately. Or that limeade I'd had with dinner might have been full of caffeine, I'd never thought to check. Regardless, after a few hours of trying to sleep, I gave up at four a.m. and got up, drawn, as always, to look at the lake. A full moon hung low in the sky, radiating beams that laid a silver carpet over the waves. As frigid air kissed the top of the warmer water, spouts of mist spun up from the waves. Spindles of fog bobbed and weaved over the waters, drifting in invisible air currents. The hazy shapes moved in sync, glowing from within.

"One of the few benefits of these drastic weather changes," Bob's voice whispered out of the dark.

"Yikes, Bob!" I yelled in shock. "Don't sneak up on me like that." I used my mantra again. *Deep breaths, deep breaths.* "You could have told me you were back."

"Just got here, and I saw you. Are you ready?"

"What the hell are you talking about?" This reunion was not getting off to a good start.

"To join me at the ball."

"You've got to be kidding me." I like a sense of humor but, really, at four a.m.?

"What do you think you're looking at out there?" Bob persisted.

"Mist. Blowing in wind currents."

"How prosaic. Use a little imagination." He pointed out the window. "See those spools of fog spinning in the middle of the lake? What do you think is making that? All of my ghost buddies dancing away."

"There's all kinds of ghosts out there?" I bent closer to the window trying to see details. "Dancing over the water? Huh."

"So? You coming or not?"

I straightened and asked, "Aren't you going to tell me what happened in Manhattan?"

Bob seemed to be in a rush, and he brushed my question aside. "Of course I will. Later. But we've got to hurry. These balls never last very long. So, are you in or not?"

"Right. I'll just put on a fancy dress and walk out there on top of the water." So far I'd only heard of one person in history who could walk on water, and it sure wasn't yours truly.

"As long as you're with me, and you keep this ring on, you don't have to worry about it." Bob slipped a gold band with intricate carved figures onto my middle finger. The ring was a little big, but I could keep it on if I kept my fingers curled. "Don't worry about your clothes, either. The music will take care of it. This is your payoff for putting up with me all these months."

"All right, sure. I'm probably still asleep, but let's see how this plays out. What should I wear?"

"Moonlight."

My eyebrows shot up.

"Now just stand there, in that ribbon of moonlight," Bob continued. "Don't move."

I walked to where a moonbeam illuminated the floor, and felt silk-like slithers drifting around my body. A grayish, silvery light covered me. I was dressed, but I couldn't see what I looked like.

"What kind of a dress is this? I don't see a style."

"Of course you don't," Bob replied. "The dress can't really style itself until we hear what kind of music they're going to play."

"Whatever you say. This is one heck of a dream." I couldn't take my eyes off the gray light floating around my body.

"Come on, Roz," Bob said in a low, urgent voice. "Take my arm and let's go."

My bedroom, the stairs, my house streamed by, and we headed toward the lake. Whispers of a waltz wafted by, and my dress started shaping itself into floaty, swirly skirts that drifted like dandelion puffs in the slight breeze. I noticed a pair of elbow-length gloves, and my usually short hair lengthened and styled itself into a classic French twist. Was that a tiara? I reached up and felt around the top of my head, and pulled off a metallic item. Gracious, a teeny tiara with moonlit diamonds and dangling pear-shaped pearls. Lordy, lordy, lordy, I could get used to this. I resettled the tiara on my hair while Bob's customary smoking jacket whispered into a tux—white tie, of course.

As we walked onto the water, the mists melted away and the ballroom opened up in front of us. Tuxedoed musicians played in the corner while the mist thinned, revealing dancers waltzing elegantly in a clockwise circle. Moonlight flooded the scene. Skirts fluttered. It was like a ballroom in old Vienna, with Strauss's "Vienna Woods" frolicking with the dancers. My album cover come to life.

"It's like a movie, Bob," I whispered. "Or *Dancing with the Stars* if everybody on that show knew what they were doing."

"Would you like to waltz?" he asked, holding out his hand.

"I'd love to," I replied uneasily, reaching for it. "But I have no idea how to do this kind of waltzing. I only know the basics and this is pretty fast."

"Don't worry. Your dress will take care of it. Just relax and enjoy."

Like many large people, Bob was a light-footed dancer. And was it really me in his arms or a memory cloaked in my moonbeam ball gown? I actually held my own on the dance floor, and I felt like Scarlett O'Hara waltzing with Rhett Butler. Perfection.

After several waltzes, the orchestra shifted to a series of foxtrots. I was hardly bothered when my skirts tightened into a slinky long sheath, and my sleeves slipped off my shoulders. My tiara melted away, leaving instead a classic strand of pearls around my neck. The décor of Greek columns slowly shifted into Art Deco, and many in the audience waved around cigarettes in long holders.

"Is that Glenn Miller? Wasn't he killed in World War II?" I asked, a little confused.

"That's him. In person, so to speak. You're going to see some fun things tonight." Bob stood tall and straightened his shoulders. I think he even puffed out his chest a bit, as if he was very proud of his accomplishments tonight. "I put in a couple of requests I thought you'd like. Just wait until Fred and Ginger show up. We won't have a lot of time, though. These winter mists usually burn off right after sunrise, so we'll only have an hour or so," he said.

But what an hour. Imagine the perfect dance. You look perfect, your dress is perfect, your dancing is perfect. This was the kind of hour you'd sacrifice a life to have. You know how it is. You slog through seemingly endless days of work and cooking and cleaning and laundry and paying bills and then a moment catches you that makes it all worth while. The sunbeam hits the lilac in full bloom. The baby laughs. Your coffee is perfect. Your husband hugs you, and you remember why you married him. Your child wins a long-struggled-for award. Your client thinks you're brilliant—and says so. You settle into your favorite chair at the beginning of a book, knowing it will be a long and enjoyable read. Moments of perfection. I was living a solid hour of them.

Questions bubbled in my brain, but the dancing put them all to rest. When you can watch Fred dance "The Way You Look Tonight" with Ginger, who cares about the mechanics behind it?

After a few dances, I needed a breather. Bob, the perfect escort (who knew?) offered to get me champagne and trotted off. When he returned, champagne flutes in hand, another couple accompanied him. Young and attractive, the man wore a uniform and what almost looked like a hoop skirt swirled around the woman.

"Roz, I think you know Marcus and Felicity." Bob smiled mischievously and took pity on my bewilderment. "Remember? You were telling me about them a few weeks ago. They're over at Brebeck Winery."

"Oh, my gosh, you're the . . ." How does one put this delicately? *You're the dead ones?*

"That's right. They founded the winery over a century ago. You were telling me how much your sister liked their rieslings, remember?"

After a few awkward moments, I said, "You would be so pleased with the way your winery has turned out. It's much bigger now, and very popular."

I was having a tough time reconciling this pleasant-faced couple with the ghosts who slammed doors and terrorized overnight winery guests. Once the disconnects started, the whole dance floor started wavering, and the music became tinny and distant.

"Drat," Bob said. "The mist is burning off. We'd better get going before you get dunked."

I woke up and found myself wrapped in the comforter from my bed, freezing and buck naked, sitting in my bedroom chair around seven in the morning. My ring was gone. Beams of sunlight were just starting to peer over the bluff, and the mists had almost dissolved.

Someone started pounding on my front door and ringing the doorbell. I heard my name being yelled, grabbed my robe off the bed, and rushed to the door. When I opened it, frigid air piled in. There stood my elderly neighbor, Stan. A red-eyed, wild-haired Stan.

"Roz, you've got to come!" He pulled the front of his jacket together with trembling hands, trying to get warm.

I motioned him into the hallway and said, "Stan, calm down, calm down. What happened?"

"It's Mary. I think there's something wrong. You've got to come."

"Let me put on some clothes and I'll be right there. Have you called a doctor or the ambulance?"

Poor thing, he was shaking. He hadn't thought to call anyone.

I wrapped my robe tighter and asked, "Do you want to come in and call them? Do you want me to call 911 for you?"

Stan watched me with blank eyes. After several moments, he said, "No. I want to go back to Mary. I'll call them from home." He paused, his eyes welling with unshed tears. "But could you please come?"

"Of course," I responded. "I'll be right over."

I turned on all my houselights so he could find his way through the dark, and threw on some clothes. Splashed some water on my face. Between my broken sleep and bizarre dreams, I was a bit sluggish, but started for Stan's in less than five minutes.

I entered Stan's kitchen to find him hanging up the phone. "The ambulance will be here as soon as they can," he said.

"Can I see Mary?" I asked.

Stan motioned me through to the front room, where a solitary lamp burned in the dark. "I came in a few minutes ago to let her know I was putting the coffee on, and she didn't move or say anything. I shook her arm, and nothing happened. So I got scared and got you," Stan said.

"I'm glad you did. It's always better to have someone else around," I replied. I put my hand on Mary's cheek. Although warm, it didn't feel as warm as I thought it should have. "Did the ambulance people say how long they would be?" I asked Stan.

"Maybe ten or fifteen minutes," Stan replied.

"Why don't you stay here with Mary. I'll go make us something hot while we wait."

After Stan finally sat down, I went to the kitchen to boil water for tea. Stan had one of those old coffee percolators. I had no idea how to use it, and now was not the time to learn. I made us both mugs of hot, sweet tea, for shock, and took Stan's to him. "Here, drink this. It will help," I said.

Stan leaned toward Mary's motionless body. She'd been his companion for how many years? I couldn't imagine his fear.

"Hey, Stan," I asked. "Do you have any family I can call?"

"Why?" he responded, again with that blank look.

"To help out, you know, keep you company over the next few days."

"I've got Mary." He reached out and stroked her arm through the blanket. "She'll be better soon."

"Why don't you let me call someone, just in case."

Stan eyed me suspiciously, but pointed to his address book on the desk. "You could call my son, Aaron. He's in Corning, so he could come pretty quick."

Aaron must have been sound asleep when I reached him, because it took me a couple of minutes to explain the situation and who I was. After he understood, he said he'd call into work, get the day off, and meet us at the hospital. While I was on the phone with Aaron, Stan ran a comb through his hair and splashed some water on his face. By the time the sheriff knocked on the door, shortly followed by the ambulance crew, we were ready to go.

Stan rode with Mary in the ambulance. Judging by the bleak look on the face of the tech who had checked Mary's heartbeat, I was pretty sure of the outcome this morning, but I followed the ambulance in my car in case I could help. The weather had turned wickedly cold, and I froze all the way to the hospital. Old VWs are not known for their heaters.

Once there, I found Stan and helped him with the paperwork. About twenty minutes later his son Aaron showed up, muscular and balding, clothes thrown together like the rest of us. When Stan saw Aaron, he started to cry. Family had arrived, and he could let down his defenses.

I introduced myself, and offered to get coffee for everyone so I could get out of the way. By the time I returned with the cardboard tray of coffees, the doctor was talking with Stan and Aaron. I could tell the outcome even from twenty feet away. Aaron hugged his father while he cried as the doctor melted into the background.

Always a delicate balance—whether to stay and possibly help, or risk being intrusive during this very private time. Aaron helped Stan into a chair, and I put his coffee on the seat of the next chair. When I handed Aaron his cup, I asked, "Is there anything I can do to help?"

"Not right now, thanks," he answered. "I'll help Dad do the paperwork to get the funeral arrangements started, and then we'll head home to start calling people."

"In that case," I said, "I'll get out of your hair. Why don't I bring over a casserole for your lunch later, so that's one less thing you'll have to worry about today."

"Thanks. I appreciate it." He cradled the hot coffee in hands that were still red with cold. "And thanks for all your help this morning with my dad. He's pretty shaken up."

"Of course he is. Anyone would be," I said sympathetically. I went over to an empty-eyed Stan and kissed his cheek. "I'm so sorry, Stan. I'll get out of your way now, but I'll see you later." I grabbed my purse and sweater and walked into the freezing morning. I hadn't really been a big fan of Mary, but I could sure understand how tough Stan's new solitude would be.

At the store, I picked up enough ingredients for two chicken thermidor casseroles. And two cakes. I don't know why people think of casseroles and cakes when there's been a death, but we do.

Since it's as easy to make two as to make one, I figured I'd invite David to dinner tomorrow for the second cake and casserole. Couch Potato Days were already shot to hell anyway. I spent the morning bustling around the kitchen, which proved very cathartic, which might be why women always make casseroles and cakes in these situations, now that I think about it.

I noticed Aaron's car pull into Stan's driveway at noon, and I had my funeral meats up there shortly thereafter. Stan looked exhausted and Aaron looked pale, but he was taking good care of his dad. If I say so myself, the casserole smelled delicious, and it went over well, since we'd all missed both breakfast and lunch. There were plenty of leftovers, which would come in handy later if they got peckish.

Stan went to lie down right after he ate. I cleaned up while Aaron made phone calls. After everything had been put away, I waved at Aaron and went home for my own nap. Between my lack of sleep the night before, my imaginary ghost ball, and all the events of the morning, I felt wiped out.

I managed to sleep for a couple of hours. Since I can count on one hand the number of times I've napped as an adult, that was pretty amazing. I woke up from my berth on the sofa to see Bob sitting on the loveseat, relaxing with his arms behind his head while he gazed at the ceiling, whistling absent-mindedly.

"Did you hear about Mary?" I asked, as I swung into a sitting position.

"Oh, yeah, she's here. I haven't met her personally, but I know she got here."

"So she's going to be a ghost for a while before she goes to heaven?"

"Yeah, I guess she has a few things to work on."

I straightened out my sleep-twisted clothes and thought about my startling wake-up call this morning. "Poor Stan. He's broken-hearted. And he's going to be so lonely in his little cottage out there on the lake. I can have the occasional cup of coffee with him and take him into town once a week when I go grocery shopping, but still, that's awfully isolated. And him without a driver's license or a car."

Bob didn't seem overly concerned. "Maybe now that Mary is out of the picture Stan and his son will spend more time together."

"Maybe," I said, my voice full of doubt. "But Aaron's in Corning, which is over an hour away. He's got his work and his own life."

"Stan'll figure it out. You did." Bob brought his arms down, and smiled.

I smiled back. "I'm still a work in progress, and I've had a little help along the way."

His smile broadened to a grin.

I got off the sofa, walked into the kitchen, got a glass of water and sat down.

Bob followed me and settled into his usual seat. "What's for dinner tonight? I'm looking forward to getting back into our old routine. That sounds like a song title. We've had too much running around lately."

"It has been crazy, hasn't it?" I conceded. "Speaking of which, are you all recuperated from your Algonquin adventures?"

"The headache's gone, but I'll have to do some research to figure everything out." Bob rubbed his forehead, as if remembering how much it had hurt.

"Nothing like being dragged to the hotel kicking and screaming to give you a subtle hint about your past," I said. "You know, I've heard about some kind of group or something at the Algonquin Hotel. It rings a bell when I think about it."

"Well, please think about it some more then. I'd love to know why I was dragged crosstown."

"I'll try. We never actually talked about you being so drunk at my sister's house," I continued, curious. "What happened? I know you like a drink now and then, but I've never seen you wasted like that."

Bob's cheeks colored. "What's that expression people use these days? Ripped me a new one?"

"Excuse me?"

"You know, when someone metaphorically beats you up."

"Yes, I've heard the expression," I responded dryly. "Although I don't tend to use it much myself. Who ripped you a new one, and why?"

"My boss. Because I let your sister know about me. When I put down the candlestick."

"You weren't kidding?" I said, shocked. "It really was against the rules?"

"Completely."

"But nothing happened when I told Amy about you." It just occurred to me that Bob needed a rule book. Something he could hand his bewildered client every time he started a new assignment.

"True. You can tell anyone you want. You can appear to be as crazy as you like. But I, according to Regulation 2025, Section 22, Subsection B must not reveal my presence through any activity, appearance, or deed to anyone other than my direct assignee. I've been put on probation. One more screw up and I start back at the beginning. Ghost boot camp. And I lose credit for all my successful assignments."

"You get fired?"

"Sort of. Pretty much totally demoted to Day One of Spookdom."

"Oh, Bob," I said in dismay.

"Yeah, as I said, they ripped me a new one. So, after I left that charming session with my boss, I walked down the hall and came across that holiday party. I guess I just jumped in with both feet. You know the rest of the story."

I felt awful. Not only had I gotten Bob into so much trouble (unwittingly, it's true, but still), but then I'd been so *mean* to him when he'd had that wicked hangover. Is this what life is supposed to be like? Screwing things up with one person and then slowly fixing that situation (Amy and her Christmas gifts; Katie and the terrible dark detour; being mean to Bob) just to fall into it again with someone else? Screw up, rebuild; screw up, rebuild. Just like bobbing up and down on a lake—except a *lot* more work. How exhausting.

"Bob—" I reached across the table for his hand, but, without the ring, I couldn't feel it. He reached toward me, as well, and our hands lay on the table, almost touching, like two marooned starfish on a tablecloth beach. "I'm as sorry as can be," I continued. "I had no idea I'd get you in so much trouble. I never would have asked if I'd known."

"I'd always heard about Reg 2025, but I had no idea they were so strict about enforcing it. Usually enforcement is lax, but then *bam!* They really nailed me," he said ruefully.

"I'm really, really sorry. Is there anything I can do to make it up to you? Just name it."

"If I think of something, I will, but I can't think of anything right now."

The house's chill settled around us. I searched the refrigerator for another leftover Katie dinner, then gave up. Once more, my appetite had vanished. I'd be a rail by spring.

"Bob, before I forget, I'm going to see if David can come to dinner tomorrow night, so you and I will have to have our get-together afterward."

"Yeah, sure, that's fine. We've been clocking in lots of hours lately, so that shouldn't be a problem. Making any more progress in deciding whether to stay at the lake or not?"

"I really don't have any options with the question right now. It's the dead of winter, the housing market is busted, it's the middle of a recession, so believe me, there's nobody looking to buy this place even if I did decide to sell it. There won't be any buyers around for months, at least until springtime. I told you, that's a really lame assignment for them to give you."

"You may think so, and I may think so, but it is what it is."

More silence.

"What about that second part?" I asked. "Where you're supposed to help me to do something. Any more idea what that's all about?"

"Not a clue. And believe me, I won't be getting any more hints from Clive."

"Clive? Is that your boss?"

"For now, anyway, unless I mess up again. Or maybe I should say, until I screw up again." Bob left, not with his usual pop, but more like air being let out of a balloon.

So strange. I had never seen Bob this low. Since I'd become unaccustomed to men in the past couple of years, I didn't know what to do. How do you cheer up a depressed guy ghost? Sex was out. Mani/pedis were out. Chocolate wouldn't do much. Maybe a road trip somewhere? Bob always enjoyed them. Something to think about.

Before that, though, I wanted to invite David over for dinner tomorrow. I had a chicken thermidor casserole with his name on it. After several tries, I finally reached him on his cell. If I was hoping for a little lift in his voice when he heard mine, I would have been disappointed. All I got were flat monosyllables.

"David, hi, it's Roz."

"Hi."

"How are you doing?"

"Fine."

"Did you have a good holiday?"

"Yes."

This was ridiculous. I was getting nowhere fast. Talk about pulling teeth. I plugged on.

"I did some cooking today, and I was wondering if you'd like to come over for dinner tomorrow."

A long pause. Did he need extra time to come up with a two-word answer?

"Sure. Whatever."

Brusque was one thing; rude was quite another.

"David, what's going on? Is there something wrong?" Of course, what I wanted to say was, 'Why are you being such a jerk?' but I managed to restrain myself.

Another long pause. "It's my grapes, Roz. I'm out here, standing in my vineyard. They're all dead."

Crap! The weather. He'd told me and I'd completely forgotten. With all the running around about Mary this morning, I hadn't even thought about the impact of the cold weather on David's grapes.

"Are you sure they're all gone? Maybe they're just in shock from the cold and not dead."

"No," he said in a flat voice. "They're all gone. These vinifera I'd planted are not as cold-resistant as the native grapes, and that temperature drop was too much for them."

"Can you do anything to save them?"

"No. There's nothing I can do at this point. I'll need to figure things out in the spring."

"David, I'm so . . .." 'Sorry' didn't seem to be strong enough when a person's life's work has just gone down the drain.

I hated this feeling of helplessness. Mary dead, Bob on probation, David's crop gone. Not a thing I could do about any of them, except make casseroles and feed people. I could push myself to meet impossible deadlines in my own work, but I couldn't do a damn thing to combat Clive or Mother Nature.

It's that feeling of helplessness that makes me live by myself by the lake. What good can I really do for the people I care about? Except, maybe, to be a companion and a witness as they go through their troubles, just as my sisters provide companionship and witnesses as I go through mine. Oh, I don't know . . . these questions always feel too big for me.

After another long pause I offered, "I could bring over the casserole now and you can show me your vines before it gets dark."

"I'll meet you at the house in fifteen minutes," David said.

After yelling for Bob a couple of times and getting no answer, I bundled up the casserole and the cake, put on my heaviest winter gear, and headed to David's. Even though it was only four, it was starting to get dark. Once at David's, we put the casserole into the oven, David put a bottle of Royal Egret Riesling in the refrigerator to chill, and we went out to look at the vines.

I'll be honest, I couldn't see much of a difference, but David pointed out cracks in the trunks of the vines. His face was so serious, I didn't have to see the cold's impact on the vines. I could see the lack of a future crop in his eyes. He talked about slicing open the buds in March to see the final damage, but I could tell he didn't have much hope.

Dinner, like my lunch earlier, was a somber affair. I told David about Mary, which only added to the dark mood. David had never met Mary, but he'd heard of her. To try to lighten up the evening, I recounted some of my holiday adventures, carefully edited, and David shook off his funk long enough to describe Christmas at his sister's house. He'd obviously enjoyed himself, even though he'd spent the holiday with half of his mind on the weather.

As our glasses of riesling began to sink in, David talked about the financial impact losing the grapes would have. There wasn't much I could say, other than to be sympathetic. Starting back at square one financially—I was an expert. It happened to me all the time. That didn't make it any more enjoyable, but I could sure empathize. I just had no concrete advice or answers for him. Going bankrupt was one of my worst nightmares.

I loaded the dishwasher while David built a fire. Neither of us was much in the mood to chat, so we sat in front of the fire, with our coffee, staring into the flames. Judging by the number of times I caught David looking at his calculator on the bookshelf by the fire, I knew he was trying to figure out the impact this disaster would have on his finances, so I took pity on his preoccupation, stood up, and got ready to go. After suiting up for the cold, I gave David a hug. Really, what more can you do at a time like this? I told him I'd call him tomorrow to see how he was doing.

"Thanks for everything, Roz. I'm sorry I'm such bad company, but I enjoyed your dinner and I'll make up for it sometime, take you out or something."

"Don't worry about it at all. I'm sure you'd do the same for me."

"Yup, I would."

I grabbed my empty tray, waved goodbye, and went out into the frigid night. My thin Nashville blood was not used to this weather yet, and the cold went right through me. When I got home, I found a moderately crabby ghost waiting for me at the kitchen table and sipping his martini.

"I thought we were going to have dinner together tonight," Bob said, raising the martini glass to his lips.

"I'm sorry, Bob, I tried to get you but I had a change of plans. This cold snap killed all of David's grapes, so I took him the casserole I'd made this morning and had dinner with him. I really did try to get you."

"I believe you. I had a little situation with Lola I had to take care of."

"I'd love to hear all about Lola one of these days. She must be a pistol."

Bob smirked and nodded his head ruefully. "Believe me, she's a handful. I'll have to check the privacy laws before I dare say anything. The last thing I need right now is more demerits." Bob gestured toward his martini. "Want one?"

"It's tempting, thanks, but I think I'll stick with tea tonight." I ran some water into the kettle and put it on the flame. I sat down next to Bob and rubbed my hands over my face. "Was it only three days ago I sat having tea at the Plaza? It feels like years, since so much has happened. Then, if you add in that, in the last six months I've lost my job, moved halfway across the country, got a ghost, and now all this with Mary and David's dead grapes. What an insane year. What was that phrase Queen Elizabeth used? It's an *annus horribilus*." The kettle boiled, so I got up to make my tea.

Bob sipped at his martini. "Well, it's almost the New Year. Maybe things will look up then. Besides, I don't think getting a ghost's been so horrible for you. Didn't you have a good time last night?"

"Oh—" I stopped dead in my tracks, my teabag waving above the empty mug.

"Didn't you?"

"Well, yes, but I thought I'd been dreaming. I didn't think we really went to a ball." I turned to Bob, the teabag still dangling from my hand.

Bob sniffed, "Well, yeah—"

"Oh, well . . . it was amazing!"

Bob smiled. "I thought you'd enjoyed yourself. I had fun too. We don't get a chance to do that kind of thing too often. The weather has to be just right."

Then it occurred to me. The same cold front that had created my ballroom fantasy had also demolished David's grapes. Saddened, I said, "You mean the weather has to be extreme enough that it kills somebody's crops."

Bob paused with his martini in mid-air. "Well, I guess so. I never thought of it that way." He put his martini down. "So foul and fair a day I have not seen," he muttered.

"What?"

"Nothing."

I sat down, finally dunking my cranberry-apple teabag. "I honestly don't know how much more I can take, Bob. Just pray things go well with my Community Chest clients. As long as I have work and some money coming in, I'll figure everything else out."

"Money, money, money," Bob said, and took a long drink of his martini. "At least you're consistent. It's always the same theme with you."

"Hey, I'm not saying I have to be a millionaire," I protested. "I just want enough to pay my bills, and I don't live extravagantly. I think there's a lot of nobility in being able to pay your bills on time. I hate to think what David's going through tonight. He might lose everything because of this stupid weather."

The cold had settled resolutely into the house. I got up and turned the heater a smidge higher.

The phone rang. Angela. So much had changed since we spoke yesterday. I launched into my litany of recent woes and then, in case she wasn't bombarded enough, I recapped, maybe a little hysterically, all of my problems of the past year. Angela tried valiantly to cheer me up, but I wasn't having any of it. It was my pity party, and I dug in with both feet. Finally, both worn out from our frustrating conversation, we hung up. For one of the few times in our decades-long relationship, Angela had failed to make me see the bright side of things. I felt useless, hopeless, and exhausted, so I took a hot shower and a sleeping pill, and went to bed.

The next day was more of the same; depressing, gray, frigid cold, and blustery. I made cinnamon rolls and took some to Aaron and Stan. Judging by the number of covered casserole dishes in the fridge, word of Mary had gotten around and the food-laden condolence calls had begun, so I temporarily crossed them off my worry list.

David wasn't home, so I left some rolls with a note for him on his porch. I knew they could stand the cold and would heat up well in the microwave. I found out later he'd gone to consult with some of the long-time growers to find out how bad the damage was all around. From what I understood, vinifera grapes throughout the area had been killed, with a few minor exceptions. Root stock had been set back at least three years, the soonest vinifera grape growers could expect a crop on the new vines they'd have to plant. A bleak time for all the vinifera grape growers around Crooked Lake.

By mid-day I was home from my drop-offs. The afternoon yawned, wide-open, so I tried to get back into the Couch Potato Day spirit, with only half-hearted success. There was so much bad going on that, for one of the first times in my life, I had a hard time escaping into the oblivion of books. I persevered, though, and eventually achieved lift-off, and managed to get away from my own worries for the rest of the day.

Chapter 13
Dancing in the Dark

New Year's Eve fell on the next day, Wednesday, and the day started out with me going to calling hours for Mary. I dressed up a bit, exchanging my usual blue jeans for my all-occasion black pant suit. I added a sage green blouse, some earrings, and a gold chain to relieve its gloom, and went downstairs for my purse and lists. I made lists before going into Avondale. As long as I was using the gas, I could run a few errands as well, since stores would be closed for the next day or two. I had to replenish my shelves. All the cooking of the past few days had used up many of my staples. It wasn't easy or cheap being the Casserole Queen.

One glance through the window told me to prepare for another bitter, gray, windy day outside. I could guess that, now that it had settled in, I could anticipate a long, cold, winter, just what I'd been dreading. The car started reluctantly and stuttered the ten miles into town.

I stopped first at the funeral home to pay my respects. A picture of Mary on an easel greeted me in the hallway. A Mary I'd never known. That Mary stood tall, full of energy and life. Blond hair glinting in the sun, laughing blue eyes, dressed in full camo with a rifle held loosely in her arms. A total dish. Completely different from the shriveled-up, wrinkly carcass in the coffin. How the mighty fall.

I spent a few minutes looking at Mary's corpse. The major thought running through my head was that this was going to be the ultimate outcome of my life, and I might as well try to enjoy living a bit more before I reached the end.

After determining to be kinder to myself and to loosen up the old purse strings a bit, I looked for Stan. He sat in a far corner, gray-faced, looking like a rag doll that had most of the stuffing yanked out of it. Aaron, dressed in a corduroy blazer, sat next to him, as did a dark-haired woman who resembled Aaron enough to be his sister. In the opposite corner of the room, about ten people milled around. Younger, about Aaron's age, and in constant motion, reaching for cigarettes they couldn't smoke, pulling jackets on and off, always moving as if they were very uneasy with their surroundings.

I went to Stan, patted him on the shoulder, and shook Aaron's hand. Aaron introduced me to Jenny, his sister. If I didn't know better, I'd have said Jenny had already started drinking this morning. I motioned to the group in the far corner and asked Aaron who they were.

"Mary's kids and their spouses," he answered.

I realized since Mary and Stan had never married, the families had never blended, which meant they were in direct competition for Mary's assets, especially the lakefront property, worth hundreds of thousands of dollars. I could be looking at another Hatfield and McCoy feud here. Everyone would be on tenterhooks until Mary's will was read after the funeral. Who would win out? Mary's ex-husbands and children and grandchildren? Or her handyman of many years? I was so glad I wouldn't be in the middle of *that* discussion.

I chatted with Stan and his children for a few minutes and found out he'd be spending the next few days with Aaron, at least until after the funeral, which would be in early January. After visiting for a bit, I went to sit in one of the empty chairs in front of the coffin. I wanted to spend some time reaffirming my personal commitments to be more lenient with myself. Maybe the next time Tess called to move up my deadline, I'd push back a little. If I screwed up gift-giving again, I'd just try to make it right without beating myself up over it. Instead of wasting time trying to figure out the something I was supposed to do for Bob, I'd just ignore it and go about living my life. If it got done, it got done; if it didn't, it didn't.

A woman sat next to me, and I turned to nod hello. She looked familiar, but I couldn't place her or remember her name.

"It's Pat. Remember?"

I continued to look at her with a puzzled stare, trying to remember where we'd met.

"From Royal Egret winery. The tasting. You were with Bev."

"Oh, of course, Pat. I'm so sorry. I was drawing a blank," I admitted.

"It was a couple of months ago, so I don't blame you," she said good-naturedly. "How have you been? Are you settling in okay? Bev tells me you two have been to a few more wineries."

"We've done a couple of tastings. That's been a lot of fun," I answered. "And overall I guess I've been doing all right after the move. This morning's kind of sad, though. Did you know Mary?" I nodded toward the coffin right in front of us.

"Years and years ago. She used to hunt with my father and his brothers when they were young. What a hell-raiser she was back then. Always getting into trouble." Pat smiled to herself, as if remembering tales of long-ago escapades. "My dad still talks fondly of her, but he's in the nursing home so I told him I'd come by to pay our respects."

I nodded. I liked seeing the lines connecting people to each other in this small town, like the beginnings of a fragile web. Nothing in the world more delicate than those strands. Nothing stronger, either. I'd missed those linkages over the past decades because of my nomadic business life.

Pat stood, glanced at the coffin one last time, patted my shoulder, and said, "See you at the winery one of these days."

I nodded and, a few minutes later, left as well. On the way out I waved at Stan, his kids, and the others. Once out in the blustery late morning, I stopped at the dry cleaners, the bank, the post office, and the gas station. At the grocery store, I picked up a few items to supplement Katie's fast-fading leftovers and the ingredients to start a big beef-vegetable soup.

After unloading all my groceries at home, I changed into my blue jeans and got the soup going. Pellets of hail started falling and mist blew over the lake and enveloped the house. Since this was the last day of my Couch Potato Festival, I resisted the urge to check email and see if there was anything from my clients.

Instead, I settled on the sofa with the last half of my book. For a few peaceful hours the soup simmered away, and I got lost in Austen's Bath. Another bout of hail hit, heavier this time, and the wind seemed to pick up, moaning around the roof and whipping the lake into rugged waves that pounded loudly against the shore. The lights flickered, but I figured that would be normal in such a stiff wind.

When I got up at three to turn down the soup, the lights went out again. The power bar on my computer screeched and my electric fire alarms beeped madly. Twice the power tried to re-establish itself, with no luck. Every electric item shut down, dead. No light, no electric stove, no heat. Well, this was a fine kettle of fish, as they say.

Heat drained out of the house like water out of a sieve. After two hours, the only warm thing in the house was my rapidly-cooling pot of soup. As I struggled to squeeze my winter coat over the two sweaters I already wore, I yelled for Bob.

"I told you, you don't have to yell," he said as he shimmered in. "What are you doing?"

"Can't you feel how cold it is in here?" I asked, twisting around backward in little circles trying to find the entryway to a sleeve.

"No, as a matter of fact, I can't."

"Oh." That made me pause for a second. "Well, my power's out, and it's frigid in here. I've got to figure out something to do for tonight." After much struggling, I managed to pull on my coat.

"You could try a hotel," he suggested.

I stared at Bob balefully. "The nearest hotel is in Avondale, and it would cost a fortune. I can't keep running to a hotel when the electricity goes out. Stan's got a wood stove so I'd go there, but he said he'd be with his son for a few days."

"What about David?"

"I tried him, but his cell phone is off. He might be at the Royal Egret helping with sales. I imagine this is a big night for the winery." Bob looked puzzled. "You know, New Years."

Understanding dawned. "I used to love New Years."

I looked at the liquor-flask bulge in his smoking jacket and said, "I just bet you did."

I sat down at the table, baffled. "I know they open emergency shelters in the cities, but I have no idea what they do here. If I stay in the house, I'll freeze. There are no restaurants for miles, and the few that I could find open will probably be doing big New Year's parties, if they haven't been canceled."

"It's a stumper, all right."

"You're not being particularly helpful here, Bob."

"Am I ever?"

"Good point, although you do manage to get a good shot in once in a while." This was starting to look like a very long, cold night. Happy New Year to me. Nuts. I really did need to start making new friends.

Pounding at the front door interrupted us. *Please, no more dead bodies,* I thought, as I hurried up the stairs.

You know all those fairy tales about the White Knight riding to the rescue of the fair maiden? Well, dear reader, they're true, if you substitute a middle-aged grape grower in a beat-up pick-up truck for the knight-in-armor on his horse. And when you're as cold as I was, you don't carp over details.

I threw my arms around David, all drama queen to his knight. "You saved me, you saved me!"

"Well, somebody had to," David replied in a practical tone as he stepped out of the gloomy sleet and into my dark hallway. "At least you have a flashlight," he said. Then the wavery beam of my dime-store flashlight gave out as my battery died. "Well, almost," he said.

"I don't have power," he continued, "but I have the fireplace and that at least keeps my place somewhat warm. I didn't think you'd had your chimney cleaned yet."

I crinkled up my face in silent embarrassment at my oversight.

As David spoke, he pulled a huge flashlight from his coat pocket. Its powerful beam lit up my whole hallway.

"I'm going to have to get one of those," I said, wistfully eyeing the thing.

"If you're going to live out here, you sure will," David responded. "We don't lose power often, but you can bet we'll lose it at least once or twice every winter. Do you want to grab a few things to stay at my place overnight if you need to?"

"Thank you, thank you. I'll just get a toothbrush." I led him into the bedroom, where I grabbed my overnight bag from the closet. David shined the light so I could see what I was doing. I picked up some underwear and socks, mentally debated about bringing my big warm flannel nightgown, but opted instead for my Tweety-bird flannel pajamas. I trotted off to the bathroom for my toothbrush and a few odds and ends, and I was ready to go.

"All set?" David asked.

"Just about. I left some candles burning downstairs in the kitchen, and I need to put them out. I made some soup. Should I bring it? Do you have a way to reheat it?"

"Sure, bring it along. I'll figure something out with the fireplace."

Bob calmly sat at the table where I'd left him, watching as I filled a bag with food for dinner. Once I blew out the candles, and we functioned by David's flashlight, all I could see of Bob was his dim outline, the silk of his smoking jacket occasionally catching the light.

David picked up the bag of groceries and headed toward the stairway. I followed with my overnight bag and turned to wave goodbye to Bob. The last I saw of him was a ghostly flicker of his fingers as he lifted his martini glass.

After hours of sleet, ice coated everything outside. We skated to David's truck, and David helped to hoist me and my stuff into the passenger side. Of course the truck started right up, but with all the ice, David drove very slowly. Even though he lived only a couple of miles from my place, it took fifteen minutes to get there.

"I came to your house straight from work," David explained as we descended from the truck. "We shut down the winery early with all this sleet. People stopped coming in by mid-afternoon."

A crisp rim of ice had formed around the door's edge and it crackled as David yanked open the door. The house was completely dark, and freezing. David set the flashlight on the counter so that the beam shone toward the fireplace. "I'll get the fire going if you want to take care of that," he said, indicating the bag of food.

We both fumbled around for a bit, but in a few minutes David had built a fire, and I set out dinner on the counter. The cinnamon rolls I'd made for him yesterday were there as well, half eaten.

David found a cast iron pot and hung it from a hook near the edge of the fireplace. I put the rest of the meal, including the cinnamon rolls, onto the cocktail table in front of the fire. The room was already starting to warm, so I peeled off my coat.

"Since it's New Year's, what do you say we treat ourselves to a bottle of Royal Egret Reserve Gewürztraminer?"

"You had me at 'since.' And you won't even have to set it aside to chill. Tonight all the wines have been pre-chilled for us."

"True, true. A side benefit of a power outage in winter."

I wrapped myself in one of the quilt blankets piled on the sofa and sat in front of the now-crackling fire. David handed me a glass of gewürz, wrapped a blanket around himself, and joined me on the sofa.

"Happy New Year," he said, raising his glass in a toast.

"And may it be a lot kinder to us than the old one," I responded.

"I'll drink to that." David sniffed the wine before tasting it.

I did the same. It smelled delicious, with echoes of peach and spice. Summer captured in a glass.

We sipped for a few minutes. I thoroughly enjoyed the wine, the fire, and the respite from the storm. Amazing how much more pleasant a storm is when you're in a warm dry place, with hot soup, cool wine, and a friend.

"I never really thanked you for coming to my rescue back there, David. You were so kind to think of me in all this weather. I'd really started to get a bit worried. I wasn't sure what I should do."

"You can always come here if the weather gets bad or the power goes out. Or just knock on the door of anyone who has a fireplace or a wood stove. People are very decent around here. No one's going to let a stranger freeze to death."

"What would you have done if you were me and you weren't around?"

David stared at me over his glass of wine as he tried to unravel my question in his head. "If I was a girl? New here? In this weather with no electricity?" He thought for a minute. "I'd probably have headed toward Avondale and gone to the police station or fire department. They could've at least kept you updated on the situation. They probably have a generator, too, so it would be warm. But I think you should plan on coming here whenever possible." He smiled and winked.

I laughed and took another sip of wine.

"You know," David continued, "I have a crank radio for these kinds of emergencies. Let me get it going and we'll see if we can get an update on the power situation." He rummaged through a closet near the door and finally found the radio buried in some clutter on the floor.

We both cranked the handle for a few minutes, and eventually pulled in a very static-y broadcast from Bath, a small town to the south of us. The broadcaster, a man named Mel, read weather status reports and nearby closings and delayed openings, punctuated with occasional songs from the past. We left the radio on, and turned our attention to the soup, which tasted delicious. My grandmother had been right. Hunger makes the best spice.

After two bowls of soup, rolls and butter, and two glasses of wine apiece, we were feeling no pain. David got up and stoked the fire while I put the dishes on the kitchen counter. They'd keep until tomorrow. I was in no mood to deal with them then.

I hurried back to the warm perimeter in front of the fire. David was just settling on the sofa when a tinny version of Fred Astaire's "The Way You Look Tonight," came on the radio. I stopped dead, suddenly transported back to the ballroom on the lake where I had last heard this song. Only that time it had been sung by the real Fred Astaire, or, at least, the ghost of the real Fred Astaire.

David looked up from the sofa, puzzled by my quick stop. "What is it, Roz?"

I shook my head a bit to clear it. "Nothing. Just hearing that song again kind of surprised me. The last time I heard it I was at a dance."

David caught only the last few words. "You want to dance?" He looked bewildered, but started lumbering out of his seat.

"No, no. I just said I was *at* a dance," I clarified.

"Oh, okay, then." David settled back in, obviously relieved.

I sat next to him, huddled in my blanket, and picked up my last swallow of wine. "No, this is fine. This is really nice." Fred faded away, and I lifted my glass toward a now droopy-eyed David. "Happy New Year, David."

I could say we dozed off, awoke in the middle of the night, realized our true love for each other and ran off into the bedroom and made mad, passionate love until the morning, but we didn't. Exhaustion, worry, hot soup, chilled wine, a warm fire and we were both out for the count. The next thing I knew, my head was at one end of the sofa, and my feet were in David's lap. I'm pretty sure I kicked him awake, because I heard a "Hey!" and felt my foot hoisted in the air.

"What the . . .?" I mumbled, trying to open my eyes and get control of my foot at the same time.

"Stop kicking me. Jeez."

I creaked into a sitting position. Whatever parts of my body weren't screaming in agony were moaning in pain.

Everything hurt. New life lesson learned: Women of a certain age should avoid spending the night on sofas whenever possible. I think David was in the same shape, because I heard a little muffled cursing as he hoisted himself off the sofa, and he tried nursing the kinks out of his back all the way to the stove.

I followed suit, shambling off the sofa. I shuffled, bent over, behind him to the kitchen area, rubbing my lower back.

"Spending the night on the sofa always looks a lot more glamorous in the movies, doesn't it?" I asked.

"I'll say," David responded as he reached into the cabinet for ibuprofen. He popped off the top and shook a few tablets into his palm. "Want some?"

I held out my hand. We swallowed our pills with long drinks of water, and then I went into the bathroom.

By the time I returned, face washed and teeth brushed, coffee was brewing and the toaster was doing its magic. I stood between the two, just basking in the heat generated by the appliances. I could hear the furnace cranking away, confirming that the power must have come back on.

"Nothing like losing electricity for a while to make you really appreciate it when it comes back," David said. "I'm going to fry myself some eggs. Can I make you some?"

"Just one would be great, thanks." Between the ibuprofen, the coffee, and clean teeth I was starting to feel a lot more human. "What a night!" I said. "I don't know what I would have done without you, David. You really saved me."

"For sure if you'd stayed at your place it would have been a long, cold night. I think this worked out much better," he said, handling the eggs and frying pan with the ease of long practice.

"We'll both be fine once we've worked out all the kinks," I said. As if pulled by a marionette's strings, we both reached back and started massaging our lower backs, then noticed each other and laughed.

With a delicious breakfast in front of us, and the world outside encased in ice, I was in no hurry to leave.

After David swallowed his second piece of toast he said, "You should probably go to Avondale Hardware first thing tomorrow for a heavy-duty flashlight. They come in handy all the time."

"You're right."

"You might also want to look for a good stainless steel thermos."

"I can understand the flashlight, but why the thermos?"

"You're like me, I think. You can cope with almost anything as long as you have your coffee in the morning."

Since I was lifting my mug to my lips as he said those words, I could hardly deny it.

"And if you don't have your coffee," he continued, "nothing else the rest of the day goes right." I nodded. "If the weather is dicey, and I think I might lose power during the night, I'll brew up a pot of coffee before I go to bed and put it in the thermos. It stays almost boiling hot so if you wake up with no power, you've got your coffee and you're all set to deal with things."

"You're brilliant!" I said, and meant it.

David just laughed. "Doesn't take much to impress you."

"That's a great idea, and I'd never have thought of it. I come from generations of engineers, but I'm not very practical in some areas."

"If you live out in the country long enough, you will be," he responded with a chuckle.

I poured us each a second mug of coffee. "David, I know it's none of my business, but can I ask you a question?" His eyebrows rose, and a flash of wariness came into his eyes, but he said, "Sure."

"I just want to make sure that you were going to be okay after losing your grapes. We never really talked about it. I can only speak for myself, but I was terrified when I lost my job, and I didn't know what I was going to do, or how I was going to support myself. If you feel the same way about losing your grapes, I wanted to let you know I could be a shoulder for you to cry on. I wish I could lend you money, but I'm kind of scraping the bottom of the barrel myself. But I'm someone you can always talk to, if you wanted . . ." My voice drifted off. Even after we'd spent the night together, so to speak, I was still a little embarrassed to bring this up. But he needed to know our friendship worked both ways—I could give support as well as take it.

He cleared his throat, and took a gulp of coffee. "One of the first things I noticed about you, Roz, was what a kind heart you had. And the more I get to know you, the more I realize that, and the more I value it."

I stared down into my mug, a little embarrassed.

"Like you," he continued, "I'm probably going to be scraping by for a bit because this has been a genuine set back. Those vines were doing beautifully and losing all of them hurts, no doubt about it. But I've got my job at Royal Egret and they'll take all the hours I can give them, so I'll survive. When Bethie died, there was some insurance money that I put in the bank, so I'll use that to restock the vineyards. It's not going to be easy, but I'll get by."

A tightly-wound spring of worry in my chest loosened a bit. "I'm so glad. I didn't know if you were going to have to sell and move, or what."

"No, no." David shook his head. "It won't come to that . . . I don't think. You never know what curve balls the universe is going to throw you, but, so far, I'm okay. Lots of beans and franks in my future, though."

I snickered. "Believe me, I know what you mean."

Eventually we chipped our way out of the house to the truck. The sun had already started melting the ice. In a few hours, if it warmed up enough, there'd be nothing but slop.

With the bright sun glittering on the landscape, the previous night's fire and shadows felt as unreal as my ghost ball from a few nights before.

David drove to my place as carefully as he had to his house. As we pulled into my driveway, I said, "You know, last night could have gone very differently." I was thinking about how I could be lying frozen in my bed right now.

Judging by the wicked gleam in David's eye, he was *not* thinking about the same thing when he said, "No, it couldn't have." He opened his door and circled around to help me out. Once he had me firmly in his arms, halfway between the seat and the ground, he continued. "I don't let wine and a power outage do my seducing for me. When I set out to seduce a woman, she knows she's being seduced!" David smacked a loud kiss on my astonished 'o'-shaped mouth, plopped me onto the ground, and headed back to the driver's seat. "See you later, Roz!" he yelled, then grinned, gunned the motor, and shot off.

"Well, really," I huffed to myself, pretending to be miffed.

Everything in the house looked fine. The heat cranked away, and I appreciated it, probably for the first time. I took a quick shower, changed, and headed into the kitchen for another few cups of coffee.

What a cozy night it had been, even though my back might need a few days to recover. What a great guy David was. Imagine finding such a decent man out here in the wilderness so far from everyone and everything. Who'd have thought?

And Bob. Bob who, in his own bumbling, useless way, gave me a lot of laughs. Life for this solitary woman, living by herself on the shores of a lake, was starting to look up. Who would have known?

Nights of dancing or broken, crumpled sleep took their toll. Wakes and power outages added their own stress.

Horizontal ghosts and miffed family members didn't help matters any, or did my surprise smooch that morning. That kiss offered a whole level of complication I didn't want to think about. I needed a few days of quiet and routine to get back to normal. Thank goodness Tess and Amanda would be back on the job soon, and we could start strategizing the Community Chest America Wins! entries. Between strategies, collecting and analyzing data, and writing up the submissions, I'd be busy for several months. Exactly what I needed right now.

Mary's funeral had been delayed until after the New Year's holiday. I looked out my window and checked Stan's house. No smoke coming out of his chimney, so he must have remained with his son.

I usually try to review my pitifully tiny retirement stock portfolio over the New Year's and Fourth of July holidays, but I wasn't in the mood. Too restless to read, I decided to cook a few meals that I could freeze for when I'd be a lot busier with work.

After a quick check-in call with Katie (her shrieks when I told her about my night with David were still making my ears ring) and a brief "Happy New Years" call to Pop and Milly, I turned on the football games to burble in the background.

People have tried to teach me the game of football for years. I even have a book called *How to Watch Football* on my bookshelves. The most I've ever learned is that one team gets four tries to get the ball a certain distance, and if they can't do it in four tries they have to kick the ball, or something. It really doesn't matter. I just like the noise of football games. Everyone sounds so *excited* for hours on end, it's always amazed me.

I grew up in a household where the men would have football on every Sunday, all afternoon. I guess I like it so much because in many ways, it's a soundtrack of my childhood. There are few other sounds that make me feel as protected and taken care of. I use football games now as cheerful background noise when I cook or pay bills in the winter. I think, every year, that I should record a couple of games so that I can play them for background noise all spring and summer, but so far I've never gotten my act together enough to do it. One of these days . . .

With the football game on in the background, I chopped vegetables for soup, made a meatloaf, and put a ham in to bake, then started a couple of loaves of oatmeal bread. By three p.m. the kitchen smelled wonderful, and by six my freezer was stuffed full of single-pack freezer bags that I could pull out for months. I poured myself a well-earned glass of wine and sat down to my dinner of ham and cheese and vegetable-stuffed baked potato. Just as I finished up the last bite, Bob shimmered in.

"Hey," I said.

"Hey, yourself," Bob tossed back. He settled into his chair, and pulled out the flask of rye. "How'd things go last night? Did you stay warm?" He shot me a wicked grin.

"Yes, thank you very much, I was just fine," I replied rather primly.

His grin broadened. "Well?"

"Well, nothing."

"Nothing?"

"We slept on the couch." Speaking of which, I reached over to take a couple more ibuprofen while I had a full stomach.

"If you play it right, a couch can be lots of fun," Bob continued.

"Well, we slept. We were tired, and we're not eighteen anymore." I sounded like a cranky school marm.

Bob studied me with an appraising stare. "Too bad."

"Look," I said irritably. "Could we get off my love life please?"

"Or lack thereof, you mean."

I glared at Bob for a few seconds. "Anyway, hotshot, what have you been up to all day?" I started to clear the table.

"I've been trying to figure out this Algonquin thing. Not a lot of luck. Our files are a mess."

I turned, dishes in hand, and stared at him. "You're kidding me. You're still using paper files in the afterlife? That's craziness." After opening the dishwasher, I loaded my dishes into it. Then I said, "Since you bring it up, though, I did a little digging on the Algonquin myself, this afternoon while everything was cooking. I had a vague memory of something famous at that hotel, so I jumped online and found out that a bunch of people used to hang out at the Algonquin in the nineteen-twenties and thirties. They called themselves the Algonquin Round Table. The people in it were writers and publishers and actors and critics. It seemed pretty famous. Maybe you were one of those people?"

"Huh. Interesting. It feels right, but who would I have been?"

I shoved the dishwasher closed with my hip, turned it on, and started wiping down the counters. "I have no idea. There were tons of people in and out of the group. It wasn't anything official. People would drop into the hotel for a meal and sit at this big round table. That's why they called it the Algonquin Round Table. We'd have to do lots of research to figure out which person you were. Does it really matter?"

"I don't know. But the fact that the hook dragged me across town makes me think it might." Bob glanced at me, an expectant look on his face.

"Well, maybe." Counters clean, I sat down again. I probably should have been interested in this Bob identity issue, but I really wasn't. Especially if it meant a lot of extra work for me, which I suspected was the issue at play right now.

Who would ever have dreamed the afterworld wasn't computerized? I had no intention of pounding a keyboard as Bob's Gal Friday in my off hours, at least not until I was convinced it was important to know exactly who he had been. I already knew he'd been a writer in the early days of movies and he'd had a couple of kids. And he'd probably hung out with a gang of folks at the Algonquin in the early decades of the last century. All these facts were interesting, but I didn't exactly see how they'd be relevant for a woman of a certain age trying to keep body and soul together in the opening years of the twenty-first century.

"Good luck with your research project," I said, politely trying to distance myself from it. "I'm going to be really busy with my Community Chest entries for the next few months, so I'm afraid I'm not going to have a lot of time to help you out."

"No problem," Bob said, but I'm pretty sure I heard a note of disappointment in his voice. He continued, "If I'm supposed to find out more about the Algonquin, I'll figure out a way to do it. Maybe you could show me how to use your computer?"

"Maybe, but I'm on it all the time when I work." I really didn't like the track this conversation was taking, so I tried to steer it in a different direction. "Mary's funeral is tomorrow. How's she settling in at your place?"

"She's still just wandering around, trying to get the lay of the land. She'll be like this for a while. That's why they need to get going on that orientation program I was telling you about."

"It's not me you have to convince, it's Clive. I think it's a fine idea."

Bob took another slug from his flask. "Frankly, I'm keeping my distance from Clive these days."

"Probably just as well, all things considered. You know, I think I've figured out the thing I'm supposed to do."

"Really?" Bob looked up, curious.

"I bet it has something to do with these Community Chest campaigns. They help tons of people live better lives throughout the country, so the strategies I help develop in them could have a huge impact."

"Hmm." Unimpressed, Bob took another sip. "Could be. It seems to me that usually the assignments are a lot more simple and personal. But you could be right," he added, as if trying to console me.

"In that case, we might be almost done, right?" I should have been filled with happiness at that, but I wasn't. I began to suspect I'd miss this pain-in-the-butt spook when he finally vanished out of my life.

"It doesn't really feel that way to me but these days I'm a little shaky about my job so, who knows?"

"David's shaky about his vineyard, you're shaky about your job, I'm shaky about my finances. Whatever happened to job security, long-term marriages, pensions, and the white picket fence?" I shook my head, discouraged. "I'd go down the road of everything's gone to heck in a hand basket, but I vowed to be more optimistic and positive as one of my New Year's resolutions, so I'm going to stop myself right there." I stood and walked toward the living room. "Want to watch some TV?"

"Not tonight," Bob said. "I've got to check in on Lola. The holidays can be tough on people." Bob looked dismayed at having said something almost personal about another client—a violation of other-side privacy laws?—and disappeared.

Turned out there wasn't anything worthwhile on TV, so George R. R. Martin and I finished out the night.

Chapter 14
Good Vibrations?

Friday, January second, dawned clear and cold. Between the plows and the salt, the streets were clean. Shoveling the few feet between my car and the roads took only minutes. I headed out in plenty of time for the eleven o'clock funeral.

Stan and his children were there, as were all of Mary's ex-husbands and children.

I'd never been to a funeral in a funeral home. I'd always been to a church for them. I remembered my grandmother's funeral. She'd raised ten children in the middle of the Depression so when she died, sometime in the nineteen-eighties, generations of descendants had packed into that quaint New England church. After her family was grown, she'd been very active in the community, so townspeople added to the crowd at her services. My grandmother had six sons, including my father, and when they carried her casket out of the church, it rested only on the shoulders of her sons. As the six men walked past me, openly crying, I remember thinking, *She has a catafalque of her own sons, and that is not a sight I expect to see ever again in my life.* And so far, in this age of two-children families, I haven't.

Mary's funeral was a much less-populated affair, just family and a few neighbors. As I sat watching the services, I mentally renewed my vows to try to be a little kinder to myself. Seeing the sparseness of the crowd, I also decided to start looking into doing some volunteer work. I wanted my grandmother's funeral, not this one. I wanted to leave a hole in a community, not just in a family or at a workplace. As the services concluded, I gathered my winter paraphernalia, paid my condolences to Stan, who invited me back to his house at two, and went over to the hardware store. Sturdy, heavy-duty flashlights and steel thermoses were not cheap, but I remembered my new kindness resolution and paid the bill without wincing, much.

As I drove the ten miles back to my house, the sun shone brightly, melting off the last of the sleet. Although the trees were winter-bare, the lake they surrounded burst with the blues of summer. No boats were out, of course, but miles of waves glittered restlessly. The last thing I expected to find was a strange vehicle in my driveway. I pulled into the driveway of my Florida-vacationing neighbors, picked up my hardware store bags, strode over to the unfamiliar car, and rapped on the dark-tinted window.

It wheeled down, and there she sat, my sister Angela, all the way from Mississippi. Shocked, I dropped my bags. Thank goodness nothing was breakable. Angela! Out of the blue! She jumped out of the car, and we hugged and screeched and danced around with excitement. Eventually the cold started to get to us, so we grabbed bags and suitcases and lugged everything into the house. We plopped her luggage on the guest bed and, chattering all the while, headed down into the kitchen.

One reason I was so stunned to see Angela in an ordinary airport rental car in my driveway is because when I imagine her coming to visit me, I always see it in terms of Glinda's Big Bubble descending in the *Wizard of Oz*. I'm a Munchkin in that scenario, and Angela is Glinda in a big puffy dress and sparkly high crown.

I've always had a sneaking suspicion that Angela's a little more evolved than I am, a few rungs higher on the food chain. She's unfailingly kind and always thoughtful. I try to be unfailingly kind and thoughtful, but I'm restless and edgy and judgmental, full of awkward angles and impulses, where Angela is full of disciplined good will.

I'd told Katie once about my suspicion that Angela was more highly evolved than I, and she'd rolled her eyes and sighed. "For Pete's sake, Roz, haven't you ever heard that comparisons are odious? Besides, it's a lot easier for Angela to be kind and thoughtful all the time. She's had the same husband for years, and he adores her. She's spent much of her life at home raising two wonderful kids. She's never had to spend one minute as an adult worrying about money. I love Angela with all my heart, and she's had many of her own challenges to contend with," Katie continued, "but I don't know if she could have survived all the stuff you've juggled, much less thrived the way you have. Look at you, divorced and on your own, no job security except your own wits, and you've done well enough to have your own business and your own home on a beautiful lake. I don't know many people who could pull that off. So don't waste time thinking about more evolved. That's stupid."

Stupid it might be, but it had always been in my mind when I interacted with Angela. Her life reminded me of a quote from Thoreau: "Kindness is the only investment that never fails." Angela believes that the Universe, or God, is always presenting us with lessons and until we learn them, the Universe will keep giving the same lesson to us in different guises. I think the lesson the Universe—or maybe it's the Economy, I'm always getting those two confused—keeps sending me is to learn how to live with loss. Have a great job? Lose it. Get another great job? Lose it. Have a great marriage? Lose it. Have lots of money? Lose it. The one coping skill I've learned is humor. When the Universe seems determined to have you set up housekeeping on the lower floors of Maslow's pyramid, all you can do is laugh, plant geraniums for color, and lay in a goodly supply of chocolates. A few happy DVDs might help. You'll need them all.

As kind and thoughtful as Angela was, she was fed up. Fed up with depressing conversations with me. Fed up with Katie telling her how I was spinning out of control, seeing ghosts, and dragging her daughter down dark Manhattan streets. Fed up with rumors about me drinking too much.

"You've got to put a stop to all of this nuttiness, Roz. From what Katie tells me, there's a very nice guy up here who you might get something going with. You need a companion, someone who can help you out when things get bad. This ghost fixation is stopping you from building something real with David. You've got to pull yourself together, Roz, and get your life back under control. This Bob, if he even exists, is not helping you at all."

"Didn't Katie tell you about the candlestick? She knows he exists now."

"That's neither here nor there, Roz."

I needed to defuse this whole encounter. "Angela, you must be hungry after being on an airplane all morning. How about a sandwich?"

"Yes, I'd love a sandwich, but we're not finished talking about this, Roz. I didn't fly all the way up here just to eat a sandwich, you know."

"I know, I know, sweetheart, but it's been a busy morning for both of us. Coffee?"

"Yeah, sure."

For a few minutes we turned the conversation to happier matters, discussions about our mutual holidays and respective projects, my work and her kids. But inevitably Angela brought the conversation back to Bob.

"Don't you see how bad Bob is for you, Roz?"

"Bad? No, I don't see that at all."

"Dragging you down dark streets in Manhattan? Pushing you into shelves of glass at the mall? Being a constant drinking buddy? You could have frozen in here the other night if David hadn't come by. Bob was no help then either."

"You make it sound like Bob actively does bad things to me, and he doesn't," I tried to explain. "He's just in the vicinity."

"Exactly my point!" Angela slammed her hand on the table for emphasis, and I jumped. Angela *never* slammed anything. "If Bob wasn't around, these kinds of things wouldn't be happening to you, Roz. They could be dangerous."

"Life is dangerous, Angela. Whenever you step out of your door, bad things can happen to you. You know that. You've sent two kids off to college and out into the world."

"I'm not stupid, Roz." Angela rubbed her forehead as if she was getting a headache. "I know the world's a dangerous place. I'm just saying you don't have to invite danger to sit down and eat dinner with you every night."

"But Bob can be so much fun. He makes me nuts a lot of the time, but we have a lot of laughs. And I want laughs more than almost anything else. I'd miss him if he wasn't here."

"So if you missed Bob, you might be a little more motivated to spend time with David and develop a real relationship."

I'd never heard Angela be quite this logical. Even though it disconcerted me, I started to get angry. I blurted, "My relationship with Bob *is* real! It's just not the *regular* kind of real. You know, I am so sick of people telling me I'm not leading a regular life, that I need a husband to take care of me. I can take care of myself. Well, for the most part, anyway. And what I can't do for myself, I can pay someone to do. Bob *is* a companion. He's just not a *regular* kind of companion. But our relationship works for me. Angie"—I put my hand over hers on the table—"I like David. He's a fine man. But these are early days, and I'm not going to rush into something just so my family can heave a collective sigh of relief. I tell you, Angie, my attitude pretty much is that, as long as I can pay my bills and I don't hurt anybody, I can pretty much do whatever I want!"

"I knew this was going to be a tough conversation." Angie sighed. "So I came prepared." She reached into her purse and pulled out a letter I'd written her shortly after my divorce from Matt. She opened it up and read these words from my younger, much unhappier, self: "The loneliness, Angela, digs into your bones like a damp chill in winter. Wherever you go, it follows like a desperate beggar. You can't outrun it, and you can't distract yourself from it. I hope you're never as lonely as I am right now." She put down the letter. "And now you're trying to tell me you're just fine living by yourself up here. You can talk until you're blue in the face. I don't believe you."

I poured more coffee and tried to figure out what I could say so she'd understand me. Finally I tried, "Angela, I meet women who have been married for decades. So much of the time it's awful. They stay married for the financial security and the kids. So many of those women have given up growing and learning and exploring new worlds. The only meaning left in their lives is their grandchildren. I'm sure having children and grandchildren is wonderful, but defining your whole existence through them? It's just not for me."

"That's ridiculous, Roz," Angela said impatiently. "What on earth does having grandchildren have to do with you living alone up here?"

I tried again. "Whenever I get people in my life, I wind up taking care of them or being responsible for them. Husbands, clients, employers, younger brothers and sisters, pets. I'm sick of it. If that's what a full-time, regular relationship is for me, and it always seems to be that way, I don't want that relationship."

"Relationships don't have to be that way," Angela said, still frustrated.

"But they always have been for me. Don't you see? I was raised to be that way, to take care of people. I'm tired of being sucked dry, and apparently I don't know any other way to do a relationship. So the answer for me, as unpopular as it seems to be for the world in general, is to just not do a full-time relationship. So no husbands, no adopting children, probably even no pets. Don't you see how Bob is pretty much perfect for me? A little distraction, a few laughs, the occasional martini, not very demanding. I don't have to feed him, wash his clothes, or water him like a plant. In many ways, he's just perfect."

Angela sat back in her chair and pursed her lips while she studied me. "I think you're shortchanging yourself, Roz. Relationships don't have to suck you dry. Mine doesn't. Katie's doesn't. A good man wouldn't."

"You're right on that, Angie. I don't know what I'd do without you two. And David does seem like a very nice guy, but he has his own problems right now. This situation with all his vines being killed, he's financially back to square one. And you know how much being broke terrifies me."

Angela stood to hug me. "You break my heart, Rosie, and what breaks it even more is that you have no idea why. You've defined your life into this impossibly lonely little box, and you won't let yourself get out of it."

"But it's *my* life, Angie, and I'm not hurting anybody and I'm paying my bills, so I get to set it up any way I want."

Angela shook her head and gave my cheek a soft kiss. "Huh. We'll see."

I realized it was after two, and I wanted to stop over at Stan's as I'd promised. Angela opted to stay at my place and unpack a bit and settle in. So I walked out into the cold, completely oblivious to the debacle that was about to unfold.

A handful of neighbors and relatives were sitting in Stan's living room sharing remembrances of Mary. Many of their stories revolved around her prowess as a hunter and fisherwoman, echoing Pat's comments the other day. They described her fondness for daredevil stunts, like driving her '57 Chevy out onto frozen Crooked Lake in the middle of a long-ago January. As a woman totally lacking hunting, fishing, or daredevil genes of any sort, I was awed by these stories. They helped me see the malicious sprite I'd met only once in a kinder light. For the most part, Stan sat quietly in a corner, while his son and daughter made coffee and set out sandwiches and doughnuts. I sat with him for a few moments and asked how he was doing.

"I'm holding up," Stan responded. "She gave everything to me." He must have seen the confusion on my face, so he clarified, "Mary. She left everything to me in her will."

"Oh, that's good, isn't it?" I had mixed feelings. Mary ignored her ex-husbands, five children, and many grandchildren to leave everything to her handyman? So much for motherly love. But then again, it was none of my business.

"Yes. Now I know I can stay here. I didn't know where I was going to live before," Stan said.

"Well, that's a good thing."

"Hmm." He stared off into space, and I waited. Stan continued. "When I was going through Mary's things to get her clothes for the funeral, I found her wallet. The only picture she had in there was a newspaper clipping about me when I shot the first twelve-point buck of the season. I have no idea when she even got that clipping, it was so old and falling apart."

"If she carried that picture all these years and she left you everything, she must have loved you a lot, Stan."

"Yeah, I guess." Stan got lost in his thoughts again, so I patted his hand and went to find another cup of coffee. Just then, the front door slammed back and Mary's oldest son Harvey stumbled in.

"You *bastard!*" he screamed, pointing at Stan. "You conniving, stealing *bastard!*" Stan sat there paralyzed, while Aaron hurried to his side. One of Mary's old friends, Mark, stood up and tried to defuse the situation. "Now, Harvey, take it easy. This was what your mom wanted."

Harvey wobbled where he stood and slurred, "That bastard stole everything, and he's not going to get away with it. You want me to shut up and go away? Just give me the lakefront land, and I won't fight for anything else."

The lakefront property was ninety percent of the value of the estate. Of course he wouldn't fight for anything else.

By now all the men in the room were standing, and Harvey could see, even in his drunken state, that he was outnumbered. He started backing out the door, but had to get in one final shot. "This isn't over, you bastard. I'll be back." He jumped into his truck and gunned it, fishtailing when he swerved onto the road.

Mark closed the door, turned to the room, and said, 'I guess we should have expected something like that. Stan, are you okay?"

He wasn't. He had turned bone white and seemed to be having trouble breathing. Aaron took his arm and led him to the bedroom, where we could hear him trying to get Stan to lie down.

Those of us left in the living room started to move again, refilling cups and plates, talking in hushed tones. "It's that Montgomery blood," I heard Mark say to his neighbor. "Crazy as loons, and greedy as they come. Stan had better watch out with that bunch. They're pretty damn mean."

I couldn't wait around for any more fireworks. I had a sister at home, and I wanted to spend time with her.

After thanking Aaron and Jenny for their hospitality, I walked home, keeping an eye out for irate Montgomerys behind every tree. It was growing dark by the time I walked into the house, so I snapped on the hall light and called out, "Hey, Angie, I'm home!"

"I'm in the kitchen," she yelled, and I went downstairs.

"Want some tea?" she asked. "The kettle's still hot."

"No, thanks. I'm floating on liquids already. It was a nuthouse over at Stan's."

"Really?" So I told her about Harvey and the threats and the carryings-on. "One more thing to worry about, angry drunks with guns hanging out in the woods."

"Sounds like yet another reason for you to think about selling this place and moving," Angela said, as she slowly flipped through her telephone-book-sized *Vogue*.

"Oh, I don't know," I said, peering over her shoulder at the magazine. "I just don't know what I'm going to do."

We spent a few minutes looking at the glossy magazine, giggling at geometric haircuts, black lipsticks, and bizarre designer models. Living in the country, I have very few demands for *haute couture*, but I still love looking at fashion magazines now and then. I'm alternately attracted by some of the beautiful fabrics and lines of many of the outfits, and repelled by the excesses some designers use to make the models look as ugly as possible. Fashion is probably like football to me, a game I don't understand in the slightest, but I still enjoy getting involved in it once in a while, on my own terms.

After a few minutes of fashion excess, I went upstairs to check email. Tess had written and sent final status reports on all her national Community Chest campaigns. She'd also included a copy of the official America Wins! contest rules, so I could start working on their entry. Work, paying work at last, thank God! As a freelancer, I always breathe easier when I have my next project in my hands, and Tess's email would keep me busy for weeks. I let out a little "yippee" of joy, and

Angela yelled up the stairs, "What's up?" I started singing ABBA's "Money, Money, Money" and went downstairs to tell her the good news.

"That's great!" she said. "Why don't I treat you to dinner to celebrate?"

"Honey, you don't have to treat me to dinner. I have plenty of food here."

"I know, and I'm sure it's delicious, but I'd like to get out and see a little bit of the area before I leave tomorrow."

"It's pitch black out there," I said, pointing at the dark windows. "There aren't even any streetlights. We won't be able to see much of anything."

"I know, but let's get out." She stood, plunked down the huge magazine, grabbed my arm, and started dragging me up the stairs. "This way when you tell me about places over the next few months I'll be able to visualize them."

"Well, okay." I gave in and put on my coat. "I'll take you into Southport, but don't get your hopes up. There's not a lot going on this time of year."

"As long as I can find a good meal and a nice glass of wine, I'll be fine."

We drove south on roads that twisted along the contours of the lake. The water glistened on our left, quiet waves rustling in the moonlight. We passed empty mansions and cottages, only occasionally seeing a light or the blue glow of a television.

Southport still wore its white holiday lights, so it looked lovely. The town square was surrounded by now-quiet shops; the gazebo on the square a vision of twinkle-frosted gingerbread. Angela and I window shopped and checked out menus posted in restaurants. We finally opted for a quiet Thai restaurant on a side street. It was new since the last time I'd spent any time in town, the fateful day I'd met Terri on the square.

As always, I enjoyed eating something I hadn't cooked myself, and I loved our dinner conversation; books, music, family goings-on, great meals, and recipes.

Angela spent some time talking about her kinesiology and chakra studies. She'd gone to Denmark the previous summer to take some very advanced classes in her studies of how energy flows in and around the body. Frankly, it was all a bit over my head.

Angela is one of the people in my life that I can sit down with after a five-year separation and talk as though we'd seen each other yesterday. Physical distance would never be an issue with us. We usually chatted a few times every week. And, fortunately, the topic of Bob didn't come up once during our restaurant conversation. Maybe I'd actually been able to get my point across, and Angela had decided to let me bumble my own way through things.

After dinner we strolled across the square to the local ice-cream parlor, which specialized in hot cider and homemade cocoa during the winter. Cocoa in hand, we spent a few minutes exploring side streets I'd never seen before. Southport had a lot more going for it than I'd realized.

Angela, tired from her travels, went to bed early. I was looking forward to telling Bob about my day, but that night in my bedroom I couldn't get him. Lola again? Weird. It had been, what?, close to three months of almost daily get-togethers with Bob and now nothing. Oddly unsettling. I punched down my pillows a few times, watched a few minutes of an infomercial, but couldn't settle even though my alarm clock showed three a.m. I turned on the radio and the imported dulcet tones of the BBC announcer finally lulled me to sleep.

I slept hard. So hard that Angela had gotten up, showered, dressed, and repacked before I even opened my eyes. I stumbled downstairs in my robe and found her feeling her way through making breakfast.

"Here, sweetie, sit down and let me do this. I'm so sorry, I never sleep in like this, but I just couldn't settle down last night and once I fell asleep, I was out for the count."

"Oh, Roz, it's not a problem. But I have to be on the road to the airport by ten."

I doubled my breakfast-making speed. "Why can't you stay longer? It's crazy to head back so soon. You just got here."

Angela took charge of buttering the toast and said, "We've got a dinner party with John's boss tomorrow night, and I can't take any chances of missing it. You know how it is flying in winter. You never know where you're going to get hung up, so I have to allow lots of time to get back."

I was mystified. Why on earth had Angela come so far? Sure, she'd read me the riot act about Bob, but she could have done that over the phone. We sisters read each other the riot act by phone all the time. This visit made no sense whatsoever. But I wouldn't argue. Any excuse to spend time with Angela was fine with me. Or so I'd always thought.

We hurried through our brief, muddled breakfast. Obviously Angela wanted to hit the road, and obviously I was discombobulated by my heavy sleep. I didn't even have time to dress before Angela flew out the door. I caught up with her at her rental car, where she sat setting the GPS for the airport.

"I loved seeing you, Angie, even though it was awfully quick. I'm so sorry I'm not quite myself this morning. I never had a chance to see Bob last night, and I'm a little off balance."

"Well, Roz, you should probably get used to it," she said, adjusting the angle of the screen.

"Get used to what?" I huddled into my robe as a cold gust came along.

Angela got out of the car, opened the back door, put her

overnight bag in the seat, and turned to me. "You should probably get used to not seeing Bob."

"I'm not following you. Why wouldn't I see Bob anymore? You're not making sense, sweetie." I hugged myself in the frigid morning air.

Angela turned and looked me straight in the eyes. "I had a talk with Bob yesterday while you were at Stan's."

I froze. "You what? You saw him?"

"No, I didn't see him. But I felt him and talked to him."

"You felt him? What does that mean?"

Angela sighed. "Roz, think about it. What have I been doing all these years? Studying energies. What do you think all that time with chakras and kinesiology was all about? It's all about energies and working with them. And what do you think a ghost is? It's energy, so of course I could feel him. It's what I've been studying for twenty years."

"Oh," was about all I could manage.

"So while you were gone yesterday, I felt Bob in the kitchen. He usually comes in by the cabinets, right?"

I nodded, and she continued. "So I just told him how I thought he was hurting you by being around, the same stuff I told you yesterday, and how, if he really cared about you, he'd go away and leave you alone so you could see if things develop with David."

"Did he say anything?"

"I didn't hear words, but I could feel that he was upset. But I just kept telling him how much he would hurt your future by staying around."

"You had no right to do that, Angie," I said angrily.

"I had *every* right to do that," she shot back. "I'm your sister, and I love you. I won't stand by and watch you screw up your life. If your happiness means I lecture a ghost for half an hour, I'm perfectly serene about doing it."

"He never said anything?" I sounded like a broken record, a heart-broken record.

Angela at last looked a little uncomfortable. "I said he didn't say anything. But he did write something. Just two words." She reached into her pocket and pulled out a crumpled scrap of paper.

I snatched it from her hand and smoothed it out, trying to decipher the illegible handwriting. Finally the words unscrambled. *Everyone's different.*

"Everyone's different," I murmured. "Everyone wants different things. That's exactly what I told you, Angie. Bob knew it, too, but now he's gone."

"As soon as he wrote it, he vanished. I could feel it. It almost felt like a big hook grabbed him out of the sky."

"A hook?" I started to understand poor Bob's awful new situation. "Of course, because he revealed himself to you. Now you've put him in ghost boot camp. Great job, Ange."

Angela snapped her parka closed with firm resolution. "It's all for the best, Roz. I can live with myself and what I've done."

"I'm glad you're happy, because I'm not," I said. I looked at my watch. "You'd better get going. It's getting late. Have a safe trip."

"I love you, Roz. Remember, that's why I did this. Because I love you." Angela got behind the wheel, started the car, and blew me a kiss.

I gave her a begrudging wave and headed back into my very cold, very empty, house.

Chapter 15
Window-Mirrors

Late January

The weeks since I last saw Bob have been long, cold, and miserable. Well, no, miserable might be overstating things a bit. The Irish drama queen lives.

On the bad side, it's been frigid, dark, and blustery just about every day since early January. Between the constant overcast clouds, snow, and the virtually daily mists on the now-frozen lake, I live in a world of almost unrelieved gray, and definitely unrelieved cold.

As you might guess, with heating oil so expensive, I keep my house on the nippy side. My still-thin Nashville blood spends most days shrieking hysterically, so I walk around in so many layers I can't bend in the middle. Stripping down to actual bare skin to take a shower becomes a daily exercise in moral fortitude and self-discipline.

Since I'd heard that fifty percent of a body's heat is lost through the head, I've even taken to wearing a cap and fingerless gloves when I'm working. If anyone unexpectedly ever knocked on my door (very unlikely in this part of the world in the dead of winter), they might think they'd taken a detour into a Dickens novel. And from what I'm told, the snow doesn't even get serious until February, God help me.

On the good side, I've actually developed a bit of a social life. Stan and I do our grocery shopping together in Avondale most weeks. I see David a few times each week and Bev Miano talked us into joining the local Community

Chorus with her and her husband. It's a lot of fun, and it's free! This means David and I go to Avondale every week and have dinner out (nothing fancy—usually the Chicken Shack or pizza), and then sing for two hours, which certainly lifts the spirits.

My sisters were right. David is a thoughtful, kind, and very attractive man. I was right, too, though. He is definitely worried about his future as a grape grower, and how he will be able to survive what the community now calls the "Christmas Day Massacre." His finances preoccupy him, and just about every time I'm at his house, I notice scraps of paper covered with scribbled numbers tucked under the corners of books or coffee mugs. I know his financial situation weighs heavy on his mind.

Even tonight. Today is David's birthday, so I baked him a yellow cake with chocolate frosting and took it to his place, where we had a few of his friends over for cake and coffee. In the depths of winter, most local people avoid night driving, so Mick and Debbie came by after lunch. Mick, too, had lost all of his vinifera plantings in the massacre, so the conversation veered toward the depressing until we'd catch ourselves and steer it back to birthday cheer.

Mick and Debbie are a comfortably older, comfortably stout couple who obviously have a soft spot for David. They had taken him under their wings after Bethie died. They are lovely folks, salt of the earth, and it tickles me that Debbie seems to like me.

As we were eating, I pulled out David's surprise birthday present. "Roz, you certainly didn't have to do this," David said, while ripping off the paper. "Huh, a flask for liquor," he continued, in a puzzled voice.

"An old pewter flask," I explained. "Look at all of the animals on it!"

"Wow." David turned it over in his hands a few times, and then passed it along to Mick and Debbie to admire. "I've never had anything like this before. It sure is different!" He threw his arm around me and kissed me on the cheek. "Thank you, Roz. It's really great!"

After coffee and cake, Debbie and I cleaned up while Mick and David looked at websites for grape root stock, researching where they'd buy their next plantings. As Debbie dried the cake plates, she told me about a grape growers meeting she and Mick had been to the week before. "There's one grower, Toby, who's a real character. He was perfectly comfortable about his grapes getting wiped out because he said the new plantings would be even better. He has this theory that the whole Finger Lakes area is working its way to global prominence with its wine, and the only way we'll get there is by making mistakes all along the way and fixing them. He said one thing—now, let me see if I can get his phrasing right—that Crooked Lake pulls in what it needs. Talent, expertise, energy, and people, and that this area will attract whatever it needs to recover from the massacre and keep growing."

My thoughts wandered to me. Of course. Why on earth would Crooked Lake ever have drawn me in? A crabby woman of a certain age with the abilities to make a good soup and put a soft edge on hard-nosed business writing but otherwise, few marketable skills? When Debbie talked about Crooked Lake pulling in what it needed, the image of Bob flailing around on the bottom of that invisible hook flashed through my mind. Was the Universe full of invisible hooks that kept tugging people around? Making them fall in love? Move across the country? Make stupid investments and then try to recover from them? An interesting way to think about life, but I wasn't sure that I bought it. But, then again, I had seen Bob tugged across Manhattan. Hmm . . .

I snapped out of my woolgathering while Debbie put the plates away. Much as I would have liked to spend the afternoon at David's watching football while cuddled under a blanket on the couch, I had a fast-approaching Community Chest deadline, and I needed to put in a few more hours of writing. Yup, I am still doing a lot of work on weekends. So much for my resolution to push back on unreasonable deadlines.

I wrapped up some cake for Debbie and Mick to take home, and covered the rest for David for later. He looked up from the computer when he saw me starting to get my stuff together.

"You're not going already, Roz? I thought we could watch some football later."

"I'd love to, I really would. But I've got a deadline Tuesday, and I need to put in some more work this afternoon. I wouldn't be very good company. I've got too much on my mind."

David pushed his chair from the computer. "I'll walk you out to your car. Here, Mick, these are the vines I was telling you about."

Mick slipped into David's chair to peer at the monitor. "Hey, Deb," Mick said, clicking through the screen with the mouse. "Come here and look at these."

Debbie strolled toward him, stopping to give me a warm hug on her way.

David shrugged into a coat, and we walked out to the car. "So, are we on for Community Chorus tomorrow?" he asked. "I'll spring for pizza."

"Sounds perfect. You want to pick me up at five-thirty?"

David nodded. "I really like that flask you got me, Roz. It was quite a surprise. I haven't had such a nice birthday present in years."

"It was a bit of a splurge, but I figured we could both use a little splurge right about now. I had a lot of fun shopping for it. I bid on it on eBay. It's the first time I've ever done anything like that."

"Done anything like eBay or buy a liquor flask?" David smiled.

"Both." I grinned back.

"Something new every day, right?"

"You got it."

Even though it was freezing outside, David didn't appear to be in any hurry to get back to the warmth. He rested his hip against the side of the car.

"Speaking of splurges," he said, "how about we go out for a nice meal next weekend? Maybe head up to Rochester to a restaurant at the mall? There are some wine books I'd like to look at in the bookstore, and then we could have dinner. We could maybe even call it an official date."

"An official date, huh?"

"Yup."

"I'd love it. You'll make my sisters very happy. Me, too, of course."

As David pushed away from my car and started to open the door, he asked, "Things getting better with your sisters?"

"It's been a long, slow process, but we're getting back to normal. Lots of short answers on my part when they call, but they keep calling me, so we'll be fine. Eventually."

"I'm glad to hear it. One of these days you'll have to tell me exactly what happened when Angela visited. I'm still a little fuzzy on the details."

"Sure. One of these days." Not very likely. Cold, I scooted toward the open car door. "Okay, I'd better be off before it gets too dark. Happy Birthday!" We hugged, but with all my layers and puffy coat, he must have felt like he was embracing the Michelin Man. "I'll see you tomorrow."

"Looking forward to it, Roz."

With great effort, I bent at the waist and launched myself into my low-slung car. Waving, I pulled down the driveway and made the short drive to my house.

My front light blinked on when I got within motion detection range, enabling me to work the door locks. The house was cold and dark, and I went to the kitchen to make some tea before I settled down to work. I put on the kettle, turned up the heat, bustled with mugs and teabags for a minute, then sat at the table to wait for the water to boil. I couldn't resist thinking about my dud of a birthday present for David. Why on earth had I gotten him a liquor flask? Wine drinkers don't use them. Only hard liquor drinkers like Bob do. Stupid, stupid, stupid. Right on par with my usual track record for gifts. What the heck was wrong with me lately?

When the water boiled, I poured it into my mug and brought it back to the table. "Three minutes to let it steep," I said to myself, "and then up to the computer to get some work done, young lady." One minute led to two, then three, as I stared out the window at the lake. Against the dark outside, the window reflected back like a mirror. Usually I loved window-mirrors. Now, decades later, I still remembered the window-mirror as my night train pulled out of the London station for Oxford, and my happiness and eagerness to move to the next stage of my studies. Years of commuter bus and train window-mirrors flashed through my mind as I remembered working my way millimeters up the corporate ladder, and those nights of heading back to my home and marriage in the suburbs.

And now, this dark window-mirror to my quiet lake, reflecting back a comfortable, cozy kitchen and a quiet, thoughtful woman of a certain age who should really be working instead of wasting time. Report drafts waited to be written, and bills waited to be paid, while I sat daydreaming about a sweet, preoccupied grape grower and a bumbling, ridiculous ghost; daydreaming about laughing dinner conversations revolving around the sex lives of newts or the filing system in the afterworld; daydreaming about how, if I could pick only one thing to have right now, it would be laughter. To heck with the rest of it.

But my favorite laughing companion was dangling around on the end of a hook somewhere, and I might never see him again. So much for his assignment to help me decide whether to live at the lake and get something special done. Yeah, right. Bah, humbug.

Meditating, I sipped my cranberry tea and once more tried to motivate myself into working on my draft of "Effective Community Chest Strategies for Knobox Company." Instead, looking steadily into my inky window-mirror, I pulled the draft toward me, flipped it over to the clean pages on the back, and started writing.

"Trust me, it will hit you like a brick of gold . . ."

End of Book I

CPSIA information can be obtained at www.ICGtesting.com
Printed in the USA
BVOW03s0056241114

376271BV00005B/10/P